BLINDED

A Cade Ranch Novel

Greta Rose West

PUNK
ROSE

PRESS

ALSO BY GRETA ROSE WEST

Wild Heart: Welcome to Wisper - A short Cade Ranch prequel

Join the newsletter for this short introduction into the Cade Ranch world and for extra goodies and scenes. Sign up on my website.

gretarosewest.com

BURNED: A Cade Ranch Novel

BROKEN: A Cade Ranch Novel

BUSTED: A Cade Ranch Novel

BRAVED: A Cade Ranch Novel

BLINDED: A Cade Ranch Novel

ACKNOWLEDGEMENTS

Writing acknowledgements is usually kind of fun. But this time, I'm reflecting back over the last several years, and I'm feeling the weight of it all. I have no idea what I'd be doing if it weren't for all the people I'm about to mention. I'm pretty sure I wouldn't have published any books. I went through something really hard, and I wrote to find my way out of a place I didn't want to be. Saying goodbye to my dad seemed impossible and too hard to face, but with your help, I did it, and I've come out on the other side, still sad and missing him, but stronger and knowing that he's behind all of this. He's proud of me, and he's egging me on from above.

The following people were the railing along the staircase I climbed to get to today, and I'm grateful, more than they can ever know.

Peter Senftleben, my editor extraordinaire, thank you for taking the time to guide me, for your friendship, and for your belief in me. Thanks for always pushing me to dig deeper.

Joanne Machin, word nerd, for teaching me and supporting my cowboys, and for coming to love the twang, thank you. Converting you is a feat I'll always be proud of!

M. Whoa. Dude. Finn's book is out! Wtf do I do now? Lol. Thank you, my friend. Thanks for EVERYTHING. Here's to a thousand more books between us, and a million more DMs. ;)

Christy, you're a rockstar and I love ya. Thanks for reading my stories and for giving the most honest feedback anybody has ever received. Lol. Keep it comin' cuz you make me better.

Tracy, you're Superwoman. Thank you for ALWAYS believing in me. I believe in you, too, and I love ya, Sistah.

Aan mijn vriend, Cece, bedankt voor je vriendschap, voor je steun, en ga je ondersteunende memes! Ik hou van je. <3

A special shoutout goes to Rob Lang for his beautiful cowboys, to Sarah Kil for helping me make my cowboys come to life on my covers, and to Dawn at Austin Design-Works for the most beautiful website ever in the history of ever! ;)

Can I acknowledge and thank music, like, as a whole? I'm gonna cuz these books wouldn't exist without it. All kinds. Even country! Gasp. Did I just say that? The last two years have been filled with so many amazing artists. There are so many playlists. Music is the thing that guides the stories from my imagination to the page, and if it's possible, I've fallen even more in love with music than I was before, and that's sayin' somethin'. Gregory Alan Isakov, Bon Iver, Brandi Carlile, Foo Fighters, The Milk Carton Kids, Lord Huron, Ray LaMontagne, Clutch, Ben Howard, Nathaniel Rateliff & The Night Sweats, and Freya Ridings, just to name a ton. Thank you for your inspiring words and melodies, for your love and poetry and angst, for making me scream-sing in my car, and for lifting me up when down was all I knew.

To my ARC readers and Street team (now that I know what the difference is—thanks Christine!), your support means the world. Thanks for being excited to get my ARCs, for sharing the books, and for loving my cowboys. You're a dream team! Mwah! xoxo

And to the readers, the people out there who I don't know, and they didn't know me from a hole in the ground, but they took the chance and read my books: to you, I love you. Thank you. This one's for you…

Dear Reader,

I don't even know where to start.

Thank you.

Thank you for reading my books and for falling in love with my cowboys, all the quirky characters in their lives, and the little town of Wisper, Wyoming.

I can't believe Finn's book is out in the world. Publishing one book, let alone five, was a pipe dream. It was this huge unattainable thing two and a half years ago. I never imagined I would get here. I'll be honest, I had no clue *how* to get here. But something inside me just wouldn't be ignored, and I'm so damn glad I listened to that voice in my head.

Becoming an author has been the most fun, the most fulfilling and satisfying thing I've ever done. I've never worked so hard, but it doesn't feel like work. It feels like my destiny, and I'm not usually one to believe in that kind of thing.

Whatever it is, destiny or not, it's everything to me, and I have plans for so many more books. Some connected to the Cade brothers and some not, and I hope you'll continue on this journey with me. I promise to always bring the angst, characters who are real, and the steam. Always the steam. And I'll bring the love.

You've given me yours, and I love you right back.

love always,

greta

To my Readers:
Finn is for you.

And to my boys:
You aren't the railing; you're the power in my steps.

CHAPTER ONE

FINN

I WAS DREAMIN' of the ocean.

The waves lapped at my feet as I stood, facin' out to look at the big, wide expanse of the world, listenin' to the quiet water roll and push and pull, the moonlit night wrappin' 'round me like a hug.

The gentle crash of the surf was warm and frothy, and it calmed me from my toes up to the top of my head. I smiled, swayin' in the night air, drawin' a slow breath into my lungs, the soft scents of sand and salt water and… somethin' else relaxin' me. Somethin' tropical. No, somethin' sensual—sexy —like what I imagined a woman's skin would smell like after she'd been swimmin' in the ocean. Salty and wet, sweet sweat and desire.

Funny, I could describe what desire looked like on the outside but not what it felt like inside my body. Not really. I couldn't describe what it felt like to touch a woman who wanted what was on the inside of my mind instead of on the outside of my skin—a woman who wanted me for how I made her feel and think, instead of just what I looked like.

Plenty of women thought that was what they felt for me,

plenty had told me they desired me, but aside from the baser need to release, I'd never met a woman I desired that way either. Not one who turned me inside out with need and love and want. And, contrary to what everyone believed about me, I'd never met a woman who desired *me*. I wasn't sure anyone cared about the thoughts in my head.

But, even though I couldn't describe what it felt like to be really wanted, somehow, in my dream, I knew the scents I could smell all around me, the taste on my tongue, and the feelin' of silk on my skin—I knew the woman I would be with, when I finally found the one I couldn't live without, I knew she'd smell like this. She'd taste and feel like this.

Like the sea.

Drawin' the scent into my body one last time, I turned to walk away. It was a dream, but I still had a shit-ton of work to do in the mornin', so I figured I could hint to my dream self that it was time for a little uninterrupted REM.

But as I turned, somethin' grabbed and slapped at my feet. Hard. It stung my wet skin, tuggin' me backward gently, and instinctually, I kicked at it, but it began to climb up my legs.

It felt like a wide scratchy rope, but when I looked down to see what had stung and scraped my skin, I gasped. An iridescent, incandescent ribbon of light that changed from ice blue to glowin' pale green with little sparks of yellow wound its way up my legs, flashin' and winkin' in the dark.

It scratched and crawled its way up my body quickly, trappin' my arms to my torso, and then it wrapped itself around my chest. It didn't hurt, not really, but it was uncomfortable.

Suddenly, it stopped its trailin' ascent, pullin' itself into a tight circle around my throat. I worried it would try to choke me, but it didn't. I wanted to rip it off, but the warm and irritatin' ribbon seemed sad. Lost… Okay, yeah, this was a dream, but come on. A sad fuckin' ribbon? What the hell was my subconscious up to?

Wrappin' itself around my eyes, the melancholy marauder blinded me, cuttin' off my last advantage. It pulled itself into a tight knot behind my head, tanglin' my hair in its clutches, and fell away from every other part of my body, hangin' loose, danglin' and swayin' in the ocean breeze next to me, pokin' me here and there. It tickled my skin.

The ribbon wanted to play. Or so I thought.

But then those deceptive tendrils started hittin' me, pummelin' me in the face! They shoved themselves inside my mouth, chokin' and gaggin' me, and they dragged me back to the water, pushin' me down into it. The salt assaulted my nose and ears and burned my skin as I was dragged under.

I tried to call out for help, but really, what had I expected? I was still in la-la land—there wasn't anybody around to help me. And no sound came outta my mouth anyway. I couldn't move my arms or legs, and they felt like they weighed a thousand pounds apiece.

Somehow, in all my drownin' glory, it occurred to me that I wasn't even tryin' to fight. I didn't wanna die, 'course not, but I wanted my tiny, murderous ribbon to be happy, to feel free.

I heard Homer Simpson in my head—"D'oh!"

Had I, in about two minutes inside of some imaginary dreamscape, succumbed to some kinda kinky, inanimate-object-focused Stockholm syndrome?

Fuck. My last thought was that I was about to die in two feet of water in an ocean I'd never actually seen, and I hadn't even had a chance to perfect my mole sauce or boeuf bourguignon!

Well.

Shit.

Jerkin' awake to the distant sound of runnin' water, I heard… the shower? Again?

Someone screamed ear-splittin' bloody murder right below my bedroom. "Get this dog away from me!"

Ahh. My new houseguest.

Wonderful.

She took showers like the world depended on her body bein' Irish Spring–clean and shiny every second of every day.

It was a good body, but still.

Okay, fine. Not just good. Aislinn Burroughs was the hottest woman I'd ever laid my baby blues on, but she drove me up the fuckin' wall.

Returnin' from a tour with my band, Tennis Elbow—yes, it was a stupid name for a band, but I didn't care as long as I got to play music—I'd been excited to meet this woman, the younger sister of the man investin' in my family's ranch.

For months, I'd been lookin' forward to meetin' her, since the very first time I'd seen her picture, but much to my dismay, when I came home three weeks ago, I was greeted by the rudest, most spoiled-rotten brat I had ever met. And she was a vegetarian! I mean, if it were possible for a person to be made specifically for me, this woman was the exact *opposite* of that.

She'd already wooed my whole family in my absence. My sister-in-law, Evvie, adored Aislinn, and even my grouchy brother, Jack, worshipped the ground she walked on. They all treated her like some porcelain doll.

But she was a Chucky doll!

All she did was scream that the dog was buggin' her, or she complained about the food I cooked for her. She abhorred gettin' dirty, and she wore the most ridiculous, expensive, *white* clothes. Didn't she realize she was stayin' on a horse ranch in the middle of Wyoming, for cryin' out loud?

I couldn't wait for her to go live with Billie. My baby brother Jay's fiancée and Aislinn were best buddies, and Billie had invited the most unappreciative houseguest in the world to stay at her new house, but it was bein' renovated, and since Aislinn was visually impaired and couldn't navigate the house and all the construction supplies safely, they were both stayin' at the ranch.

Lucky me. I was countin' down the days till she left.

She screamed again, and I threw my covers to the floor, rose outta bed like the walkin' dead, and yanked dirty sweats up my legs. This woman made more noise than tinfoil in the microwave, and I was just about at my wit's end.

"What! What is it this time?" I stomped down the stairs to the bathroom, ready to rumble, but when I got there, I deflated like a little kid's birthday balloon after five days trapped in the sun in the back of his mama's minivan.

Aislinn sat sprawled on the bathroom floor, naked, tryin' to cover herself with the shower curtain, while Tony, the best rescue pit bull in the world, sat between her legs, pantin' and smilin' up at her, waggin' his butt and tongue.

"Shit. Are you okay? Did you fall?"

"No!" She screeched, and I resisted the urge to cover my ears like a five-year-old. She yanked the shower curtain, makin' sure her womanly bits were covered, and all the little plastic hoops holdin' it up popped off the bar, rainin' down on her like confetti on New Year's Eve.

"Are you going to just stand there staring at me, or do you think you might find me a towel? When I entered this bathroom"—she said it like it was less than a bathroom, the word puckerin' her mouth like sour candy—"there was a towel hanging from the towel rack. This dog breaks in every time I take a shower and steals my towel. Do you think you could maybe train him *not* to do that?"

"Maybe he's just protestin' your wastin' of resources. You take eight showers a day."

She huffed indignantly. "I take one shower a day, two if I help groom the horses because I am mildly allergic to them, and if I don't shower, I itch."

"Oh." How could I be mad at her now? "Well, do you have to be so loud about it? This is the third time your showers have woken me up."

"If you'd train your dog, there would be no noise." Tuckin' the plastic shower curtain under her arms, she clenched her teeth, seethin' at me. "May I *please* have another towel?"

When she raised her eyes to mine, my heart did a little skip. It always did when she looked at me. She couldn't see me, so she didn't know my reaction, but her eyes were the most beautiful I'd ever seen. They were an almost shockin' sea-glass green. I'd never seen anything like 'em, and incidentally, lookin' at her eyes always led me to lookin' at the rest of her, which was just as exquisite.

Her skin was the lightest brown color, silky and glowin', her features dainty and perfectly feminine. And she was tall for a woman, probably five foot ten, maybe eleven. If I were interested, which I definitely was not, she woulda been perfect for me since I was six foot five.

Her hair was black, short and pixie-like, which I totally dug. Her haircut made her even prettier 'cause it framed her face, which was definitely the star of the show.

But then, unavoidably, she would open her mouth to speak.

"If you please, *Finn*, a towel?"

"Oh, right. Be right back."

"Hmph."

What? Not even a thank you? Or maybe, "So sorry to disturb you, Finn"? Nope, there was never any of that. No gratitude, no remorse for ruinin' my sleep or invadin' my house. Jay and Billie were always off doin' some thing or another, which left Aislinn with me. Neither one of us jumped for joy about it, but Billie and Jay kept leavin'. The dicks.

Runnin' up the stairs three at a time, I grabbed a towel from the hall closet and stopped in my room for one of my flannels. I wasn't the rude one. I was the gracious host.

"Here," I said, steppin' back into the bathroom, shooin' Tony out with my bare foot. "I brought you one of my shirts too." I handed 'em to her, and she wrapped the towel around herself under the shower curtain and covered her chest with my shirt.

I tried to look away. I swear, I did. I turned my head toward the wall, but my eyes found their way back in her direction of their own accord. It wasn't my fault.

"Can you shut the door, please?" she asked, pushin' the curtain off, shovin' it between the toilet and shower stall.

"Lemme help you up first."

She held out her limp hand like I was her butler, there just to be at her beck and call. "Thank you."

I rolled my eyes but took her hand, pullin' with maybe just a tad too much muscle, launchin' her up and forward. Tony slipped in between us, playfully growlin', and he grabbed the towel and flannel with one quick nip of his teeth and yanked. They fell to the floor, and he dragged 'em both outta the bathroom before I could catch him, which left Aislinn naked as a jaybird, practically in my arms.

I looked down. "Fuck." I couldn't help it. *Sweet Jesus.*

"Get out!"

"Aislinn—"

"Get. Out!" She pushed me, her wet hands on my bare chest, and even though she was pissed as all get out, the physical contact had my dick punchin' to attention behind my gray sweatpants. "Get out! Get out! Get out!" She pushed again, and I stumbled backward, but then she advanced on me like a sexy lioness, searchin' with her hand for the door handle, and when she found it, she slammed the door shut so hard, the wood rattled in the frame.

"Sorry," I spoke to the door in my face. "I'll get you another towel. Just hang on a sec."

"Don't bother. I'm calling Billie."

Great. I was in for it now. Aislinn would blame the whole debacle on me, and I'd never hear the end of it from Billie. She was already callin'. I heard her phone 'cause she used some app or settin' that spoke to her to tell her what was on her screen. Every time I tried to talk to her, she'd pull out her phone and tap the screen, and the annoyin' voice would interrupt me.

"I'll get you another towel, and I'll put Tony outside. I'm sorry," I said again louder, like an idiot. Lookin' down at my feet, I smiled at the goofy dog lyin' on the floor on his back, rollin' on the stolen towel, his gray and white freckled belly exposed and available for scratches. "He just really likes you. He wants to play. You can't be mad at him for that."

"Oh yes, I can."

"Well, if you wanna jinx your dog karma, far be it from me to get in your way."

"What?"

"Your dog karma."

"You are utterly ridiculous. Go away!"

I shrugged. "C'mon, Tony. Let's go back to bed." Tony hopped up, waggin' his nubby tail. "Okay, I'm goin' back upstairs. Sure you don't want another towel?"

Turnin' my ear to the door, I listened for her response. When there wasn't one, I shrugged again. Miss Hoity-Toity Pants could figure it out for herself.

Tony followed me up the stairs to my bed, snugglin' in next to me while I scratched behind his ears.

"You're such a bad dog," I told him, grinnin', but it sounded more like, "You're such a good boy." He licked my face and we fell asleep.

Tony probably dreamt about gnawin' on steak bones and chasin' cats. I dreamt about uptight city princesses, beautiful in the sunlight, runnin' their hands all over my body. But suddenly, my legs were tied together with the ropey wrangler from my earlier dream, and then my hands were bound. I couldn't move 'cause I'd been tied to the paddock fence with the damn thing—trapped in the burnin' sun and naked as the day I was born—and Aislinn stood in front of me, pointin' at me and laughin' like an evil sorceress.

CHAPTER TWO

AISLINN

"WHEN WILL your house be ready? I cannot stay at the ranch with that *man* any longer."

Billie laughed. "You mean Finn?"

"Yes, I mean Finn! You knew who I meant. He's maddening. He eggs that dog on. I think they're trying to make my life miserable." Listening to the sound of the tires on the road while Billie drove me to talk to my brother in Jackson, Wyoming, I crossed my arms over my chest, breathing deeply and trying to calm down.

Theo had been released from the local hospital and was renting a house in the little town, but I'd barely talked to him since I found out he'd been lying to me for years. I was glad he was okay, but I was so angry with him, I couldn't think straight. It felt weird to live without his daily influence, but my anger did a good job of easing the pang of separation from my brother.

And I had friends now, Billie and Evvie and the Cades. But not Finn.

"I think you might be the only person on the planet who

doesn't like Finn. If you could see him, you wouldn't be so rude to him."

"Billie! What an awful thing to say."

"Sorry, but I'm just saying your reaction to him would be much different."

"Handsome isn't everything."

She snorted. "Handsome? The word does not do him justice. He's a panty melter."

"A what? Oh my God, Billie. You're so crass." Shaking my head, I inhaled, letting the country air coming in my window fill my lungs. Back home, I never rode with the window down.

The air in Wisper smelled so different than the air in Boston. Crisp and clean instead of humid and stuffy, it was sweet and earthy at the same time. I could smell the fir trees—the perfume of the needles and the clean sappy wood of their trunks. But there were other smells, too, like cows and horses and grass and dirt.

It surprised me that I enjoyed those simple scents, but something about them gave me strength and grounded me. The air all around me was invigorating. It felt electric on my skin. And big. When I was outside at Cade Ranch, I could feel and smell and *know* that I was standing at the bottom of a majestic mountain even though I couldn't see it.

At home, being outside could be so much more unpleasant than being indoors. Except for the savory scents from restaurants and bakeries lining the streets of Beacon Hill, the air smelled like car exhaust and the mud and algae from the dirty river. And people. People normally didn't smell good. And they made so much noise. I found myself reveling in the quiet at the ranch, listening to birds sing and the horses run and play. It was calming and relaxing.

Until Finn returned from wherever he'd been playing rock

star with his friends. He was loud and rude and… big. His presence sucked all the oxygen out of the room. He did smell good though. Oh God, he smelled so good. I couldn't think of the word to describe it, but I could drown in it and die content. I wouldn't ever tell *him* that though.

And his voice? Even though every single word out of his mouth annoyed me and made me want to kick him in his testicles, the timbre of his voice was a low, slow, sexy rumble, like errant thunder from a faraway summer storm. He was a solid person, and he was never nervous or stressed out—well, except maybe sometimes when he was talking to me, but usually, it wasn't hard to hear and feel his happy calmness. Even though I couldn't stand him, I had to grudgingly admit that he comforted me with his easy and affable aura.

I was the opposite, always stressed and uncomfortable. And maybe that was why he annoyed me in the first place.

"Well," I huffed, "he may be a 'panty melter,' but he is the most boorish person I have ever met. He's ill-mannered and, and… churlish." I wouldn't let Billie know it either because she would never let it go.

"Churlish? What does that even mean?"

"It doesn't matter. And you haven't answered my question. When will your house be ready? Because if it'll be much longer, I'll pay for a hotel or rent a house of my own where there will be no dog." And no Finn.

"Oh, please," Billie said, slowing her Jeep to turn a corner. "You can't fool me, Ace. Finn and Tony may annoy you, but you love being around everyone. You'd be miserable in some hotel all by yourself."

"Not true. I have spent plenty of time alone, and I was fine. That's the same kind of thinking that made Theo treat me like a child. Just because I'm blind doesn't mean I can't be alone."

"I didn't say you couldn't, I said you'd be miserable. You like being surrounded by the family."

"Finn Cade is not my family."

"I meant the Cades in general, and me. I never said the name Finn." I heard her smiling, and I wanted to pinch her. Hard.

"Whatever. How much farther? I'd like to get this over with as quickly as possible."

"You're still pretty pissed at your brother, huh?"

"I'm furious with him. Our parents died ten years ago, and the whole time, he knew the truth. He knew our mother wasn't my birth mother. He let me believe a lie. He let me mourn an imposter. He didn't trust that I could handle it. Just one more example of how he treats me like a baby." I crossed my arms again, trying so hard to hold in the hurt and disappointment of my brother's betrayal.

"What does he want, anyway?"

"I don't know. He said something about needing to speak to me about our dad's business."

For the rest of the drive, I was quiet, thinking about my birth mother. Hadn't she cared about me at all? I would never know, and it was devastating. It made me feel less than. It made me feel discarded, and I was fighting hard not to let anyone know.

When we pulled up outside Theo's house, I said, "Just once, I wish he would give me the chance to be an adult. I'm not that helpless sixteen-year-old girl anymore. Why can't he understand that?"

"Thank you for bringing her here, Billie. I appreciate it."

"I'm right here, Theo," I said, standing in the middle of

my brother's living room. It was weird to think it was his living room and not *our* living room. "I can speak for myself. Billie didn't do it for you. She's *my* friend. She did it because I asked her to drive me. It wasn't for your convenience. God, you're so self-centered."

"Uhh, okay, I'm just gonna run and get a latte. Ace, text me when you're ready. You want a chai tea?"

"Yes, please. Thank you." I used my cane to locate a chair and sat stiffly, then turned toward the sound of my brother's voice. The door closed behind Billie when she left, and I immediately felt less brave. "Why did you want me to come? I'm still angry with you."

"I know. I'm sorry, but I miss you. How are you? How's it going at the ranch? Are they treating you well? Do you need anything?"

"Not from you. What do you want? You said you needed to talk to me about Burroughs Financial."

"I-I… I lied."

"Surprise, surprise." I scoffed a laugh and Theo sighed.

"Aislinn, I'm sorry. I just wanted to see you. It's been weeks. I can't tell you how sorry I am. I wasn't trying to hurt you. I didn't like keeping the truth from you, but I just—I wanted to protect you. You've been through so much, and I thought—I wanted to spare you from that ugliness. I wanted you to have a good life."

"A good life? You mean a false life. You've been trying to protect me since our parents died, but you protected me so much that I don't—I—" The morning sun was coming in through a window, and the magnified warmth felt like it would burn my neck. My throat was dry, and I was afraid to tell my brother the truth.

"What?"

There was no noise in the house besides an annoying and

inconsistent ticking noise behind me. I thought it might've been the refrigerator, and I was pretty sure I smelled some kind of alcohol. "Nothing."

"Please talk to me. If you want me to be honest with you and treat you like an adult, then be honest with me. Tell me what you want to say."

"You want me to be honest?" I gripped the arms of the chair. "That's rich coming from you. You don't deserve it. You lied to me. For years!"

"Maybe I don't deserve it, but you do."

"I don't even know what I deserve. I have the world at my fingertips thanks to our parents and you, but how can you be sure I deserve any of it? My real mother abandoned me at birth, my parents lied to me my whole life, and my brother"—I squeezed my hands into fists—"my brother—the one person I thought I could count on, the person I thought I could trust—stole my identity from me. I don't know who I am!

"And it wasn't just the stuff about my birth mother. You never told me you were in love with Tim. I didn't even know you two had any kind of relationship other than employer and employee." I shook my head and heard him shift in his chair. "You didn't trust me with that either. You didn't tell me that he and Louise had been killed. You hid it from me because you didn't think I could handle that either.

"You didn't tell me you were in trouble. I had no idea you were alone and scared. Maybe, if you had trusted me, confided in me, I could have helped. I could've told you not to bother because I don't care! I don't care if the world knows about our father's affair or that my mother abandoned me. I don't care! Let people talk and gossip. What does it matter to me? Those people don't care about me, so why should I care what they think?" Letting out a big breath, I hung my head. I was angry, but more than that, I was disappointed.

"Aislinn, it's not that simple. You don't underst—"

"I don't understand? Is that what you were going to say? Of course you were. I don't understand because you're doing it again." Shaking my head again and feeling completely exhausted with my brother's "protection," I stood. "You're still not telling me everything. You won't explain because, to you, I'm just a powerless little girl. You expect me to put my trust in you every day. You want me to let you make decisions for me, to guide me through life, but you won't trust me enough even to make a cup of coffee on my own.

"Well, forget it, Theo. I don't trust *you* anymore. I don't want your help or your protection. I don't need it. I'm done. You're not my brother anymore. You're just somebody I used to know." Reaching into my purse for my credit cards that he paid for, I gripped them so hard in my hand, it hurt, but then I snapped my wrist, hurling them at him, hoping they hit him in his face. "I don't want anything from you ever again."

The cards clattered on the wood floor, and I heard Theo to my right, standing slowly. He was probably still in pain from the injuries inflicted on him by the man who'd been blackmailing him and who had threatened my life.

I turned, stepping forward with a little more speed than I should have. I'd only been inside Theo's rental one other time when he came home from the hospital—the day he'd given me the same sorry excuses to explain why he'd lied to me for so long—so I wasn't familiar with the furniture patterns. I bumped into something, banging my shins hard.

"Ow!"

"Aislinn, stop. Where are you going?"

"I'm leaving."

"One step to your left. You're between the couch and coffee table."

Inhaling, I stood tall, trying to preserve my dignity. I pressed the button on my cane to extend it and used it, shuffling forward to find the wall.

"The door is four steps to your right."

"I know."

"Aislinn—"

"I don't need your help, Theo. What's so bad about me finding my own way? You're just afraid it won't lead me to you, and then you'll be alone. Well, tough *shit*, to paraphrase my best friend. I'm going to live my own life. Without you." Finding the door and feeling extremely relieved it hadn't taken me forever and that I hadn't tripped on anything or fallen on my butt, I yanked it open.

The October sun warmed my face, and the air was cool, but this time, the heat felt good on my skin. I knew there were two steps leading up to the porch, so I found them with the end of my cane and made my way to the sidewalk, following the edge of the lawn. I could hear Theo behind me, wincing as I stumbled, chasing after me and wanting to tell me where to go, what to do. How to live. Who to be. But I was done listening to him.

I would figure it out on my own.

CHAPTER THREE

FINN

"WHY YOU SO TIRED?" my brother Kevin asked when I yawned for the umpteenth time. "You slept in. I had to pull your ass outta bed again this mornin'."

We'd driven over to Bob's Feed and Tack for supplies. Since my youngest brother, Jay, had taken over management of the ranch, he'd ordered all kindsa new shit. This time it was an order for some monogrammed saddle blankets with the letter C stitched everywhere in big, bold script, and new leads and bridles.

"Not gettin' much sleep lately." I climbed outta the truck, yawnin' again and draggin' my feet into the store.

"How come? Billie and Jay goin' at it all night long? Whoever woulda thought Jay would turn out to be the sex fiend of the family? Have you seen the way they look at each other? Shit's intense."

I groaned. "Don't remind me. No, it ain't Jay and Billie keepin' me up. It's the *other* person stayin' in my house."

"Aislinn?"

The bell on the door jingled when we entered the old,

dusty farm supply store, and the man himself, Bob, looked up.

"Who else?" I said to Kev, rollin' my eyes, then threw a tired smile at Bob. "Hey, Bob. How ya doin' today?"

Bob was sittin' in his campin' chair behind the counter, readin' *People* magazine. He had to have a steady stream of gossip to be satisfied. Didn't matter where it came from. "The world's endin', boys."

"Oh yeah?" I asked. "What's the word on the street today?"

"Hold on, lemme just go tell Linda to bring your order out."

"Bob," Kev said, chucklin' and shakin' his head, "you know it's wrong you make your wife do all the heavy liftin', right?"

"Please. That woman drives a forklift better'n anyone. Those boxes are heavy. Be right back." Heftin' himself outta the chair, he yanked his jeans up, though they wouldn't stay up since his big belly was in the way and he was obviously allergic to belts.

Bob disappeared in the back room, and Kev asked, "How's Aislinn wakin' you up? She's quiet as a mouse." He picked up a packet of Bob's prize-winnin' tomato seeds from a basket on the counter, studied it for a few seconds, then dropped it back in.

I snorted. "Yeah, a mouse on steroids and the whole house is a ginormous block of cheese. She makes so much noise. I can't even tell you how many times I've been ripped outta sleep."

His eyes snapped to mine. "Jeez, Finn."

"What?"

"I'm just surprised you're bein' so insensitive."

My mouth fell open. "Insensitive? Me? You, Kevin Christian Cade, the rudest person known to man, are callin' *me* insensitive?"

"Yeah. She's probably havin' a hard time navigatin' through the house. Be a little nicer."

I rolled my eyes again and opened my mouth to tell him all the ways Miss Hoity-Toity Pants was navigatin' through my life—she navigated just fine—but Bob interrupted.

"Okay, boys. Linda will meet us outside. Need anything else today?"

"Yeah," Kev said. "Dean wants more beef jerky. Give us one of them big jugs of the stuff."

"Get it yourself. Aisle five."

Kev nodded, turnin' to hunt down the jerky, and I followed.

"Think it's okay to use the business card for beef jerky? Jay didn't say nothin' about buyin' food."

"Can beef jerky from a farm store *really* be considered food?"

Kev shrugged. "That's an existential conundrum for another day."

"And you know it's bullshit."

"Beef jerky's bullshit?"

"It's bullshit 'cause Aislinn can find her way around just fine."

"Oh, we're back to that." Kev smirked, and I smacked the back of his annoyin' head.

"Yeah. We are. Y'all baby her. She's fully capable, but she's spoiled rotten. She expects me to wait on her hand and foot, she complains about everything, and she doesn't like Tony. That's a red flag right there."

"Yeah, but Tony loves her, so that kinda negates your point. Dogs have a good sense of people. Come to think of it, Iggy loves her, too, and Sammy. All the animals do. You're the only one left out in the cold on this one. Wonder what that says about you?"

"Shut up, dick."

Kev laughed, grabbin' two industrial-sized buckets of spicy beef jerky for Dean, and we checked out, usin' our brand-new, shiny Cade Ranch credit card, courtesy of Jay.

We helped Linda load the heavy boxes into the bed of our rusty, red beast of a truck while Bob talked Wisper gossip.

"Jessup Anderson's closin' the newspaper. You know, everything's online now. He shoulda done it years ago, but he's a stubborn ol' man."

I lifted the tailgate, slammin' it closed. "Oh yeah? He retirin'?"

"Yessir. Must be nice, eh? Wish Linda would let me retire."

Miss Linda snorted. "Yeah, right, Bobby, you'd go outta your mind. Where would you get your gossip if you weren't here every day, meddlin' in everybody's business?"

"I have my sources. Anyway, word is somebody's already bought the buildin' from Jessup. They'll probably build some garish strip-mall monstrosity."

"Well, who bought it?" Kev asked.

"Dunno. Jessup won't say."

Laughin', I said, "Bob, your gossip ain't thorough. That right there's the start to the end of the world."

"Ah." He shooed us away. "Gimme time, boys. Have a nice day now. Go wrangle somethin' or other. C'mon, Linda, drive that fancy lifter back to the garage. I think it's time for some of your famous sweet tea."

"Bye bye, boys." Miss Linda winked and beeped her squeaky horn, drivin' away at one mile an hour, and Bob followed her on foot, naggin' her for speedin'.

We drove back home and parked at the end of a long row of trucks. Construction had begun on the arena, and there were workers buildin' it out. They'd already ripped the gray sidin' off of the west-facin' part of the structure, poured the new foundation, and were busy settin' up the new framin'.

Workers were everywhere, every day from nine to five. The addition to the arena was gonna open a world of possibilities for Cade Ranch, startin' with the EveryBody Rides program, an equine therapy and adaptive ridin' program for kids. And we'd already started plans for a veteran program too. Big things were happenin' for us, and it was excitin' but kinda scary at the same time. Changes were comin'. Massive ones.

Jack was handlin' it better than I thought he would. He seemed a little grumpy, but he had Evvie now, so not much mud stuck in his eye for too long these days. Dean was happy with Oly, still awaitin' the birth of their twin girls. Guy was happier than a pig in shit. And Kev and Jay were both happy and in love too.

Apparently, I was the holdout. Go fuckin' figure.

Kev pulled up in front of the house, then skulked off to the barn, and I went into the kitchen for yet another cuppa coffee. Bein' woken up a thousand times a night was gettin' old.

I was one lip length away from takin' a swig of that delicious life-savin' nectar when I heard the loudest, screechiest scream. I ran outside toward the noise, jumpin' the porch railin' like an Olympic hurdler, sprintin' to the side of the house.

Aaand of course it was Aislinn.

The big ol' black stallion, Mad Max, had Aislinn

cornered against the house. She screamed again and tried to deck Max, her arm swingin' five miles shy of hittin' its mark, thankfully.

I wondered errantly if I could find a way to inject the coffee instead of havin' to go through all the trouble of drinkin' the stuff.

"Aislinn? What're you doin' out here by yourself? How'd you get out here? How did *he* get out here?"

Her voice shook when she said, "I walked out here. I do have legs."

"Right," I said, feelin' a little bit guilty, though not too much 'cause I was too exhausted for that. "You okay?"

"I'm fine." She gritted out, clenchin' her hands around the hem of her off-white silk shirt, and I rolled my eyes at the ridiculousness of her choice of attire yet again.

Walkin' over to grab Max's halter, I yanked, but the sucker wouldn't budge. The horse didn't seem to wanna go—he looked happy to be nose to nose with Aislinn. I pulled with all my might, but Max dug his hooves into the grass.

"What I meant was"—I grunted, tryin' again to persuade the giant to back up—"what're you doin' out here without your cane? Don't you need that to know where you're goin'?"

Smoothin' her shakin' hands over her hair, she said, "That stupid horse made me drop it. It chased me and I ran."

Finally, I got Max movin'. He backed up, nearly steppin' on my foot. "You're a beast," I told him.

Aislinn scoffed. "Excuse me?" She was flat against the side of the house still, holdin' her breath.

"I was talkin' to Max," I said, and I rolled my eyes again, whisperin' to him, "Good thing she couldn't *see* you chasin' her."

"I heard that. I'm blind, not deaf."

I inhaled slowly, methodically, as if I could breathe in patience and good manners. "Well, how'd he get out?"

"I have no idea! I was taking a walk, and all of a sudden, he was there, following me. He pushed me. You know, he's a lawsuit waiting to happen. This whole place is. Without my cane, I could have broken my ankle in twenty different holes on this property."

I sighed. "Sue me then. Wait here. I'm gonna put Max in the paddock and find your cane." I led Max away but turned to make sure she was really okay. She slid down, ploppin' onto her butt on the ground. "Oh boy, Max, what kinda trouble'd you get me into today?"

When I got back, I slid down, too, sittin' next to her.

"Did you lock that monster up?" She tried to act like she hated Max and Tony, but I knew the truth. She was a sucker for animals. They crowded around her whenever they could, like she was Noah on the Ark, and somethin' told me it was the reason she didn't eat meat, not 'cause of some political-point-of-view nonsense.

"I put Max back in the field, yes. I think he mighta jumped the fence. Seems like he likes you."

"Well, I don't like him." She crossed her arms over her chest. "Where's my cane?"

"Oh, here." I passed the long white cane to her, and she pressed a button and the thing retracted to a fourth of its size. "Aislinn, why don't you and I start over? We're kinda stuck together. Might as well get along."

She didn't say a word, and the sounds of construction, the horses, and my brothers ridin' and workin' in the fields filled the space between us.

"I'm sorry I annoy you," I tried again. "I'll try not to do that so much."

Still, not a word, but I turned my head to look at her. She

looked so determined. Determined to do what, I had no idea, but I felt the urge to ask.

I puffed out my cheeks, blowin' the air out real slow. "You wanna go for that walk? I'd be happy to escort you."

"No. I want to be alone."

I also felt the urge not to be treated like her staff. "Okay, then. I tried. Don't break your ankle." Poppin' up off the ground, I dusted the cut grass off my ass and left her sittin' there, stewin' in her own juice.

Groomin' my best girl, Gertie, in front of the barn, I watched Aislinn. She hadn't moved from the side of the house in almost half an hour. She sat cross-legged like a kid and picked at the grass for a few minutes, then she lay down with her arms behind her head for about thirty seconds but sat back up, clearly uncomfortable 'cause the woman couldn't seem to relax to save her life. I had just been about to go back up there to try to convince her to go in the house when Jay called to me from the arena.

I released Gertie in the front paddock, lettin' her run off her mani/pedi, and looked back at Aislinn one last time. James Brockovich—Brock, the local heartbreaker and damn hard worker—had found his way to the one beautiful and single woman in a five-mile radius and had struck up some kinda conversation.

It was easy to see he was flirtin' when he leaned with one arm against my house and one leg crossed over the other. Aislinn stood, too, laughin' politely and smilin' at him. She'd put her sunglasses on though. I'd noticed she did that some-times when she wanted to appear at ease about somethin' but wasn't. I was pretty sure it had nothin' to do with her lack of sight.

The construction guys were on a break. A group of 'em sat on hay bales, eatin' packed lunches, drinkin' pop and talkin'. But Brock was with Aislinn. It annoyed me. And it annoyed me that I was annoyed about it.

"Finn!" Jay hollered. "You comin'? Ms. Bell's here for her interview."

Shit, I'd forgotten. "Yeah. Be right there."

I threw one last glance toward Aislinn, shook my head, and stalked off in Jay's direction. When I joined him in the arena office, he introduced me to a Ms. Shonda Bell.

"So, Ms. Bell, tell us a little about yourself. You're new to the area. What brought you to Wisper?" Jay sat at the head of the table, normally Jack's seat, and I sat next to him. I was proud of my baby brother for takin' the reins of our family business. He was doin' a good job. Kid knew his shit.

"Oh, I don't live in Wisper. I just moved to Jackson about a month ago. I lived in northern Nevada for years. Just looking for a change, I guess. I live on the west side of Jackson, though, so getting here every day wouldn't be a problem. It's not far and I have a car."

"That's good," Jay said. "Do you have family in the area?"

"No."

"Oh, okay. Well, your resumé says you have office management experience. Tell us about that."

Jack knocked on the door and opened it, stickin' his head in. "Sorry I'm late."

"We're just gettin' started," Jay said. "Ms. Bell, this is our oldest brother, Jack. Jack, this is Ms. Bell. She applied for the office manager position I posted online."

All the proper introductions were made, and Jay said,

"There are five of us runnin' the ranch. I handle the non-profit stuff, and Jack oversees the breedin' program, but all non-horse-trainin' issues go through me, so you'd be workin' mostly with me."

Ms. Bell nodded. She was quiet as could be, and I wondered if she had the personality to deal with five hooligans.

"You were just about to tell us about your management experience?" Jay sat back, lookin' over her application while she wrung her hands in her lap.

She was an older lady, maybe late fifties or early sixties. Her curly black hair was pulled tight into a bun and had already started to gray around her temples, but otherwise, her age was told by the worry lines set into the skin around her deep-brown eyes. She was polite, and she smiled easy but didn't say a whole lot.

She did have plenty of management experience, though, and she assured us she could deal with all our different personalities. She and Jay discussed specific computer programs she was trained in while Jack and I sat there, probably both wonderin' why Jay had wanted us in the interview in the first place. I couldn't be any kinda help to him, at least not with the office side of things, and he knew it. But he wanted us to make certain decisions together, and the hirin' of new staff was one.

Jay promised to call Ms. Bell with a decision soon, and she left. She seemed kinda uneasy, but nice enough.

"You sure about her, Jay? She's awful quiet."

"Have you ever been on a job interview, Finn? It's nerve-wrackin'. Plus, there's so much noise from construction, so many people hangin' around. She was just a little nervous, but she's very qualified. She's the *only* qualified applicant. The only other person to apply was Sissy Melton, and she only applied—meanin' she called the house phone to tell me I was to give her the job—to be close to you every day. She even said that. She also said she was"—Jay raised a hand, scrunchin' two fingers in quotations—"'qualified in the Facebook and Tweeters,' but not with actual office work. She didn't even know what Excel was."

I sniggered. Sissy was harmless, though I'd bet she was fibbin' about Facebook and Twitter since she was at least eighty-six years old if she was a day, but she'd been tryin' to get her hands on my behind for years. "Don't you go doggin' Miss Sissy. I can't help that she adores me. I am irresistible. Plus, I always buy the best veggies from her stall at the farmers market."

"Uh huh." Jay rolled his eyes, and he and Jack walked outta the office.

"Well, so, are we hirin' Ms. Bell?" I asked, joggin' to catch up.

"Yeah, I think so. We need someone quick. Jack, whatcha think?"

"I think she'll be fine. Might take her a minute to warm up a bit, get comfortable, but Jay's right. She's qualified, and the paperwork's already pilin' up. We're gonna need someone to do all that stuff soon. I'd like to have her on the job before we go up to Montana for our equine therapy trainin' next month. Since we're goin' in shifts, it'll be really nice for me to have help while you're gone and vice versa."

"I had the same thought," Jay said. "Alright, let's give it the weekend, and then, if we still feel good about it come Monday, I'll give her a call."

"Sounds good," Jack said. "Oh, Finn, before I forget, I want you to work with Aislinn, teach her how to handle the horses."

"What?" My eyeballs popped outta my head. "No. Ain't doin' it. Nope. Nuh uh."

"Yes. She already knows how to ride, but she's used to English saddles. Just get her familiar with Western. She hasn't ridden since her accident."

"Why?" I stomped my foot like a fourteen-year-old girl.

Jack sighed. "Why does everyone question me around here? Because I said so." He turned to walk away, and I followed, whinin'.

"Jack, come *on*. I have to live with her. Why do I have to work with her too?"

"What is your deal? Aislinn's an angel. She wants to learn. She wants to find a way to be useful on the ranch while she's here. She asked for a job, but she doesn't know what she'd be good at. She needs to get comfortable bein' in the barn and bein' around the horses. You're good with people. You got a problem with that? You really that insensitive?"

My jaw dropped to the floor. I was utterly stupefied at my brothers. All of 'em!

How had I become the jerk of the family all of a sudden?

CHAPTER FOUR

AISLINN

"JUST GRAB THE HORN. Hoist yourself up."

Finn held Sammy still for me, guiding my foot into the stirrup of the saddle currently strapped to Sammy's back. I felt the heat from his hand behind me, but he didn't touch me.

"I would grab it if I could see it. I've never ridden Western before. I don't know where the horn is. English saddles don't have them." I hadn't meant for my words to come out in a bite, but they did, and the closer he got, the sharper my teeth.

"I know that, but I thought you at least woulda seen— sorry. Here."

He took my hand gently, guiding it up and to my left, wrapping it around the hard leather protrusion on top of the saddle. "That's the horn. Hold it tight, push up in the stirrup, and throw your leg over. Don't worry," he said, finally touching me tentatively on the small of my back. "I gotcha."

"I'm *not* worried."

He sighed, and I was sure he rolled his eyes. "Ready then?"

Pushing with my left foot in the stirrup, I did what he

said, reaching with my right leg and at the same time trying to feel with it so I didn't throw myself completely off the horse on the other side.

When I was seated, I situated my hips, rolling them to find my center of balance, and Finn wrapped his hand around my thigh to steady me. The saddle felt clunky and cumbersome, and the leather creaked, rubbing against itself with every little move I made. English saddles were much more comfortable.

"See? Western saddles are way comfier than English. It's like your very own La-Z-Boy on top of a horse."

"I don't 'see,' and I don't like it."

Under his breath, he said, "'Course you don't," but his hand still gripped my thigh.

"It's so much wider and heavier than an English saddle."

"There's a reason for that. Western saddles are designed to distribute the rider's weight more evenly over the horse's back. When you ride English, you're usually only ridin' for a short time, for whatever sport you're into. But Western saddles are used for ranchin', leadin' stock out to pasture, workin'. You spend a lot more time on the horse, so you want him to be comfortable for longer periods of time."

He took one step away, his feet shuffling on the floor, and his voice moved a few inches closer to Sammy's head. The warm weight of his hand on my leg disappeared, and he said, "Pick up the reins."

"I don't know where they are."

"You know where they should be. Find 'em."

Finn didn't baby me like everyone else. He expected me to do my part, to figure things out for myself. I acted like it was all beneath me or that I couldn't do a lot of those things without help, but it wasn't that I didn't think I could do them. I was scared. It had been a long time since I'd really lived or tried anything new. I whined and yelled at Theo for sheltering me, but the truth was that I was terrified. Not that I'd ever let Finn know, but I loved that he treated me that way. No one else did, other than Billie sometimes.

It made me nervous, and that was where all the biting came from.

I adored the horses, and Evvie and the guys let me help with grooming and watering, but I really wanted to ride. I had such wonderful memories of riding with my mother when I was young. I remembered feeling so free, and I wanted to feel that way again.

I wanted to feel the way I had before everything changed.

Reaching forward slowly, I found Sammy's mane and felt for his neck, then inched my way around until I located the leather reins, grasping them firmly in my hands and lifting them, but not pulling. I remembered that much from my long-ago riding lessons.

"I haven't ridden since before…"

Before the accident that changed my life completely. Since my parents died. Since I lost my sight and lost myself. It had been ten years.

"That's okay. Western's much easier than English. It won't take long for you to get the hang of it. Alright now, reins in both hands. Sit up straight. Got your right foot in the stirrup?"

"Oh yes." I toed around, feeling for the stirrup, and slipped my foot in. "Okay."

"Heels down. Sit on your pockets."

"What?"

"You know where back pockets are on jeans?"

"Yes."

"Pretend you're a normal person who wears 'em, then sit on 'em."

"I wear jeans," I said, scoffing. "I'm wearing them right now." Couldn't he feel them under his hand?

"I was jokin'."

"Oh. Whatever. Is this good?" Sitting as straight as I could, I tried to sink down into my heels.

"Yep. You got good posture."

"Thank you." What a stupid thing to thank him for, but his closeness made me nervous. I felt his breath caress my arm, and goosebumps broke out all over my body, but it was confusing because I still wanted to kick him.

Finn instructed me on how to aid the horse in the direction I wanted to go. With his hands on mine, he taught me how to hold the reins in different positions, but then he would rest his hand on my thigh again while I practiced.

"Now, remember not to pull. Small movements will do."

"I know."

"Okay. Last thing. Trust Sammy. He knows where he's goin', and he'll do what you tell him. He's very intuitive." He removed his hand from my thigh again, and it tingled where he'd touched. "And Aislinn?"

"Yes?" I said, a little bit breathless from that touch—the only touch a man like him had ever given me.

"Relax."

Before I even had a chance to take a calming breath, he clicked his tongue twice, and Sammy loped forward.

"Oh, fuck!"

Finn made a very unbecoming sound in the back of his throat, laughing at me. "You're fine. Hold the reins straight." He chuckled, walking along beside Sammy and me, and I tried not to smile. I hadn't meant to curse, but I wasn't used to anyone or anything else being in control of my body. I didn't allow most people to touch or guide me. I wanted to do it by myself. But I did trust Sammy and, admittedly, Finn.

"There you go. Feel that sun on your face? You're outside now."

"Yes, and I felt the difference in Sammy's gait."

"Good. Pay attention to things like that. That's how you're gonna know where to go, and Sammy will signal with his body. Listen to him. But if you're ever unsure where you are, tell him, 'Sammy, take us home,' and he will. 'Home' is the barn."

"Okay."

A light wind danced across my skin, probably coming down from the mountain from the strong scent of pine and fir I could detect. I did feel the sun. I knew it was still morning, around nine, but I tried to file away how the sun felt, to catalogue in my memory the location of its heat and the smell outside the barn. I wasn't used to relying on myself, but I was bound and determined to start, and knowing where I was and how to get around by myself was a beginning at least. I wouldn't depend on other people to do it for me ever again.

Sammy slowed, then came to a stop, shifting his weight from his right to left front leg.

"Alright," Finn said. "You're at the paddock gate. The paddock closest to the barn. It's a kind of rectangular shape, but Sammy will walk in a long oval around the edges. Don't be nervous about gettin' lost. It's all enclosed."

"I'm not nervous," I said, trying to feign confidence, but everything I said to him sounded conceited.

"'Course not."

A whistle pierced my ears, startling me, and I jumped in the saddle and Sammy nickered.

"Damn, girl, you look fine on toppa that there pony." It was one of the construction men, but I didn't recognize the voice.

"Shut up, Boyd, you're gonna ruin her concentration."

That had come from James Brockovich, the man who brought me orange sodas every afternoon when I sat on the porch, listening to my audiobooks and to the sounds of everyone working on the ranch. Orange soda was disgusting, too sweet and sticky, but I always accepted.

I smiled at the sound of his voice and heard him return the smile when he said, "Lookin' good, Miss Aislinn. You can do it," like I was five. I scoffed silently. How condescending.

"Yeah, he's a tool," Finn whispered. "Don't worry about them. They won't distract Sammy."

Well, I thought I had been silent.

"Thank you."

Finn's voice moved away from Sammy and me, and the metal gate creaked open. "Okay, off you go."

"Wait, what? You're not coming with me?"

"I am. I won't be far, but you already know how to ride. Listen to Sammy's body. He won't lead you into trouble."

"Finn?"

"Yeah?"

It killed me to admit it to him, but I couldn't stop myself from saying, "I-I'm… afraid."

"Want me to ride with you?"

"N-no." I shook my head. "I want to do it."

He paused, and I felt him staring up at my face, like he was measuring my determination. "Okay then. Nothin' worthwhile ever comes easy."

"Right," I said, faking confidence as much as I could, and I clicked my tongue, nudging Sammy with my heels. He walked forward slowly, as if he could feel my nervousness. He really was the most gentle animal I had ever met. He would get extra apples from me later.

I listened to Sammy's body, like Finn had said. It was difficult to keep count of how many times we walked around the paddock because I couldn't see any landmarks to know where my starting point was, but after a few rounds, I could hear the difference in Finn's voice based on where I was. He gave small encouragements: "Just a smidge to your left," and "Heels down, back straight. Imagine there's a ball between your shoulder blades and you have to keep it up by sittin' as straight as you can, upper arms at your sides. That's perfect."

Sammy's gait was so even, it lulled me almost into a trance. I felt so relaxed.

And strong. Every movement I made told Sammy what I wanted him to do, and he listened to me. He had faith in me, even if no one else did. Even if I didn't.

The men catcalled and whistled, and then James would scold them, but I ignored them, only listening to Sammy and for the sound of Finn's voice. I knew if I could hear Finn, I would be fine.

After a while, I felt so confident, I nudged Sammy into a trot. Finn didn't freak out and yell at me. I heard him coming a little closer, telling me, "Steady," and "Heels down," and "Let your body move with Sammy's."

It was terrifying and it was *exhilarating*. And knowing Finn's eyes were on my body made me feel heady. I felt beautiful from head to toe.

"That's it. You can rely on the saddle a little more, let it do some of the balance work. Relax."

Sammy's trot was fast but even, and I quickly became accustomed to the rhythm. Eventually, I even remembered to post every other stride to avoid the jostling, making riding the trot much more comfortable.

I was so confident, I led Sammy into a canter. *Oh my God*, it was so scary. But I tried to remember to trust Sammy. He hadn't deviated from his oval path the whole time I'd been riding him, so I trusted he wouldn't now. I used my legs more, sinking down into my heels, though it would take a lot more riding for my muscles to become strong enough to withstand the workout. I knew I'd be sore later, but I didn't care.

The feeling was indescribable. Amazing. The wind whipping against my face and being so in tune with an animal like that again after so many years, his hooves pounding the ground beneath me. I felt it in my spine, in my muscles, and in my soul. It felt good, and I let my body rock when Sammy's rolled.

Without thinking, I let go of the reins, using my thighs to hold me up, spreading my arms in the air, feeling that freedom, that *joy*, and seeking more of it… and then fell right off his back. One second I was above Sammy, and the next, I was below him. I heard him jump over me and felt it when he kicked dirt in my face, trying to avoid stomping me to death.

"Shit!" Isaac, the young ranch hand, came running toward me.

Someone else yelled, "Call an ambulance!"

None of the voices yelling were Finn's.

I was a little dizzy, a lot disoriented, but okay. I hadn't hit my head. My butt and shoulder would be bruised later, but other than that, I thought I was fine.

"Goddammit, Finn, what did you do?" That was Jack's extremely angry voice. I'd only heard it once before, but it was easy to recognize.

Multiple people hurried toward me, their heavy boots thudding on the ground, closer and closer, and more dust filled my nose and mouth.

"Aislinn, can you hear me? It's Brock. You okay?"

"I'm fine," I said, but the wind had been knocked out of me, so my voice was weak. I tried to catch my breath, sitting up and listening for Finn.

He never spoke.

"I'm here, Miss Aislinn. You're okay."

"Yes, James. I know."

"Oh, thank God. She's coherent."

Isaac snorted.

My cheeks heated with embarrassment, and I was sure they were red as apples. "Of course I'm coherent."

"Here, I gotcha." James was right above me. "You're okay."

"I said I was fine."

He came closer, leaning down, and he lifted me into his arms, trapping me against his chest. "You're gonna be okay."

"I said I'm *fine*. Put me down. I am not a child."

Standing still, James stopped his chivalrous rescue. "Oh, uh, okay. Sorry."

"Thank you for your help, James, but I'm okay. I'm not hurt. Please, put me down. I would like to walk." I was mortified. Where was Finn? Had he seen me fall? Why hadn't he tried to help me?

James set me on my feet, and after all of that—my big declaration that I was fine—I realized I had no idea where I was. I began to panic when James backed away from me, the starchy detergent smell of his shirt and the heat from his body dissipating, and I was just about to relent and grudgingly ask for his help back to the barn when something wet nudged the back of my arm—Sammy's nose.

Straightening the hem of my shirt around my waist, I took a deep breath and reached up, clutching his mane with my fingers, and said as confidently as I could, "Sammy, take us home."

Everyone quietly backed off, and Sammy led me to the gate and then stood, waiting, while I felt my way forward to unlatch it. I did and found my way back to him, and when we passed through, finally, I heard Finn. He was three feet away from me.

He whispered, "Atta girl," and I smiled the whole way back to Sammy's stall while Finn followed silently behind.

"FINN! Get your ass in the office, now!"

"Shit. Here. Here's your cane. You good?" he whispered, placing my cane in my hand.

"Yes. I'm good."

He touched two fingers to the inside of my wrist, sliding them up my skin when he turned, and then he was gone.

CHAPTER FIVE

FINN

"WHAT THE FUCK WERE YOU THINKIN'?" Jack boomed. "I told you to help her, not try to murder her! What if she'd broken her goddamn neck? Think her brother would still be frontin' us that money? Think, Finn. Why can't you think before you speak and act?"

"I did help her."

"Yeah, right onto her butt," Isaac said, slumpin' into a chair next to me. Smartass.

"She already knows how to ride. You said so yourself. You didn't see her before she fell. She was… magnificent. She and Sammy were one."

Jack sighed, pinchin' the bridge of his nose and collapsin' down into the fancy new desk chair Jay had bought for him. "Isaac, mind your business. Ain't you got somethin' to do? If not, lemme know. Shit needs shovelin'." Jack dropped his hand, threatenin' Isaac with raised eyebrows, and Isaac rolled his eyes but sighed and slunk off to finish his work. "Finn. She is blind. You can't just let her loose on a horse and hope for the best."

I stood my ground. I may not have been the smartest guy on the planet, but I knew people, I knew ridin', and strangely, I thought I knew Ace. "And you can't keep coddlin' her. I was right there the whole time, and you know Sammy can handle it. She's capable, Jack. You don't live with her. You don't see. She's been stuck in her bedroom or a hotel room for years. All she needs is the will to live a little. Once she finds it, she could take on the whole world. And it ain't like I coulda stopped her from droppin' those reins. She didn't ask my permission."

"Did you go to life coach school when I wasn't lookin'?"

"Did you see the monster smile on her face when she walked herself and Sammy back to the barn after she fell?"

"She was smilin'?"

"Yeah. Big. She was proud of herself. The worst happened, and she survived it all on her own." I snorted. "And she told that moron, Brock, off. The guy was all, 'I've got you, baby. I'll save the day,' but she wasn't havin' it. Heh. Classic."

"Well, that's good, I guess. But still, Finn, what you did was dangerous. You never woulda forgiven yourself if she'd been hurt."

I thought about it, and Jack was right. I'd known Ace could handle it, and I knew she could be brave. But no, I wouldn't have been able to forgive myself.

And my heart was still poundin'.

When I walked into the house after evenin' chores, Aislinn was sittin' at the kitchen table by herself, holdin' a baggie filled with ice to her shoulder.

"Hi, Finn."

"It's creepy you know it's me every time."

She laughed. An actual laugh, not a judgy, haughty bark or a condescendin' snort. It stopped me in my tracks. When Aislinn laughed, she was transcendent. Otherworldly beautiful. Her perfect brown skin glowed and crinkled around her eyes, and her face lit up like… maybe she really was an angel.

"Do you have any idea how loud you are?" She giggled a little and shook her head. "You complain about me making noise, but you breathe louder than Tony. And you have big feet. You walk loudly. And I can just tell. I… *feel* it's you. And I can smell you."

Now, I was laughin', tryin' to act like she didn't just say she could "feel" me. I was also tryin' hard not to think about what "feelin'" her would be like. "Well, I won't deny I'm probably pretty stinky after work. Sweat and horses and hay. Maybe not the best combination."

Her cheeks pinked, and she dipped her head a little. "Actually, you smell good."

She said it so softly that I didn't think I was meant to hear, so I didn't acknowledge it, but man, why did that little confession fire me up? "Are you hungry? I, um, I haven't had dinner." Washin' my hands in the sink, I peeked back at her.

"Me either. I'm starving. Where is Tony anyway? He isn't slobbering all over me for once, trying to trip me."

"He's havin' a sleepover at Luuk and Kevin's place. We share custody." Yankin' the fridge open, the condiments clattered in the door, and I quickly remembered I hadn't had time to go to the grocery store yet for the week. The contents of my old Frigidaire were pretty meager, but I had bread. And PB&J. I looked on top of the microwave. Ooo, looky there—

the perfect secret ingredient. "So, what's goin' on with Billie? She and Jay tore outta here after work today in a big ol' hurry."

"Oh, nothing. They went to Jackson to look for furniture for the new house. They invited me to go, but I'm pretty sore." She chuckled a little. "And besides, they need time alone. I'm always tagging along. Plus, they kiss loudly, and they are *always* kissing."

"Don't I know it." Pullin' six pieces of white bread from the bag, I set 'em on a paper towel on the counter, spreadin' the creamy, peanutty goodness on the soft slices. "Like, if they aren't connected at the lips, they'll die."

"What are you making? Smells sweet."

"PB&J."

"Oh."

"That okay?" I turned my head to look at her and my body followed, and I leaned back against the counter, watchin' her.

She shrugged but winced a little with the movement. "Yes. Honestly, I'm so hungry, at this point, anything's fine. Thank you."

"How's your shoulder?"

"It's okay. Just sore. I hadn't ridden in so long, my whole body hurts. I'll have to work up to it, strengthen my quads and core."

"Yeah, it does take some muscle, but you did great. I was impressed."

She smiled. "You were?"

"Yeah." Resumin' my gourmet sandwich preparations, I spread the jam evenly—not too much, not too little—then stepped back, checkin' my work, and bumped into Aislinn 'cause she'd walked up behind me. "Oh, sorry. Didn't hear you." I turned, my hands reachin' for her arms to steady her without my brain givin' the command to do it.

"Why are you being so nice to me?" she asked.

"I'm always nice. You're just usually too irritated to notice." But her question raised one for me. "Why you bein' so nice to me?"

"I-I don't know," she said, but then she stepped forward, closer to me. "I like how you… how you treat me, how you expect things from me. Everywhere I go, people almost trip over themselves trying to cater to me. It makes me feel like a child. Sometimes, it makes me feel like maybe I shouldn't even try to do things for myself. Maybe they know something about me that I don't. Maybe I am incapable."

"That's bullshit. You can do anything you want. You know that. It's written all over your face." I could see it. It was that determination I'd noticed before, radiatin' outta every pore on her beautiful body, peekin' out like the sun tryin' to shine through some heavy storm clouds.

She didn't acknowledge what I'd said, but instead, she whispered, "Today was amazing."

"Yeah," I whispered too. "It really was—*you* were—but I'm sorry you got hurt." Hangin' my head, I closed my eyes. She coulda been *seriously* injured. "Jack's right. It coulda been a helluva lot worse."

"I know, but it wasn't your fault." She didn't move away from me. She stood there with her arms at her sides, lettin' me hold her in place, and it felt like she was lookin' right at me. It was the first time I was glad she couldn't see me 'cause she'd be able to see the shame on my face, but she surprised me by takin' responsibility for her own actions. "It was my fault. I shouldn't have done that. Trotting was enough. Pushing Sammy into a run was foolish. I don't know what came over me."

"I do." I meant to say it in a normal voice, but it was just a breath. She was so close to me, and I was still touchin' her. My big, clumsy, rough hands still held her soft, warm arms. "You felt that freedom. The power. I understand."

"Yes." She tilted her head up to mine, her eyes twinklin' and her warm breath washin' over my face. She had the most mysterious golden flecks in her light green eyes, and against her dark skin, they were arrestin'. They shimmered and winked at me, and I wanted to kiss her so bad.

Steppin' back, I removed my hands from her body. I had to remind myself I couldn't stand her. Plus, if Jack was pissed about a bruised shoulder, he'd kill me for a broken heart.

I cleared my throat with a half-assed attempt at a cough. "Grab the milk. I'll get the glasses."

Pressin' her lips together, she nodded, and I turned away from her. *Shit.* My heart thudded behind my ribs, my dick was hard as a rock, and my lungs felt frozen solid inside my chest. This was not good.

I heard her searchin' through the fridge and the thunk of the door closin', then her chair at the table scrapin' over the linoleum floor. When the construction of our sandwich stacks was finished, I carried 'em over and set a plate in front of her, and she sat forward in her chair with her hands below the table. Her cane lay on top, and her ice pack melted next to it.

"So, um, dig in. This is me and Kev's favorite late-night indulgence."

"Thank you."

Pourin' milk into two glasses, I set one in front of her, then watched as she touched her fingers to the bread.

"Wait. I thought this was a peanut butter and jelly sandwich. Why is it so tall?"

"It's a double decker. That there's the Cadillac of PB&Js.

Organic creamy peanut butter, Miss Sissy Melton's home-made blackberry jam, and one very special ingredient. Try it."

"O-okay." She lifted the sandwich to her lips, testin' the weight a little, turnin' it to try to find the right angle for a bite.

"Just open your mouth and shove it in. Ain't no other way." I groaned internally. *Watch your mouth, you idiot.* And then I couldn't stop imaginin' the very thing I was scoldin' myself for. Oh God. *Cut it out, asshole!*

And then she did what I said and took a big ol' bite, chewin' for a minute, and her face scrunched in confusion.

"What—?" She set the sandwich on her plate and chewed some more. "What is that? What did you put in there?"

"It's good, right? Do you like it?"

"It's delicious. What is it?" She laughed, lickin' the jam from her fingers.

Oh, good grief. I tried to clear the finger-lickin' lust from my throat and wet my lips with my tongue, suddenly feelin' hungrier than I'd ever been, watchin' her reaction with way too much interest, considerin' we were only talkin' about PB&Js. "Chips."

"Chips… potato chips?"

I smiled. Her voice always did this thing when she asked a question, a kinda high-pitched squeak at the end. *Stop thinkin' about her voice, and her fingers, her shoulders, thighs, face, lips… Ugh.*

My voice was a tad shaky when I said, "Yep. Genius, right? The salt from the chips cuts the sugar in the jam, and they make it crunchy, which is always a bonus."

Her eyebrows raised almost off her head, but she kept eatin'. I dug in, too, washin' my simple masterpiece down with a chug of milk, feelin' overly thankful for any distraction at that point.

We ate in silence then, and I watched every single move she made. Her fingers held the bread so carefully. They were elegant and thin, with perfect bare nails, not too short, not too long, and I imagined those fingers wrapped around—I smacked myself upside my own head.

"What was that?"

She lifted her head a little, and I wondered what she would think if she could suddenly see me. Would she like me then? Would she giggle and flirt the way most women did? Sometimes, the shit that came outta their mouths in their attempts to woo me was ridiculous. I felt embarrassed for 'em most of the time. Sure, I flirted back, but only 'cause it was what was expected of me. Who was I if I wasn't good-time Finn?

"Oh, just a mosquito." In late October? *You idiot.*

She ate the whole sandwich, even the crusts. "Thank you. That was really good. I haven't had peanut butter and jelly since I was a kid."

"Oh, well, I am a kid so… But glad you liked it."

"I-I think I'll go to bed. Maybe my shoulder will feel better tomorrow."

"Here." I popped over to the cupboard and grabbed the pain reliever. Holdin' two in my fingers, I said, "Open your hand." She did, and I dropped the pills into it, makin' sure not to touch her again. "It's ibuprofen."

"Thank you." She swallowed 'em down with the last of her milk, then set the glass on the table. "Good night, Finn."

"Night, Ace."

Smilin' a little at the nickname, just a quick twitch of her lips, she reached for her cane, extended it, and made her way to the downstairs bathroom. I watched her go, watched her walk, the sway of her hips, her ass in her jeans. Oh, she wore jeans *well*, but I still imagined pullin' 'em off her long, lithe legs.

Shit. Shit. Shit.

When she was safely locked in the bathroom, I slid down the wall between the kitchen and the livin' room, groanin' and tryin' to ignore the pain in my own jeans, right in the middle, directly behind the zipper.

CHAPTER SIX

AISLINN

MY BED WAS lumpy and uncomfortable. The ache in my shoulder felt better after the ibuprofen Finn had given me, but still, everything was a little sore. I sighed, rolling onto my back, trying to snuggle into a better position.

I couldn't stop remembering Finn's touch this morning. His hand on my thigh. Two fingers to my wrist. What a weird way to touch someone. It was strangely intimate, almost like he'd been feeling for my pulse, but it was softer than that even though his fingers were rough and callused.

And then I remembered his hands on my arms in the kitchen. I wasn't sure why I'd gone to him. I wasn't thinking. My body just carried me there, but he'd pulled away. Of course he had. We couldn't stand each other. I annoyed him and he annoyed me. He probably saw me as an irritating little sister.

I was sure he did. It wasn't like I was nice to him, and Billie kept saying he was gorgeous. He probably had a line of women waiting for him when he was on tour with his band. I could imagine droves of them showing up to his concerts every night. I'd bet he had sex with a new woman after every show.

I couldn't blame the women. I couldn't see him, had no idea what he looked like, but if his voice and scent were anything to go by… And his presence? He was so nice to everyone. He was nice to me even when I screamed at him and treated him like he was a lowly footman and I was Princess of the World. He got mad at me. A lot. But he was always kind. And he was witty and funny and sweet. Maybe that was why he irritated me so much. I was the opposite, and I hated that about myself.

I sighed again. I couldn't stop sighing. But then I heard him upstairs, playing his guitar, and I smiled. I loved when he played. Somehow, the sound relaxed me. I could feel my shoulders easing and my breath slowing when the low, quiet sound wound its way around me in the air. When he played, it was the only time Finn wasn't loud, and sometimes, I could barely hear it at all. He probably did that for me so he wouldn't disturb me. But it didn't bother me; in fact, it was the opposite. Finn's music evoked a strange feeling inside me. It felt like… home. It was pretty, the woody acoustic sound and the slow strum of his fingers across the strings…

Sometimes, it lulled me to sleep, but tonight, when I imagined his fingers on the strings, it woke me up, and then I was really uncomfortable.

But it wasn't the bed or the sheets or blanket, nor the pillow. They weren't the twelve-million thread count I was used to, but it wasn't them keeping me up. It wasn't the old silent house or the trees creaking outside, and it wasn't the perfect cool night air sneaking in the window, caressing my heated body.

No, the angst came from inside me. I was uncomfortable in my own skin, and I wanted to break out of it. I wanted to jump out of bed and run free and wild, playing and laughing and living, like I had this morning.

But I didn't know how. And now, there were so many limitations for me. Every time I imagined myself trying something new, I became angry because something or someone always stopped me.

Maybe if I asked him, Finn could help me. He knew how to live, to have fun. To be alive. And he wasn't so careful with me, not like everyone else. Like my brother. Like my parents had been. Even before I lost my sight, they'd treated me like precious glass. Theo had been the golden child with perfect grades and perfect behavior, and even though I never compared, in their eyes, I could do no wrong. I was spoiled and pampered and I had reveled in it, soaked it up like the brat I had been. The brat I still was.

Finn didn't treat me like that. Not once, since the first day we'd met. He'd let me go today, let me make my own mistakes. He was there in the background in case I needed him, but he didn't force his help on me.

He trusted me and he expected things from me.

When he played faster above me, my breath quickened to the tempo.

Imagining it was Finn's fingers, I touched the skin between my shorts and shirt and gasped, then laughed at myself, feeling silly. He would never want me like that. I'd made sure of it with the condescending way I treated him.

But what if Finn had touched me like that? What would it feel like? Pushing my silk nightshirt up, I caressed the skin below my breasts, feeling embarrassed and maybe a little ashamed about wanting to touch myself with him in the house, but when I imagined Finn lying next to me, his fingers warm and his voice a quiet rumble, caressing my skin, that shame fell away.

Holding my breast in my hand, I rolled my nipple with my thumb and finger pressing hard, wishing I could feel Finn's tongue there. His wet mouth. The hum of his voice against the sensitive bud, peaking it when he licked and sucked.

Imagining his hair brushing across my skin, the sound of his breathing, his body sliding over mine to kiss me, and his tongue slipping over mine, our saliva mixing together, I groaned, rolling my nipple harder.

I didn't know what his body looked like, but I could imagine what it would feel like against mine. Hard and sturdy from all his hours of rough ranch work, his skin would be warm over the dense muscle underneath.

He'd seen me naked, and every single time he was near, I wondered if he remembered. I wondered if he liked what he saw.

He hadn't been wearing a shirt that day in the bathroom, and when he'd pulled me up, my hands had landed on his chest. I could still feel it, slick under my wet skin. His chest hair had been coarse under my fingers, but the defined muscles underneath were smooth, and when my hands slid lower to push him away, his hard stomach muscles had tensed and released.

In the moment, I imagined sliding my hands lower, beneath his sweatpants.

I'd never admit it to him—to anyone—but I wanted to touch him again. Sometimes, my hands ached to touch him. It was an odd feeling, and when he was close, I found myself having to work to keep my hands from reaching for him.

I'd never really paid attention to men's bodies before I lost my sight, and now the only references I had were from books. I wanted so badly to know what Finn would feel like under my fingers. What his angles and edges felt like and where he was soft. Was he ticklish? I wanted to make him laugh and squirm. But if I ever had the chance, I'd work my way slowly from his stomach to his cock, and his laughter would turn to heavy breathing, and he would moan.

I wanted to know what it would feel like to turn Finn on. To be the reason he was hard.

Pushing my other hand underneath my sleep shorts, I slid one finger between my thighs and sighed loudly. There was no resistance. I was soaking wet just imagining him touching me, imagining touching him. Tentatively, I rubbed, trying to visualize Finn's fingers creating the friction, his long, callused, strong fingers. It was wasted effort—I couldn't "see" it—but I could feel it. I rubbed harder and faster, whimpering because it felt so good.

I'd only had sex a few times back in high school, before everything… But I knew, with Finn, it would be so much better than little Taylor Hornsby fumbling around down there. No, with Finn, it would be erotic and so… *so satisfying*.

He was experienced. He'd know how to make me come alive. I hadn't felt sexual attraction to anyone since my accident. The only action I got was from my romance audiobooks, and that was all imagined. Wolf-shifters were hot, what could I say?

I felt that burn, the signal from the outside of my body to the inside, the rush from my clit, telling me to let go. I tried. Listening to Finn play his guitar, I tried to imagine what he would feel like moving inside me and slipped two fingers deep inside myself. My body was slick and hot, and with the sounds of his playing above me, I was tensed and ready to come.

"Ohh." *Oh God, that was loud.*

The guitar stopped. Had he heard me?

No. It was impossible.

But maybe I wanted him to.

Sliding my fingers in and out, again and again, I rubbed faster, harder, rocking against my own hand, and there was movement above me—just a step, then slowly another.

Oh. I was so close, and I panted and gasped for air. Spreading my legs and kicking the blanket down, I sucked my finger into my mouth, coating it with saliva, then trailed it slowly down my body and rubbed my clit with the wet fingers of one hand while fucking myself with the other. I was getting wetter by the second, and my body squeezed in on itself, desperate to be filled, to be broken open, and to release.

Another step. His bedroom door squeaked open, and I imagined him descending the stairs to come to me.

I laughed. I couldn't stop the sound, and it was breathy and needy and wanting.

But now he *was* descending the stairs. I heard the old wood creak and crack with his steps, and I fucked myself so hard that my hand cramped.

The thought that no one knew this side of me urged me on. Not even Billie—the best friend I'd ever had who knew me better than even my brother—would ever guess that I could be so uninhibited, even if it was only in my thoughts and imagination. My cheeks heated when I thought about anyone finding out.

But I didn't stop.

"Oh yes." My hips lifted off the bed to meet my hand and, rubbing harder still, I imagined Finn entering my room, ripping the sheets away, and covering my naked body with his. I imagined what he would feel like, hovering above me, his warmth, his flexed abdomen, his cock, hard and hot between my thighs…

And then he would kiss me, begging me to kiss him back,

his smooth tongue searching my mouth, and he'd thrust his cock inside my body with one punch of his hips. He would moan into my mouth and drown in my taste…

I cried out, loudly, and came so hard, I felt dizzy.

There was a soft knock on my bedroom door, and even though I'd heard him moving around, the surprise of the noise made my head spin harder. And maybe it was embarrassment too.

"Aislinn? You… okay?"

My lips were dry from the breath rushing past them over and over, and I licked them. I was breathless. "Yes."

I didn't move, didn't pull the blankets back up. No one else was in the house with us. If he opened the door, I wanted him to see me like this, undone on the bed beneath his bedroom with my fingers between my legs, wet with my own cum. I wanted him to want me.

"You sure? I thought I heard…"

But I didn't have the guts to tell him to open the door.

"I'm sure. I-I rolled onto my shoulder. It hurt, but I'm… fine."

I heard his hand on the doorknob and thought I could hear the rustle of him pressing his big body against the door, and my heart raced.

"Okay." There was silence for twelve seconds. I counted. "You sure?"

"Yes."

"Night then."

"Good night."

Oh.

CHAPTER SEVEN

FINN

'COURSE I JACKED off to thoughts of Aislinn. I mean, honestly, it wasn't nothin' new. Yeah, she could be a regular royal pain in my ass, but goddamn, she was beautiful. And now, I'd touched her. Not just to lead her from one room to another or down the lawn to the barn, but I'd wrapped my hands around her arms in the kitchen, and my fingers had gripped her thigh earlier in the barn.

Fuck, her thighs were perfect. They were soft and warm, and I pictured 'em wrapped around my hips, the heat from her pussy inches away from my dick. I couldn't think of a good enough word to describe Ace's thighs. Svelte was the only one to come to mind, even though I wasn't sure what it meant and wouldn't bother lookin' it up in a dictionary 'cause I probably wouldn't understand it anyway.

She pranced around at night in these sweet little silk night shorts, and it was a damn good thing she couldn't see me 'cause all I'd been able to do since she'd moved into my house was stare at her thighs. Her ass was tight and round, and good goddamn, what I wouldn't give to have those juicy cheeks in my hands. Was it pervy that all I could think about was rubbin' my hard-on between 'em? I wouldn't even need to fuck her. I could just rub myself off between her thighs.

Unghhh. Yeah, that was enough to get me hard as wood. Unfortunately, made-up fantasies were all I had to go by, but I wanted her. I imagined pushin' up into her wet heat, and my eyes crossed in imagined pleasure. *Oh yeah*, and the soft, slow glide of my cock in and outta—

It was automatic when I grabbed my dick and pumped. I'd sworn I'd heard her cry out a few minutes ago like somethin' was wrong, but it was different than that. More than that. My sex-obsessed brain turned it into somethin' sexier than that—more obscene that that—and I imagined her below me, makin' herself come with her own fingers, and I had to go to her. There had been no decision to do it, and I was descendin' the stairs before I'd even known what the fuck I was doin'.

Spittin' in my hand, I fucked my fist faster, thinkin' about her openin' those long legs for me, thinkin' about what her face would look like when she came. I wondered what sex would feel like to her, how different it would be for her without sight. Would that make it different than it was for other people? Maybe it would be better because, since she couldn't see, she'd feel it more.

She'd feel me more.

She'd feel my face, my shoulders, my stomach, rub her hands down my legs and back up so slowly. Would she cup my balls in her soft hands? Would she grip my dick like I was now? Would she suck my cock in her mouth, between her plump lips, and tease me with her tongue? Oh fuck, I'd die if she did. I was about to pass out now as it was, 'cause just thinkin' about the possibility was so damn erotic, I could barely hold back from jizzin' all over myself.

My whole body strained, and I was sweatin' in my sheets when my imagination took me back between her legs. Would she let me eat her out? I'd give anything I had to taste her, her soft lips and the cum that would soak 'em. I'd swallow it down when I made her come with my tongue deep inside her, or my fingers while I kissed her, my tongue plunderin' her mouth like I was a fuckin' pirate.

Oh yeah, that image hit the spot like a Mack truck, and I twisted my own balls in my hand, jerkin' myself off still with the other. And then I imagined her makin' that noise again, that soft cry. Then I'd really get busy when I pounded my cock in her—

"Ohughhh!"

Shit. That was loud.

And hot.

And fuck, I came all over myself like a garden hose that got loose, sprayin' everywhere. Good thing I slept naked.

I really needed to stop thinkin' about masturbation. I swore, everytime I did, I got caught. Case in point: "Cadence! Hi, baby girl." My tiny friend appeared in front of me in my kitchen, and I patted her head while I set my spatula on the counter. "How ya doin'? How's school goin'?"

She shrugged and I smiled. Cadence was smart as a whip, but she hated school.

"Your daddy outside with Jack?" Mr. Williams brought Cadence out to visit our horses at least once a week, and she was my favorite visitor.

She nodded.

"Well, you hungry? I made black cherry pancakes this mornin'. Wait, why you here on a Sunday? You usually visit after school."

She shrugged again. Cadence wasn't much of a talker, but

finally, she sat at my table, and in the smallest voice, she asked, "Who's that lady on the porch?"

"Oh, that's Ace. Wanna meet her?"

Cadence didn't answer, just looked up me kinda sheepishly.

"You know how you and me are a little bit different than other people?"

She nodded.

"Well, Ace is different too. She's visually impaired."

She scrunched her eyebrows, thinkin' for a minute. "Does that mean blind? She can't see?"

"Nope, at least, not like you and I do."

Cadence looked toward the kitchen door.

"C'mon, lemme introduce ya."

She followed me out to the porch silently, but when we stood in front of Ace, Cadence stared at her.

"Ace, I'd like to introduce you to my friend, Cadence."

Ace didn't say anything, but she turned her body toward the sound of my voice. She wasn't wearin' her sunglasses, and her eyes in the mornin' sun were breathtakin'. They were as bright green as a piece of sea glass on the beach. I shoulda been used to 'em by now, but every damn time those eyes met mine, I was shocked again. They were just so fuckin' beautiful, and outside with the sunshine makin' her brown skin glow, I was mesmerized.

Cadence stepped forward. "You have pretty eyes," she said to Ace.

"Thank you."

"Do they hurt?"

"Does what hurt?"

"Your eyes. Because they're broken."

For a minute, Ace said nothin'. But then, "No. Not

anymore. They used to, when I first lost my sight, because I was in a car accident, and I had a lot of head injuries."

"I'm sorry," Cadence said.

She looked sad for Ace, and Ace surprised me when she spoke again. "Thank you, Cadence, but you don't have to feel sad for me. I'm okay. I healed, and even though I can't see anymore, I was lucky."

Cadence blurted, "I have autism."

"You do?"

"Yes, but I'm lucky, too, 'cause it makes me really smart, and it makes me have lots of good ideas. Sometimes I don't like it because people make me uncomfortable, but lots of times, I don't mind."

I'd never heard Cadence say so much. I was proud of her for openin' up to a stranger like that, and I kinda felt proud of Ace too. There was no hint of Miss Hoity-Toity Pants anywhere. She was just Ace.

"I'm gonna finish the pancakes. You girls hang out, and I'll let you know when they're ready."

Neither one responded to me. Cadence sat in the chair next to Ace's, and I listened a minute more once I was inside.

"How did you go to school if you couldn't see?"

"I didn't. I did school from home on a computer. My brother helped me. But I was lucky there, too, because I was able to finish high school early, and the rest of my friends still had months to go."

"That is lucky. I hate school."

"How come?"

"People. The teachers always want me to talk, and I don't like that. I get anxiety and it makes me feel bad."

"Oh, well, I understand that. But is there anything you do like about school? I liked reading. My teacher always assigned books to read, and then I'd have to write a book report after, and I loved it."

"I like reading too. My favorite is when there's a mystery. My daddy gets me Nancy Drew books from the library. Have you ever read them?"

Ace laughed a little. "I have. I loved them too."

"You have? Which one is your favorite?"

"Oh, I don't remember, it's been so long…"

They kept talkin', and I went back to my pancakes, thinkin' about what Ace woulda been like at Cadence's age. She lived such a different life than I did, and her upbringin' had probably been worlds apart from mine, but I could picture her as a ten-year-old curled up on a couch somewhere in Boston with a book. I wondered if her hair was short back then, too, or if she wore it in long braids or ponytails.

She listened to audiobooks now, and she always had a set of earbuds in her ears. Sometimes, I wondered what she was listenin' to 'cause she stiffened and clicked her books off when she realized I was in the room with her. Maybe my presence ruined her concentration, or maybe she was listenin' to some cheesy romance books—hot cowboys gone wild… Or no, she'd probably be into stories about bankers or gazillionaires with French accents and Ferraris and yachts. Billionaires gone wild? Yeah, probably somethin' like that.

It was no wonder why we didn't get along. We were too different. I was silly and goofy—never had a straight face— and she was as serious and intense as they came. She probably thought I was a clown. It was the mask I'd chosen to wear my whole life. I'd kinda had to, but it was partly my personality too. I'd never been much for sulkin'.

Things around here had been hard, and everybody struggled when our mama left us and when our Granny and Uncle Jon died. My dad was a wreck, and he changed into a stranger. He'd never been the most sensitive guy, but he turned into a big dick. Some father. He didn't care that I practically failed my way through school. As long as I was here on the ranch to cook and work for him, he was happy. Or, well, that was probably wrong. Nothin' made the guy happy, but he got what he wanted.

And me bein' shit at school meant I could work more if I wasn't busy doin' homework or involved in sports. It meant I was here to cook him dinner every night and prepare lunches for the next day. It meant I was here to clean the house, sweep the barn, do the grocery shoppin'. I got sick of that shit real quick, and in protest, I hadn't cleaned my bedroom for years.

It was stupid. He was dead and didn't have an opinion anymore, and bein' a slob was only causin' me strife, but it was the principle of the thing.

When I set my scrumptious pancakes on the dinin' table and called everybody in to eat, Ace smiled at me when Cadence led her inside. She did that sometimes, and I wondered if she realized she was doin' it. And I wondered if she could hear my sharp intake of breath every time 'cause when she was open like that and her whole face brightened like the sun, she made me weak in my knees.

But Cadence noticed this time, and she looked back and forth between Ace and me, then smiled an itty-bitty smile, and I made a silly face and stuck my tongue out to distract her. Hopefully, it was enough and she wouldn't mention to Ace that she'd caught me eyein' her.

Again.

"Mama? You there?"

The sound of my mama's hair rustlin' against her cell phone filled my ear. "Hi, Finnie. How're you? What's up?"

I sat back in my computer chair in my bedroom and kicked a pile of dirty clothes away from my feet. "I'm good. Everything's good. How 'bout you? You busy right now? Got a minute to talk?"

"I'm never too busy for you, chitterbug."

Ugh. I hadn't heard that nickname in over twenty years, and I wasn't thrilled to hear it now.

"I'm great. I just bought myself a new car. Well, new to me, anyway, and I think I'm ready to move out of the room above the diner."

"Oh, well, that's big news. Congrats. But where you movin' to? You ain't leavin' Wisper, are you?" It occurred to me after I'd said it that I sounded like a five-year-old kid, worryin' about his mama leavin' him, but, like, that was par for the course with her.

But she was still my mama, and I still wanted her in my life now that we'd finally gotten her back. Sittin' up a little straighter, I realized her answer was a lot more important to me than I might've thought.

"No, honey. I'm staying in Wisper," she said, and my shoulders dropped a little, and I relaxed, leanin' back in my chair. "Actually, I wanted to talk to you boys about it. I'm moving in with a roommate, and I wanted to make sure it would be okay with you."

"Why wouldn't it be okay? Wait—who's the roommate?"

"Um, it's… José."

"You're movin' in with José? Like as friends and co-workers, right?"

"Well, now, no. As lovers."

"Ughhh. Don't ever say that word again. And when did this happen? I mean, like, you're datin' him?"

"Yes. We're in a relationship, but I've been afraid to tell you. I know it was hard for you and your brothers to hear about the man I was with when I was overseas, and I wasn't sure how to broach the subject. Are you angry?"

"No, Mama. That wasn't about you datin' a man or livin' with him. It was about you leavin' us. But that's in the past. We know why you left, and José's a good guy. But isn't it kinda soon?"

"Well, not really. I've been back now for almost a year, and I've worked for José the whole time. We've really gotten to know each other. He actually asked me to marry him, but it is too soon for that. But I love him, Finn, and I think we'll be good together."

"He asked you to marry him? Seriously?"

"Yes, seriously. What's wrong with that?"

"Nothin', it's just, you're my mama. It sounds weird. Why do you need to get married?"

"Finn, I'm a woman, too, not just your mama. I'm in a good place in my life, I'm happy, and I still want things. I want love. Sex. I want a life."

"Oh *lawd*, Mama. Don't say that word either. But I thought you had a life. I mean, we're all gettin' along, me and the guys and you. We ain't enough?"

"Of course you are, and I love being in your lives again. It's all I've dreamt of for the last twenty years. But now that I'm back and we're working through it all, I'm realizing I still want the things I wanted when I was a young woman. That's all. It won't affect my relationship with you. Do you believe me?"

"Yeah, well, I mean, I guess I do." I thought for a minute, wonderin' how in the world she could be so certain. All the decisions she'd made in the past were bad ones. What convinced her now she was makin' a good one? "But how do you know?"

"How do I know what?"

"I mean, how do you know you'll be good together? You probably thought that about Dad, but look how that turned out. He was an asshole. So did you know that goin' in, or did he change?"

"He changed. I suppose we both did, but there was a time when we were deeply in love. But running the ranch and fatherhood made him into a different man. We were so young when we married, though, and I think that was our first problem."

"So then, how do you know José won't change, too, or that you won't take off again if things don't go your way?" I kinda felt like a dick askin' that question, but I really wanted to know.

"Oh, honey, it's completely different. José is nothing like your dad was, and *I'm* different. I'm not the same woman I was back then. I know myself better now, you know?"

"No. I don't get it. I know myself. I've always known myself. I'm Finn. Just Finn. No more, no less. So how come I can't figure this shit out for myself?"

"Figure what out?"

"You know, like, if a… a relationship will work. If I should go all in. If I won't end up with my damn heart in my hands, bleedin' and broken. I need to know. You're doin' a shit job of explainin', Mama."

She chuckled. "There's no guarantee, baby. You just have to take the chance if you love the person. If it's not right, you'll know. It's how you deal with it that makes the difference." Mama cleared her throat. "So, may I ask, who are we talking about?"

"Oh, uh, that don't matter."

"Finn, you can tell me. You can talk to me."

"Yeah, but that's still a little weird, to be honest, and, well, it ain't common knowledge yet. I mean, I'm not actually in a relationship. I was just wonderin', is all."

"So, you're interested in a woman, but it's new and your brothers don't know?"

How the fuck did she get all that from "I was just wonderin"? "Uh, definitely not, and they can't." Under my breath, I said, "Jack would kick my ass six ways to Sunday if he knew I was even thinkin' in this direction."

"What'd you say?"

"Nothin'. Nevermind all that. So, when's the big move? Are you movin' into José's house, or are you guys gettin' a new place?"

"Oh, well, we'll probably just move into José's house at first. He has a little two-bedroom over on First Street. It's a little—well, it could use a bit of TLC. A woman's touch. He's lived alone his entire adult life, so it's like a shrine to chili and beer." Mama laughed. "But it's cozy, and I don't have a lot of stuff, so it's the perfect size for the two of us."

"A two bedroom? So you can have your own room?"

She laughed under her breath. "No, Finn. We'll share a bedroom because we—"

"No! Nope. Please, for the love of God, don't finish that sentence. I get it. It makes me wanna hurl, but I get it."

"Sweetie, if you love someone and they love you, then take the chance. Yes, it can end up hurting you, but it could also be the best decision you ever make. If you don't try, you'll always wonder. And you're smart, Finnie. I think you know what's best for you. Trust yourself. You've always known who you are, from the moment you were born."

"Well, duh, Mama," I boasted, smilin', tryin' to hide the wince in my voice when she said I was smart, 'cause she'd left when I was still little, so she didn't know I wasn't smart. "'Course I did, 'cause I'm Finn Cade. Ain't nobody better." No point in tellin' her now. It wasn't like she could help me with my homework anymore.

"No, there ain't," my mama agreed, chucklin' again. "There never was and never will be. Whoever this woman is, she's a lucky one."

CHAPTER EIGHT

AISLINN

"AFTERNOON, MISS AISLINN. BROUGHT YOU A POP," Brock said, and a can of what I could only assume was orange soda clunked on the porch railing. "How you doin' today?"

"I'm fine, thank you." I clicked my audiobook off and took a deep breath, inhaling the fresh mountain air. The afternoon sun was bliss on my face, and someone was burning leaves nearby, the smell a direct, grounding connection to the land around me.

"You're not sore after yesterday? Girl, you really took a tumble."

"A little sore," I said, feeling uncomfortable because there was no noise just then. No horse whinnies, no hammers hammering. There was just quiet, still, fall air around us.

"Oh, well, I'm sorry about after. I didn't know about the etiquette."

"Etiquette?"

"Yeah. I looked it up online. I didn't know I wasn't s'posed to touch you."

"You didn't know that?"

"Yeah, I mean, 'cause you're visually impaired or, I mean, um, blind. I didn't know they don't like that."

"No, James." I rolled my eyes, but he couldn't see it because I'd put my sunglasses on. I always put them on when I heard his boots stomping and bumbling toward me. *"They don't."* I wondered if he could hear the condescension in my use of his first name. Everyone else called him Brock, but that was too intimate. I didn't want to be intimate with him even though he tried to be that way with me every time we spoke. He was trying to create a connection where there was none.

He didn't seem to hear the ire in my voice, though, and he was trying to be kind. I knew that, and I felt bad for my reaction.

"I won't do that again, unless I ask first."

"Ready to hit the road, Ace?" Billie interrupted, and the screen door creaked when she opened it. She stepped onto the porch, and I could tell she was investigating James, probably giving him the evil eye. Oh, my best friend and protector. I'd never had a friend like her, so bold and unapologetic, and I hoped I'd never have to live without her. She yelled into the kitchen. "Evvie, get your butt moving!"

Evvie's voice rang out from the downstairs bathroom. "I'm coming. Jeez."

"I'm ready." I stood, dusting off my pants. I was wearing my favorite silk wide-leg palazzos with a tank top and a long large-knit sweater. All designer. All bought by Theo. "Wait. I want to change."

"Oh my God," Billie complained. "Okay, but hurry up."

Handing her my phone and earbuds, I side-stepped past her still standing in the doorway while she interrogated James.

"Who are you?"

"Uh, I'm Brock. James Brockovich, but everybody calls me Brock."

"Hm. This for Ace?"

"Yeah. I bring her a pop from my lunch every day."

"Nice." Billie popped the top on the soda can and glugged soda down her throat loudly. "Yuck. It's so sweet."

I closed my door silently, smiling. Leave it to Billie. James would probably never bring me soda again. *Thank you, Billie.* He was trying to be sweet, I knew, but I hated soda. I never drank it. And if he thought of all visually impaired people as "they," well, we would have some fundamental differences to overcome.

Besides, I wasn't attracted to him. His energy was nervous, like mine, and when he was around, I was never at ease. I felt like he was always staring at me, and his voice was rough, but not in a good way. It was a jagged sound. It wasn't soothing. Not like…

Evvie had helped me organize my clothing into an old, clunky wooden dresser in the downstairs bedroom. I'd been living out of my suitcases, and this was much easier. The cedar smell was something I'd had to get used to at first, but I didn't mind it anymore. And Oly had given me little sachets of coconut essence and sea salt to put in them.

Evvie was doing my laundry, but she said she'd teach me how to do it myself. I'd never been made to do chores as a child, and then Theo or our staff had done it for me after the accident. Louise, my maid and cook, had been frustrated with me before she'd died, because I couldn't do these simple tasks, but it was more like I refused to do them. She'd threatened many times to stop doing my laundry so I'd be forced to figure it out, but she never did, and I barely remembered what a washing machine looked like. I had this memory of an old movie they'd made us watch in middle school of a frontier woman washing clothes in river water and rubbing them on some kind of board to get the dirt out, and that was what I thought of when I tried to picture doing laundry. So, obviously, I'd need help to learn now, especially with some of my clothes that couldn't be dried in the dryer or needed to be hand washed—which was most of them—but I wasn't looking for them now.

Tonight, I wanted to look like everyone else.

Finding the jeans Billie had picked out for me with holes she'd said were "artfully shredded" in horizontal strips down the front of the legs, I changed into them, then dug through another drawer, looking for a T-shirt. I found a stack of them in the second drawer and lifted the one on top, but they were all adorned with logos and band names. Evvie had lent me a few to wear when I helped in the barn, but besides the coarser feeling of the cotton, so different from my designer silks, I had no idea which was which.

Evvie called through the door. "Aislinn, want some help?"

"Yes, please."

My door creaked open. "Oh, you look good."

"Thanks, but which shirt is this?" I held the T-shirt in front of my chest, feeling the neck with the pads of my fingers for the print on the tagless tag, making sure I was showing her the front.

"Uh, I think it says Meshuggah. I'm pretty sure that's, like, a hard metal band. It's a black shirt with white and red writing. The picture's kind of disturbing, actually."

"Oh, it must be Billie's. Can you find me a different one please?"

"Sure," she said, and I heard her rifling through the drawer. "Oh." She laughed. "You don't want this one. It's Finn's. I don't know how it got in here."

"What does it say?"

"It says, 'fuck,' but the 'u' is a pound sign. And on the back it says, 'Sorry, Ma.' It was a joke. I bought them last year for all the guys because Ma was always yelling at them for cussing."

"I'll wear that." I tossed the shirt in my hands toward Evvie. "What color is it?"

"It's heather gray with black letters," she said, bending to pick up my shirt from the floor in front of her like she was my maid. Damn it. I was a bitch without even having to try.

"Sorry," I said, and she handed Finn's shirt to me. I rubbed the thin, well-worn material between my fingers, and I wanted to bury my nose in the fabric to see if the shirt smelled like him. "Wait. Finn won't be offended if I wear it, will he?"

"Offended? No. It'll be pretty big on you though."

"That's okay. But, I mean, it won't upset him? I've heard them talk about Ma. She was their grandmother, right?" I pulled the shirt over my head and tied the side into a knot on my hip. Evvie wasn't weird about me changing in front of her. I wasn't really shy. I'd always been confident about my body before the accident, and now, what did it matter? I wasn't sure why I was shy in front of Finn. When he saw me in the bathroom that day, I was mortified, but maybe that had more to do with him seeing me helpless than it was to do with my body.

"Kind of. Kind of like a mom too. They weren't actually related, but she took care of them. No, Finn won't be upset if you wear his shirt."

"Okay, good," I said, leaning over to find my sweater on the bed. I didn't want to wear any of my old clothes, but the sweater was warm but not too hot, and it really was perfect for October in Wyoming with the big knitted holes. Finn's flannel shirt was hanging in the far back of the little closet in the corner of my room, and it would probably look better with my outfit and keep me warm, but I didn't want anyone to know I'd kept it. "Where are we going again?"

"We're going for an early dinner in Jackson, and then Oly's meeting us after she gets off work to get mani/pedis. Then we're going to Manny's Bar."

"Okay. I'm ready."

We walked out to the porch, and Billie offered me her arm. I took it. I always accepted her help because I trusted her. She led me down the porch steps, handing my phone and my sunglasses back to me, and Evvie followed.

"Bye, Brockie," Billie called over her shoulder, then whispered to me, "Oh boy, Ace. That guy has it bad for you. Here, wave to him." She grabbed my hand, trying to make me wave like a schoolgirl.

"No. Billie!" I whispered, digging my nails into her arm.

"Fine. I will. See you later, Brockie."

"Bye now. You girls have fun."

I scoffed. "He speaks to me like I'm a child."

"In case you can't tell, I'm rolling my eyes at you," Billie said, exasperated with me.

"What? I'm tired of people treating me like I'm five."

Billie opened the passenger door for me. "Two steps straight ahead."

"Thanks."

Evvie sat behind me. "Uh, yeah, I'm pretty sure Brock is quite aware you're *not* five. He looks at you like you're a popsicle and we're in a heat wave."

"He does?"

Evvie laughed. "Oh, yeah."

Billie opened her door, and I heard smooching. I rolled my eyes behind my sunglasses. "Hi, Jay."

"Hey, Ace. Alright, I got some stuff to finish up, but I'll meet you in a bit."

"'Kay. Love you," Billie told him. She'd become as sweet as James's orange soda. But only to Jay. To everyone else, she was still the sarcastic smart mouth I'd claimed as my best friend.

"Love you too," Jay said, and I heard a smack and was pretty sure he was grabbing her ass.

"You two are worse than me and Jack," Evvie said.

"Whatever," Billie snapped. She was embarrassed.

"Jay's coming with us to the salon?" I asked when she shut her door and started the engine.

"No, he's meeting us at Manny's later. All the guys are. I doubt Oly and Dean will stay long though. She said she'll be too tired after working all day. Man, I can't even imagine trying to grow one human, let alone two."

The SUV bounced and jerked when Billie drove onto the gravel lane, and I realized that the pop and crackle under tires had become one of my favorite sounds. It made me feel safe.

"Finn's going too?" I asked, trying my hardest to sound uninterested.

"Uh, yep, Finn'll definitely be there. He's playing tonight."

My heart dropped into my stomach, and Billie whooped out her window, honking the horn, and the construction workers called back, whistling and some yelling, "See you tonight!"

"Okay," she said, "Ladies' Night has officially arrived. Let the crying begin!"

"I don't know about this," I said when Billie parked the Jeep.

We'd gone for pizza in "the city." I didn't usually care for pizza, but the place we went to in downtown Jackson, Wyoming had several vegetarian options, and it was delicious. I still felt full because I'd eaten three slices. Then we got manicures and pedicures. I'd been worried since you had to let people touch you to get mani/pedis, but the woman who had done mine was gentle and soft-spoken. She asked all kinds of questions about Boston, and I found myself eager to answer them.

When Billie turned off the engine, I could already hear the live music inside Manny's Bar.

"Why not? It'll be fun." She opened my door, waiting for me to step out.

"For you. For me, it's going to be too loud. And people will be brushing up against me. I won't like it. And aren't we late? They're already playing."

"We're only a few minutes late, and I'll be your bodyguard," Billie said. "Besides, Jay and his brothers are here to watch Finn. I say, let some creeper try to put the moves on you. He'll be flat on his ass in no time. Oh, here. I got you these earplugs. They won't cut the sound completely, but they'll soften it if it bugs you."

"Great, just one more thing for people to notice about me." I turned in my seat, dropping my feet to the pavement, and stood. Adjusting my jeans, I smoothed my hands down my thighs, slipping Billie's ear plugs into my front pocket when she tucked the tiny box into my hand. "Thanks."

"Ace, I'm not sure you understand just how hot you are. Yeah, they'll notice your cane when you use it, but it won't be what they're looking at."

I scoffed. "Whatever."

"Quit feeling sorry for yourself."

Evvie clicked her tongue. "Billie."

But I liked that Billie didn't hold back with me. I liked that she wanted me to be like everyone else. She expected me to be a strong, independent woman. I wanted that, too, so when she challenged me, it reminded me to stop acting like a jerk.

"Okay, ladies, let's get this over with," Oly said when she pulled into the parking lot behind Billie's Jeep and climbed out of her loud truck. "I've got a date with my pillow, and now that my feet have been pampered, Dean will massage them, which will lead to other things. God, you'd think this big ol' beachball on my stomach was the hottest thing since sliced bread. He can't keep his hands off me lately."

Evvie laughed. "Hold on, Oly. Ace is nervous. But Billie's right. You look amazing. That shirt is really cute on you. The way you tied it into a knot on the side shows off your butt. If you take your sweater off, I guarantee they won't be looking at your cane." She giggled. "And your makeup looks professional. You did a good job, Billie."

"I know," Billie said, and I was sure she rolled her eyes. Evvie laughed again at Billie's overconfidence, but it was the thing we all liked most about her. It was how I used to be, and how I aspired to be again. Maybe not overconfident, just not underconfident.

Fake it till you make it, right? "I'm not nervous."

"You look like a famous person, Aislinn," Evvie said, trying to be supportive, "like an edgy supermodel. But if you really don't want to go in, we can do something else."

"N-no. I want to. I hear Finn playing his guitar at night, but I've never heard him sing. I would like to."

There was a ten second lull, and none of them spoke.

"What?" I fidgeted with the hem of my shirt. No one moved or made noise, and I couldn't read their energies.

"Nothin'," Oly finally said. "C'mon. Let's do this. We got

your back. Besides, I already have to pee again." She bounced left, right, left, on the hard pavement, her voice weaving back and forth around me.

I took a deep breath, cursing myself inside for agreeing to this girls' night. I hadn't been so nervous since—scratch that. I'd *never* been this nervous. "Fine."

The cacophony inside the bar assaulted my ears at first. I was tempted to use the ear plugs but decided against it. Wasn't I the one saying I wanted to live? What was a little noise? Except, it was confusing. There were so many sounds and smells.

I held onto Billie's sleeve, following closely behind her, and Evvie was behind me. Oly disappeared as soon as we entered the small bar, to the restroom, I assumed. I could tell it was small because the sounds bounced off the walls so close together. I heard glasses clinking, bottles thudding on the bar top and lower tables, the low hum of people talking and laughing, and the music.

I focused on that. It was loud, but not screechy or obnoxious, and I recognized Finn's guitar just as Billie stopped at the bar to order drinks. He wasn't singing yet though.

"Well, hello, Evvie," a big booming voice said. Whoever was speaking was tall and large. His voice reminded me of a bass drum in a marching band. "Who're your friends?"

"Hi, Manny. This is Billie"—Evvie raised her voice over the din of the noise—"and this is Aislinn."

"Howdy, ladies. What'll it be?" he asked. "Now, Billie, you look like a beer kinda girl to me."

"Good guess. But don't give me that piss water everybody around here drinks," Billie said, and Manny laughed.

"Give me an IPA. Surprise me, but just one for me. I'm DD tonight."

"Yes, ma'am." I imagined him saluting her. "And you, Miss Aislinn?"

"Oh, I-I don't like beer."

"Hmm, okay. How 'bout wine? Maybe chardonnay?"

I shook my head. "Can you make a piña colada?"

"Well, sure I can. Ain't no drink I can't make."

"Make it strong," I said, feeling a little brave. I liked Manny. I could hear the smile in his voice, and he reminded me of my brother, the way he spoke so I could hear him clearly.

So far, so good. I was hopeful I could actually enjoy myself.

"Comin' up," he said. "Evvie?"

"I'll have a piña colada, too, please. That sounds good."

"Alright. Head on over. I think Jack and the guys already have a table in front of the band. I'll bring your drinks."

"Thanks," Billie said. "Here. Take my card. Start a tab."

My confidence deflated. It was the second time in one night that someone else had had to pay for me. I was embarrassed and ashamed. I didn't have any money—I'd thrown all my credit cards at Theo's head—but Jack had said I could have a job at the ranch, so I would keep track and pay Billie back. I'd never had to pay for anything. I had no idea how much a piña colada cost, but I'd ask Evvie later. I knew Billie didn't expect to be paid back, but it was important to me.

How was I supposed to be independent if I went from relying on Theo for everything to relying on Billie or Evvie? No. I needed to learn to rely on myself.

They led me to a table, and as we walked, I imagined every head in the bar turning to look at me. I had never actually been inside a bar. I was sixteen when I lost my sight, and since then, I hadn't really had friends. Not ones I could hang out in a bar with. I'd had alcohol before, usually when Theo and I traveled. I loved the beach, and whenever we went to one, which wasn't often, I ordered a piña colada. But loud places could be very disorienting, and the loss of control from getting drunk usually made it worse. My anxiety didn't help either.

"Ladies!" Kevin shouted. Clearly, he was already drunk.

"Kevin," Billie warned, "if you try to give me a nuggie with that fist, I will castrate you where you stand."

"You're gonna be my sis-in-law," he said. "I'm allowed to annoy you."

Billie groaned, so I assumed he followed through with the poor decision to mess up her hair. "You're a dick."

"Aww, I love you too," he slurred.

"*Hallo*, Aislinn," Luuk said. I liked the sound of his voice. His accent was sexy, and just from the tone, I could always hear his kindness and patience. He'd need a lot of that to be with Kevin.

"Hello."

"There is a chair in front of you if you would like to sit down. Shall I hold it for you?"

"Yes, please."

He waited while I removed my sweater. Even over the music I could tell everyone around me was quiet, and a nagging part of me wished I could see them. Before the accident, I would have made a show of it, dragging my movements out slowly, making sure everyone noticed me. And they would have. I would've made sure they did, with a flick of my long hair over my shoulder and a coy smirk aimed at the cutest guy I could find.

I didn't have long hair anymore, and I didn't have confidence.

I sat, draping my sweater across my knees neatly, then a chair squeaked across the floor next to me, and Luuk leaned in. "Do not worry," he said quietly in his smooth Dutch accent. "You have made them all speechless because you look very beautiful tonight."

I smiled, feeling very thankful for that Dutchman. "Thank you."

The band played on, but there were no voices still. They didn't use speakers, probably because Manny's was so small. No need. I could tell I was sitting directly in front of the band, slightly off to the left, but I could also tell many people stood in front of our table, blocking the flow of the sounds.

The music was nice, kind of alt-indie-folky. There was even a banjo, though it didn't sound country. The guitars were acoustic—there were two—and the drums were soft. People chatted a little all around me—I heard Billie talking to someone next to me, probably Jay, and I heard Dean's deep voice behind me. But mostly, people listened to Finn's band.

The song ended and the crowd clapped, then Finn spoke.

"Thanks for comin' out. This is a new project. Nothin' fancy. Manny said he wanted live music, and he *begged* us to play. I'm sure y'all know that you don't say no to Manny Perez, else he'll pound ya."

Everyone around me cheered and laughed, and Manny boomed from the bar, "Watch yourself, Finnigan."

"Yessir," Finn said, laughing. "Anyway, this song is called 'This Life, That Sea'. It's new."

Evvie and Billie whooped next to me, and Luuk clapped. Someone whistled using their fingers, not just their lips—I could always tell the difference—and then Finn strummed his guitar. Annoyingly, I again imagined him strumming my body with his fingers and felt embarrassment crawl up my neck.

So far, the song was soft, just his quiet guitar, but then the people standing in front of me moved—the sound of the guitar was more directly in front of me—and Finn took a deep breath to begin singing, but he paused. He held his breath.

The guitar stopped, and for fifteen seconds, no one made any noise. I didn't think the pause was part of the song, but there were no clues around me to explain why Finn would stop. Was there an equipment malfunction? Had he forgotten the words to his own song?

I didn't know why, but I could *feel* people looking at me, so I searched through my bag on my lap for my sunglasses and slipped them on. It was stupid, but I immediately felt more secure.

Finally, Finn began playing again and he sang. He seemed a little shaky, like maybe he was nervous, which surprised me, but I could hear him clearly.

Is this my life?

Is it me?

You're the sun shinin' on the mountain, the light in the sea.

I hear you reachin', callin' out to me.

The banjo joined the guitar, but subtly in the background, and the drums were a gentle, rolling sound. A cello joined in from the right side of the stage, slowly, weaving and blending with Finn's guitar, and it was beautiful. It lulled me into this dreamy, romantic trance. I was transported to the inside of Finn's mind, and I never wanted to leave.

His voice was utterly beautiful.

Salt burns my eyes, but you can't see,

What you're doin',

Oh, what you're doin' to me.

Masculine but so soft and steady, Finn's voice was a low,

luring rumble, somehow dirty and gritty, but in the sexiest way. It was ridiculous, I knew, but I imagined he was singing to me.

"Miss Aislinn, I'm on your right," Manny said, and I jumped in my seat. Listening to Finn, all the other sounds had faded away. "Sorry to startle you. I put one of them cute little umbrellas in your drink so you'll feel like you're at the beach."

"Thank you." So I would know which drink was mine, but he didn't say it, and I appreciated that.

When the band was done playing and I'd finished two piña coladas, Billie led me to the restroom. I wanted to talk to Finn, to tell him how much I loved his music—I thought maybe it could be my next step toward goodwill with him—but he wasn't near me, and I was too much of a scaredy cat to ask Billie to take me to him, even with the alcohol fueling my confidence a little.

"Billie, I do know how to go to the bathroom by myself," I said when she opened the door for me and followed me in.

"Right, I know. Sorry. You're okay though? Having fun?"

"Yeah, I am actually. The band was really good. Is Finn around? Maybe I'll tell him."

"Yeah, he's out there. I'll go flag him down for you."

"Thanks."

She left me in the bathroom, but she was probably outside the door, guarding it like my very own Viking warrioress.

I finished peeing and washed my hands in the sink. Public restrooms grossed me out because I used my hands to find my way around, but I always carried hand sanitizer in my purse, Maui sun-scented. It reminded me of the month I'd spent in Hawaii with my parents before the accident. Theo had been in his first year of college.

My mother had been trying to connect with me on that

trip. I thought then that it had just been because I was a whiny, demanding teenager and we'd grown apart, but now I wondered if maybe she'd been trying to tell me something back then. Maybe she'd wanted to tell me about my real mother, but I'd blown her off, instead spending my days flirting with my way-too-old-for-me surfing instructor, shopping with my rich, adulterous daddy's credit cards, or sneaking out of our beach house at night to meet local boys.

When I left the bathroom, I listened for the sound of Billie's voice. She wasn't posted outside the door like I'd thought, but I heard her only ten feet or so away. And then I heard Finn.

He sounded angry. "Why is Ace here? Why'd you bring her, Billie?"

"What?" She sounded confused, and then she was angry, too, probably getting ready to defend me somehow. "Finn! What the fuck?"

Oh. I turned quickly. I was so embarrassed. Of course he hadn't wanted me there. Who wants their blind, whiny house-guest to follow them around, drooling over them and latching on like a groupie? There were probably hordes of beautiful women waiting to talk to him, to flirt with him, trying to lure him to their beds.

I had to get out of there.

Not even using my cane, I walked in the opposite direc-tion of Finn and Billie, hoping desperately to find a door, but instead, I bumped into a man, his rough, wide frame blocking me from my escape.

"Miss Aislinn?" The voice was instantly familiar, and I sighed in relief.

"Oh, James. Can you help me, please?" I sounded like I was about to cry. Which I was.

"'Course. You okay?"

"Yes, but is there a door around here? I n-need some air. I want to go outside, but I don't want to go back through the bar."

"Oh, uh, yeah, here." He grabbed my arm, but this time it didn't make me angry. I grasped his forearm with my other hand and squeezed. "We can go through the kitchen. There's a door back there."

"Thank you."

"Wait, shouldn't I tell your friend you're leavin'? I don't want her to beat me up." He laughed nervously.

"I'm not a child, James. I don't need her permission." Even though I knew Billie would be so mad at me because she would worry.

"O-okay. Follow me."

When we were outside, I stopped walking, yanking on James's arm.

"What's wrong?"

I wanted to leave. I couldn't go back in there, but I didn't have anywhere to go. I didn't have any money, and I'd left my purse at the table with Luuk, so I didn't have my phone. I knew Theo's cell number, but I was not about to call him.

"Um, I want to leave, but I-I don't want to go to the ranch. I—"

"Aislinn, lemme just go get your friend. I'm sure she'll take you wherever you want."

"No. Can you take me? Please? I don't have money, but maybe we could just drive?"

He was quiet for a moment, the only sound his loud breaths. "I think I might get my ass handed to me on a rusty platter for this but… okay. C'mon. My truck's over here."

I didn't bother telling him that I had no clue where "over here" meant. I just clutched his arm and followed. We stopped and he opened a truck door, the sound of it creaking above me at twice the height of a normal car door.

"Okay, um, step up. The runnin' board's about two foot high."

"What's a running board?"

"It's just the step, like a stair."

"Okay." Reaching out in front of me, I felt for the door. I slid my hand around until I found the inside handle and grabbed it, then stepped on the running board. James's hand stayed on my back to steady me, and I knew he was trying to be helpful, but he was pushing me. After a minute, I finally pulled myself into his truck, but I misjudged the distance to the seat and landed on the floor.

"Ah, I'm sorry, Miss Aislinn. You okay?'

"I'm fine." I felt around to get my bearings, then climbed up into the seat and crossed my arms over my chest.

What the hell was I doing? Billie would kill me for leaving, and I was making an utter fool of myself. But I couldn't go back into that bar. I was humiliated. I'd let Billie do my makeup even though I couldn't see it. I probably looked ridiculous. I was wearing clothes that weren't me, and my nails were painted. How stupid.

And the whole day, the only thought in my head had been, "Will Finn like it? Will he look at me?"

I couldn't even see myself, and I didn't like how I looked. And what did looks matter anyway? After the way I'd talked to him and treated him, how could I ever have thought Finn would have one ounce of interest in me?

He didn't. That was clear.

The truck dipped and creaked when James got in, and I smoothed my hands down my thighs.

"Where you want me to go?"

"Away from here."

CHAPTER NINE

FINN

THE GUYS and I finished our set—it was a short one, only five original songs and a few covers—and I rushed to the bar for my free beer, almost droppin' my guitar into its stand.

Shit. I was so nervous. I didn't get nervous, didn't get stage fright. Usually, music was the thing that calmed me down. It was the tool I used to stop my pacin', to say what I wanted to say when regular words failed me.

"What the fuck is wrong with you tonight?" My drummer and friend, Spade, walked up behind me, smackin' the back of my head.

"Nothin'."

"Nothin'? You've never frozen like that before. What'd you do, forget your own fuckin' lyrics? You played the wrong chords."

I'd come up with that song thinkin' about my weird dream, the feelin' I'd had when I woke up, before Aislinn had screamed and thrown a fit. But when I saw her sittin' at the table in Manny's with my family, listenin' to me play— wearin' my shirt!—I froze. I realized right then and there that the dream had been about her.

The song I wrote was about her.

And she could hear it all. She could hear every single breath I took. Maybe it was stupid, but I thought there was no way she didn't know that song was about her. My heart pounded, and my fingers fumbled over the strings. She could hear it, and she focused on it 'cause it was the one sense she relied on most.

I didn't know what to say to her. Should I say somethin'? Should I not? Maybe I shoulda just run screamin' from the bar. Or maybe she couldn't have cared less. It was no secret I wasn't her favorite person. There was an attraction there, but it didn't mean she liked who I was as a person. In fact, I was pretty sure it was the opposite.

Fuck. I felt like a fifteen-year-old kid playin' his first set at the local VFW. My voice cracked, and my hands sweat and shook. On top of all that, I hadn't been able to stop starin' at her. She couldn't see me, but everybody else could. They all noticed. There was no way they hadn't.

"Fuck off, Spade. I said it was nothin'," I warned, chuggin' my beer when the bartender handed it to me. I tried to breathe a little through my gulps to calm my racin' pulse, but I was *still* nervous. I looked around but didn't see Aislinn anywhere. But I saw Billie, and she was headed straight for me.

"Whatever, man." Spade disappeared, chuggin' his own free booze—the glamorous perks of playin' bars.

I had forgotten the lyrics even though I knew 'em down to my soul, like they'd been tattooed on my face and were the only things I saw when I brushed my teeth in the mornin'. But I wouldn't tell Spade that, and I wouldn't tell him that seein' Ace had stopped me cold.

"Hey, Finn, Ace wants to talk to you. She just went to the women's room. She'll be right out."

Billie smiled, and I wanted to run. Why did Aislinn wanna talk to me? Did she know the song was about her?

"Why is Ace here? Why'd you bring her, Billie?" I was so nervous, I thought I might throw up. Naturally, I chugged more beer.

"What? Finn! What the fuck?"

More beer. I handed the empty to the bartender, Dede, and she replaced it with a freshie, silently judgin' me with her oddly-wise brown eyes. She shook her head, rollin' those eyes.

"Why would you say that? What's the matter with you? Ace just wants to tell you she liked your fucking music. When did you become such a dick?"

"No, it's not that. I just—" I looked around again but still didn't see her. "Um, where is she?"

"I told you, numbnuts, she's in the bathroom. What is your problem? Why shouldn't Ace come to Manny's? Why, because she's blind? That is so ableist, Finn. She can do anything anybody else can—"

"I know that, Billie," I grumbled, lookin' around again. "How long does it take for her to pee? Jeez." I was still wonderin' if I had time to grab my gear and split.

"Oh my God, you are so insensitive."

There was that word again.

Dede interrupted, "You talkin' about that tall drink of water with short dark hair and perfect tight"—she arched just one eyebrow—"jeans? The blind chick?"

"Yeah," Billie said, "what about her?"

"Oh, nothin', but she just escaped out the back door with that guy—the orange pop guy. Whiskey and orange pop. Yuck."

"Brock?" I asked. Guy had an unhealthy fixation with Fanta.

"Yeah, that's the one." She looked at me, both eyebrows raised now while she wiped down the already clean bar top with a wet rag. "She heard what you said."

"Shit."

"Finn, you dick. Now look what you've done." Billie speared Dede with her eyes. "You didn't think to stop her? Where's the back door?"

"Ain't my job. Back there," she said, noddin' over her shoulder.

Billie stomped off and I followed. *Shit, shit, shit.*

We pushed through the back door, and Billie cussed. "Great. She's gone. Nice, Finn, way to go." She sighed, pullin' her phone from her back pocket. "I'm calling her."

"Em, excuse me, Billie?" Luuk stuck his head out the back door. "You cannot call her. She has left her purse. Her phone is in here," he said, holdin' it out to Billie. "It was just ringing. I was looking for her."

Billie growled. "Finn!"

"Brock's a good guy," I said, but I wanted to strangle him. "She can take care of herself."

"I can't even tell you how many bags of dicks you suck right now, Finn."

Yep. I didn't think I could feel worse if she was hittin' me on the head with those bags of dicks.

Luuk and my brother had to drive me home 'cause I'd inhaled three more beers and two shots of whiskey (not mixed with orange pop) in the span of about five minutes, worryin' the whole time about where Aislinn was and what she was doin' with Brock. I knew he wouldn't hurt her, but how much had he had to drink? I had no idea.

And what if he thought he was gonna get lucky? The guy was a popular choice for local women, always had been. I was sure he had the moves to woo Ace to his bed, or maybe he'd try for the bed of his truck. I didn't think she'd go for that, but would he try to push himself on her? He wouldn't force her but—

I wanted to scream when I thought about 'em fuckin' in the back of his truck. The freakin' orange pop guy!

Standin' on my front porch like I was Aislinn's overly protective father waitin' to yell at her for comin' home after curfew, I chugged another beer but, halfway through, realized I probably looked like my alcoholic dad, chuggin' beers to avoid his feelin's. I dumped the rest over the porch railin', sighin' and feelin' disgusted with myself. I was already drunk. I didn't need to be drunker.

If she'd hated me before, she really would now.

Damn. And we'd just been warmin' up to each other. I snorted at myself. Yeah, I was warm alright. My warm hand gripped my dick every night when I jacked off to thoughts of her below me, tossin' and turnin' in her bed.

I paced in the kitchen till I made myself dizzy, then collapsed on the couch to wait. I tried countin' sheep to relax, but I guess I passed out 'round about the seventeenth sheep mark.

An hour later, or maybe five—I had no clue 'cause I was still drunk—the screen door clattered open, and I jumped up off the couch. "Aislinn?"

"Yes."

Jesus, the relief I felt seein' her home and in one piece— she didn't look like she'd had sex—except, what the fuck would that look like?

I searched behind her for Brock. "Where's your date?"

She laughed—the haughty, condescending one. "None of your business."

"Right, sorry. I-I was—but you're okay?"

"I'm perfectly fine. I had a wonderful time. Please excuse me. I'm tired, and I'd like to go to bed."

"Ace—" Hurdlin' the back of the couch, I almost fell on my face when my leg got stuck between two cushions. I stumbled to stand in front of her and said, "I'm sorry you overheard me."

She stiffened, surprised by my closeness.

"I didn't mean it that way."

"I don't know what you're talking about. I didn't overhear anything. Brock asked me out so I went with him. He's a very nice man. Very romantic. In fact, he's taking me to dinner tomorrow. Good night."

She bit her lip, waitin' for me to move 'cause she knew I was blockin' her exit.

"Aislinn, I—"

"Please." Closin' her eyes, she said, "Excuse me. I told you, I'm tired."

I stepped to the right, and she walked past me, usin' her cane to find the way, but stopped outside her door. She didn't turn around. "But your… your music was lovely." I watched her shoulders rise and fall with a deep breath. She said, "Good night," and her door thudded shut behind her.

Billie ran halfway down the stairs in her Bugs Bunny pajamas and bare feet. "Was that Ace? She's home?"

"No, that wasn't Ace. That was Miss Aislinn Burroughs," I said. "But yeah, she's home."

If I'd thought the last month had sucked balls, the next month was somethin' out of *The* goddamned *Bell Jar*. I hadn't actually read it, but I'd seen the movie, and it was depressin' as shit.

I watched daily as Brock won Aislinn over. She relaxed with him, and she'd stopped wearin' her sunglasses when he was around. She and Brock had gone on double dates with Jay and Billie, and anytime she and I were alone in the house, she was in her bedroom, or she'd put her earbuds in and turn on one of her audiobooks.

And when I tried to talk to her, she was polite but curt. Impersonal. And she didn't laugh, except for when Brock was around, and then it sounded forced. Fake. It felt like she was puttin' on a show for me, but why would she do that?

Oh yeah, 'cause I'd opened my big mouth and made her feel so uncomfortable.

The reno at Billie's house was finished, but she had to leave town for a job while Jay and Kevin went up to Montana to learn about equine therapy at a big successful non-profit barn up there. So Aislinn was still stayin' at the ranch. She hadn't ridden much since she'd fallen that day. She didn't seem to wanna do anything that had anything to do with me.

Jay and Ms. Bell had been trainin' her in the office to help out. Ms. Bell was workin' out well, and she seemed to really enjoy havin' Aislinn around to help her. They spent their lunch breaks with their heads together, chattin' and gettin' to know each other.

Walkin' in there one mornin', I bumped right into Aislinn.

"Sorry. I was lookin' for Ms. Bell." I steadied her with my hands on her arms again, just like that night in the kitchen.

"She left to run to Jackson for office supplies."

"Oh. Okay then."

"What do you need, Finn?"

Ah, shit. I was still holdin' onto her. I dropped my arms. "Oh, nothin'. It ain't a big deal. I can get it later."

"Get what?"

"I just wanted to look up the history on Surely. I know she came from a rescue, but I was hopin' there was a little more info about her past in her file. She's really skittish. I was just wonderin' if maybe it's 'cause I'm a guy. Maybe she'd do better with a woman. I dunno. I've tried all my usual tricks, but she still hates me."

She scoffed. "You're surprised? Not every woman is going to swoon at your feet."

Uhh. Okay?

"I know that, but what's that got to do with Surely?"

"Nothing." She turned, extendin' her cane out in front of her, and made her way to the desktop computer in the corner. Clickin' a button on the mouse, the screen came to life, and she said, "Find file 'Surely A Winner.'" She tapped the mouse again, and the printer came to life, and I stared at her ass in her tight jeans as she leaned over the desk. I couldn't stop my stupid brain from imaginin' myself between her legs.

Finn! You. Are. A. Perv!

The printer spit out three pieces of paper, and Aislinn took 'em from the tray, then spun around and handed 'em to me.

"Thanks. That was impressive. How'd you do that?"

"Billie set it up."

"Genius."

She cocked her hip, and I noticed the line of buttons down her pink-and-purple flannel shirt. She'd left the top two open, and the curve from her chin to her neck and lower disappeared from my view, and it had my eyes on a wild goose chase for more dark silky skin. Plus, it didn't help that she looked drop-dead gorgeous in a flannel. I liked when she wore jeans and T-shirts or flannel shirts instead of her uppity silk stuff 'cause she seemed more relaxed that way. "Is that all you need?"

"Uh, yeah, I guess." I glanced at the papers, and the letters blurred on the page like they always did. I wished Jay was here. He always helped by readin' to me. "Thanks. I said that already. Okay. I'm gonna go."

"Buh bye." She turned, fiddlin' with stuff on the desk, and I walked away, laughin' to myself 'cause she sounded more like Billie and Oly every day.

Sittin' on the floor in Surely's stall, I read through her file slowly. That was an understatement, unless slow meant the same speed molasses dripped when it was frozen. Without Jay's help, it was gonna take me all day to read the stupid papers. I'd never been good at readin', and my attention was always interrupted by somethin' or other. I'd pretty much flirted my way through high school. If graduation had been based solely on my academic performance, I'd still be stuck at Wisper High.

I cut up an apple with my pocketknife and held the chunks in the air the whole time, tryin' to tempt the mare to come closer and to relax, but she wouldn't.

The poor horse had been found on a farm about fifty miles away. Surely's former owner, an elderly lady who'd been a bit of a recluse and a little bit of a hoarder of animals, had passed away from natural causes, and the animals hadn't been found till more than two weeks later. Animal control had rescued Surely, two llamas, fifteen pigs, a shit-ton of chickens, and a dog from the farm. We'd only had Surely a few weeks, but so far, nothin' seemed to make her happy. Jack was convinced she'd make a fine therapy horse, though, so I kept tryin'.

"She likes Tony."

"Shit!" I dropped the papers and jumped straight up in the air when I heard Aislinn's voice, and Surely reared. "Whoa, girl." I stood and grabbed Surely's halter but let go 'cause she side-eyed me and stomped her hooves. She really didn't like me. "Damn, Ace, you scared me. It's so quiet in here with Kevin gone and construction on hold."

"Tony comes in here when no one's around. I hear him sniffing around and rolling in the hay. She whinnies when he's around. A happy whinny."

"Really? Jack said she lived on a farm with a buncha different animals. I wonder what happened to 'em all."

Aislinn pushed the stall door open a little, edgin' her way in, and Surely took one step toward her. "I could make a few calls. Maybe we could find them. What does her file say?"

"Oh"—I looked down at the papers on the ground—"I haven't read it yet."

"So read it."

"I, uh, I can't."

"Why not?"

"The ink's real light. You probably need new cartridges." *Ah*, it made my stomach sour to lie to her like that, using her blindness as a way to hide my shortcomin's.

"Oh. Well, why didn't you say so? I could've called Shonda and asked her to pick them up. It's too late now, she's already on her way back. I'll order them online."

"Sorry, forgot."

"Okay, well, we can read it on the computer."

"No. That's—just forget I asked. I don't need it." I tried to distract her. "You thinkin' what I'm thinkin'?"

"I highly doubt that," she said, and she huffed a laugh.

"Aislinn? I know you're still pissed at me, and I'm sorry, but are you okay? You seem… I dunno, different lately."

"I'm fine." Surely took another step toward her.

"Things goin' okay with Brock? You guys gettin' along okay?" I winced. That wasn't what I really wanted to ask.

"That's none of your business. What were you thinking?"

"Huh?" I inched closer to her too.

"You said, 'are you thinkin' what I'm thinkin'?' What were you thinking? I can't read your mind."

"Oh, right."

She lifted her head toward my face, surprised at how close I'd gotten. It had been forever since she'd had an actual conversation with me. I couldn't stop the attraction drawin' me to her, and since she kept her sunglasses on around me now, I hadn't seen her eyes in weeks.

Except for now. Now I could see the shiny jade color, and I loved it. I imagined cradlin' her face in my hands, kissin' the edges of her lips when she spoke so I could feel her breath across my skin.

"I, uh, I was thinkin' maybe if we found Surely's friends, they might be available for adoption. I'm pretty sure Jack won't let me adopt 'em all, but maybe the dog. Might make her feel more comfortable."

She blinked, and her eyelashes fluttered like tiny butterfly wings when I spoke.

"Whatcha think?"

"Why do you care what I think?" She stepped closer to me, too, and Surely turned away, nosin' through the hay in her feed bucket hangin' on the stall door.

"I care about pretty much everything you do or don't do."

She scoffed and shook her head. "Right."

"Ace…" I breathed her in, her beachy, coconutty scent mixed with hay and dirt. "I didn't mean what I said at

Manny's that night. It's not that I didn't want you there. You bein' there made me nervous. I didn't know you were comin', and I wasn't prepared for it."

"Why would you need to prepare for it? There were a hundred people there. Why would I matter?"

I swallowed loudly. "'Cause I'd never played that song before. I-I wrote it about… about you."

"Me?"

"Yeah. Maybe that sounds stupid to you. I dunno. But you made me nervous." It sounded like there was a microphone in front of me now when I swallowed and said, "You make me nervous."

"I do?"

"Yeah." I hadn't realized I'd done it, but I was inches from her as she tilted her face up even closer to mine. I whispered, "Yeah, you do."

She closed her eyes, sighin'.

"I wanna kiss you so bad. I've wanted to kiss you for months."

"You have?" she whispered, too, and her breath rushed over my lips.

I was one measly inch away from shovin' my tongue in her mouth when she pulled away.

"I have a boyfriend."

"Oh. Right. Brock." I breathed, "I'm sorry."

She licked her lips. "But it wouldn't matter if I didn't."

"Why's that?"

"Because I don't like you."

Ouch. That hurt more than I woulda imagined. Most people did like me, and maybe I took that for granted a little. And maybe I wanted Ace to like me more than I was willin' to admit. But the truth was, she wanted me just like I wanted her, whether she liked it or not. From the way our bodies couldn't stop themselves from pullin' together like magnets, that much was clear.

"Aislinn?" Ms. Bell called from outside the barn. Ace and I stood an inch apart, breathin', and I tried with all my might to control the desperate need pourin' outta my body so I didn't grab her by the hips and take her down to the wood chip-covered, dusty barn floor. "Are you in here, dear?"

"Yes, Shonda. I'm here," Aislinn said, takin' a step back.

Ms. Bell appeared in the aisle. "Oh, there you are." She eyed me warily through the stall door. "Everything okay in here?"

"Yes, ma'am," I said, and Aislinn reached back, lookin' for the door handle, and when she found it, she yanked it open.

"Excuse me. I'd like to get back to work." She backed through the open stall door, then extended her cane, turned, and walked away, leavin' Ms. Bell and me alone.

"I don't know what that was I just walked in on," she scolded in a low voice, "but I don't think I should have to tell you it's unprofessional. You better not be trying to take advantage of her, young man."

"'Scuse me?" What the fuck? When had Ms. Bell turned into Headmistress McGonagall? But I couldn't be mad at her 'cause she was lookin' out for Aislinn, and I realized I cared more for Ace than I dared to admit. Duh, it'd been starin' me in the face now for over a month, every time I was jealous to see her with Brock.

"You heard me. She doesn't need you fawning all over her. She's just trying to work and learn how to support herself. She doesn't need you coming in here with all of this"—makin' a stank face and bobbin' her head from side to side, she waved her hand in front of my chest like she was washin' a car—"trying to distract her."

I laughed, completely offended. "Oh, you're lookin' out for her, huh? But you'll just stand by while that other guy gropes her in plain sight of everybody."

"That man means nothing to her. You know that. She flirts with him to irritate you because she's infatuated with you."

My eyebrows shot through the roof.

"Oh, please," Shonda said, plantin' a hand on her hip. "Don't act so surprised. But I'm watching you, and I'm warning you: keep your hands to yourself."

"Finnigan Sasquatch!"

"Hey, Bigsy," I said when my brother Dean's best friend pulled up outside the barn in his wife's orange Nissan Sentra, yellin' out his open window. "You know that thing looks like a clown car?"

"Suck a dick."

"Why does everyone keep tellin' me to do that?"

"You must look like you need a good, stiff—never mind. What crawled up your butt? Where's your brother? We were supposed to go to lunch."

"Oh, you ladies had a lunch date? Was that before or after you were gonna go hat shoppin'?"

Bigsy snorted, climbin' outta the car and pullin' his forearm crutches from the back seat. "Good one."

"I think he took Oly to the doctor."

"Something wrong with the pregnancy?"

"Nah. I think they were just late for the appointment. Oly came tearin' in here about an hour ago. He probably just forgot to call you. They go every week now. The babies are due here pretty soon."

"Hm. Well, I guess I can forgive him for that. Especially

since Annie and me are gonna be rushing off to see the doctor soon ourselves."

"What? You—"

"Yeah, man! I'm gonna be a papa!"

"No shit? Bigsy! That's amazin'. I'm so happy for you."

"Thanks. Well, so you wanna be my lunch date? I'm fucking hungry. You're nowhere near as cute as Dean, but I'll survive."

I laughed. "Sure. Lemme just get my heels."

"Shit, if you wore high heels, your head would get lost in the stratosphere."

"If you knocked your ol' lady up, you can't be sufferin' from erectile dysfunction, but I thought everybody with little-man syndrome had that problem. Ooo, or was it the mailman who stuffed a bun in her oven?"

Bigsy pushed me with the end of his crutch in the middle of my chest, and I stepped back, laughin', but I tripped over my own feet and landed on my back in the dirt. Bigsy cackled, and Aislinn sighed, suddenly standin' over me.

"I'm sorry, Miss Aislinn."

"It's not your fault that Finn's an idiot, Marcus."

"Well, I know that. He achieved idiot status all by himself. We're going to lunch. You wanna come with us?"

"No, thank you." Aislinn stepped around me, whackin' me in the head with her cane when she passed. "Finn, the new gelding will be here in two hours. Make sure you're back by then."

I sat up, mutterin' under my breath, "Yes, ma'am," and I saluted her behind her back.

"I heard that."

Bigsy laughed while I stood and dusted myself off, and I couldn't help myself from watchin' her walk away. Goddamn, she filled out those tight jeans so good.

"Is that fear in your eyes or just flat-out lust?"

"Shh, shut up. Get in the damn car."

———

"So, you got a hard-on for Aislinn?" Bigsy said when we grabbed a booth at José's Diner for lunch.

I sighed.

"You sound like your broody brother."

I rolled my eyes. "Pretty sure she hates me."

Bigsy laughed, then his eyebrows shot off the top of his head when Jules Markham walked up and stared at me, ignorin' him completely.

"Hi, Finn."

"Hey, Jules." She smiled and just kept starin'. "Oh, sorry." Slidin' outta the diner booth, I stood. "You wanna sit down? This is Bigsy. Bigs, this is Jules Markham, Oly's best friend and Isaac's sister."

"Hi." Jules flicked a glance in Bigsy's direction but looked back at me. "I was just talkin' to Oly and Dean the other day about bringin' my class out to your ranch."

Jules didn't make any move to sit, so I stood there like an idiot. I didn't know what to do with my arms. Should I keep 'em at my sides? Cross 'em over my chest? Clasp 'em behind my back? I felt like a big ol' piece of ribeye everytime I ran into her. She stared at me like she wanted to lick my face. "Oh, is that right?"

"Yeah, I'm teachin' the kids about animal husbandry, and Oly thought it might be fun to take 'em on a field trip instead of just bringin' a dog to school."

"Oh, sure. That sounds fun."

"Yeah? You think so?"

Hadn't I just said that?

"Well, you wanna help me? Here, gimme your number. I'll text you."

"Okay. I mean, yeah, I can help, I guess." She handed me her phone, and I put my number in. I glanced at Bigsy, and he sat, starin' up at me with the smuggest smile on his damn face. "Here."

She took her phone from my hand and smiled up at me again, starin' really hard into my eyes. "Thanks. Okay, well, I've gotta get back to school. I'll text you."

"'Kay."

"Nice to meet you, Migsy."

Bigsy snorted when Jules walked away without even a polite look in his direction. "What was that?"

"What?"

"Hi, sweetie." My mama walked up, delivered a plate full of my usual order—spicy fries—and lifted up on her toes to kiss my cheek. "Marcus, how are you and Annie doing?"

"We're good, Daisy. How are you?"

"I'm good too. Busy." She looked around the diner and smiled back at Bigsy, then me. "What would you boys like to eat?"

"Uh, couple burgers, all the fixin's, and more fries. Sound good, Bigs?"

"That'll do," Bigsy said. "And a water. Annie won't let me drink soda anymore."

"Yeah, me too," I said and smiled at my mama 'cause she looked genuinely happy to be providin' me with food. She'd missed so much of that bein' gone for twenty years, and I had to admit, I liked how it felt to have her here again to do it.

Her eyes shined and she winked up at me. "You got it. I'll come say hi if I get a break."

When she walked away, José met her at the swingin' kitchen door and kissed her cheek when he didn't think anyone was watchin'. She'd come out to the ranch to sit my brothers down for a talk about movin' in with José. They all groaned 'cause it was weird thinkin' about our mama in a relationship, but that had nothin' to do with the man himself. We all liked José. He was a good guy, and it was easy to see they were in love. It made me happy for my mama, and I smiled, but Bigsy interrupted, "That Jules chick's already imagining having your babies."

"What? No, she ain't."

"Oh yes, she is."

"Shut up." Wait? Really? Jules Markham?

"Finn, are you really that dense?"

I slid back into the booth. "I mean, I thought she was just a little bit of a flirt."

"You didn't see the hearts and stars in her eyes?"

"Whatever." But if he was right… "Hm. I think I'll ask her out."

"Really? I thought you had a thing for Aislinn," he said, shovin' a handful of my fries in his mouth.

"Who said that? I didn't say that."

Through a mouthful, he said, "This town's better than watching the Lifetime channel."

"Whatever," I said again, but in my head, I was already plannin' it out. I could ask Jules on a date and then suggest that we all go out—Aislinn and Brock and me and Jules. *Ha. Let's see how Ace likes that.* She was havin' the time of her life, throwin' Brock in my face. Well, checkmate.

Except, I wasn't very good at chess. In fact, I'd never played it.

Bigsy's tongue fell outta his mouth, and he fanned it with his hand. "Shit! What the fuck do they put in these fries? Ghost peppers?"

CHAPTER TEN

AISLINN

"ACE, YOU LOOK FINE."

"Fine? I can't look fine. This is a date."

Billie's voice was tinny and echoing, coming through the video call on Evvie's phone. Jay and Kevin had returned from Montana, but Billie was still out of town, and I missed her. "Yeah, but on your last date with Brock, you wore the purple sweatpants I bought for you."

"Only because it was cold outside."

"Didn't he take you to a restaurant?" Evvie asked.

"Yes, technically, but it was a food truck. That doesn't count, and we sat outside, so it was cold."

Billie sighed into her phone, and Evvie fidgeted on my bed. In her no-nonsense way, Billie said, "Ace, just admit that you're getting dressed up 'cause Finn's bringing a date too."

"I don't care what Finn does. Who cares?" I stomped my foot. "Please be more constructive than 'you look fine.' Do I look hot?"

The bedsprings squeaked when Evvie stood. "Yes. You look beautiful, but wear jeans. Your ass looks fab in jeans. Those baggy silk pants leave too much to the imagination."

I practically ripped the middle drawer of the dresser out trying to find jeans. I'd barely spoken to Finn in two weeks, but now I was sweating and my heart was flopping around in my chest like a fish out of water. Finn had said he wanted to kiss me. He almost did kiss me, and now he had a date?

Okay, so fine, maybe I'd pushed him away with my "Because I don't like you" comment. But that was it? He was giving up? Just like that?

He made no sense, because why would he want to kiss me? Just because I looked good to him? Because I was a woman living in his house and he was a man? Was that it?

I was making no sense, even to myself. And I was still so humiliated from what he'd said at the bar. Because when I lost my sight, everything changed. Everything about me changed. My identity changed.

I had been the rich, popular, perfect teenage girl. Everyone wanted to be me at my school; even people who hadn't gone to my private high school wanted to be me. I had every expensive designer bag, shoes, clothing. My father bought me a Jaguar for my sixteenth birthday, for Christ's sake, and all my friends, and some adults, had been envious. I wanted for nothing, and I cared about nothing but myself.

But the day I woke to darkness, all of that was gone. Who was I if I wasn't Aislinn Burroughs, the lucky, spoiled, pampered princess?

I was Theo's little sister. That was the only title I'd had for the last ten years. Theodore Burroughs Jr.'s whiny, needy, difficult, and blind little sister. Business associates of Theo's hated when I was forced to attend a meeting. I didn't have to see their faces to know. It was in their voices and in the air in whatever cold, sterile conference room I found myself in.

Theo made me go to those meetings to try to force me to get interested in our father's business, but all that time, I couldn't have cared less. I wanted nothing to do with it. I wanted the money it afforded me—half of it was mine—but that was it. And really, what did I need that money for? Clothes, shoes, bags? Who cared what I wore? I barely cared.

Until now.

So when Finn reacted the way he had that night at Manny's bar, it had been a confirmation to me that that was how he saw me—as a pampered little girl. And no matter how many times he apologized or said it wasn't what he had meant, it was how I felt.

I didn't believe he could really want me, and for once, I wanted someone to think that I was worth the fight. I wanted to think that about myself. All my long-lost adoring fans had scattered with the wind, and all they had ever cared about was what my money and popularity could get them. But I wanted someone to want something from me that had come from inside me. Not the outside.

I wanted to be worthy of someone like Finn, but I knew I wasn't. So every time he was nice to me, I reacted with that knowledge in my mind, and it made me mean.

And now, Finn had just casually announced he was bringing a date on what was supposed to be a quiet dinner with Jack, Evvie, Luuk, and Kevin. Oh, and Brock. And then Oly had said to Finn, "It's about time. Jules has been in love with you forever."

Jules? Who was Jules! Probably some ditzy, flaky groupie. She'd most likely be all over Finn, sticking her tongue down his throat at every opportunity. How rude. This was supposed to be a civilized dinner.

Whatever. It didn't matter. Finn may have wanted to kiss me, but he didn't actually like me. He didn't want a relationship with me. How could he?

But I didn't care.

I didn't care!

I whimpered and whined, digging through the drawer. Where were my sexy jeans!

"Listen, Ace, I've made some headway on your birth mother's case. Remember I told you I've been working on it on the side? I wanted to tell you what I've found."

I froze for three seconds but unfroze just as quickly, hoping Billie and Evvie hadn't noticed.

After finding out that I was the product of an affair my rich, affluent father had had with a lowly intern at his company, I'd wondered about my real mother every day. But she'd given me up and had walked away without so much as a glance back in my direction, and I'd been raised by my mother—Theo's mother. She hadn't really been mine. Elizabeth Burroughs had been a stand-in. An imposter. She was black, too, so I had looked the part—half white, half black. I'd fit the bill, and Elizabeth Burroughs had added me to her family like she was adding a piece of furniture.

And she never thought I was worth telling the truth to. Neither had my father, and neither had Theo.

Stiffening my spine, I lied, "I don't care, Billie. I don't even know why you're still looking into it. I couldn't care less about her. Evvie, do you see my jeans anywhere?"

"Really?" Billie sounded confused, but I didn't say anything more. "So then, you wouldn't be at all curious if I told you she might still be alive?"

"Listen, Aislinn, I, uh, wanted to talk to you."

"Okay. So talk," I said, crossing my arms over my chest when Brock parked his truck at the restaurant in Jackson.

"So, um, how do you think this is goin'?" When I didn't answer, he said, "*Where* do you think this is goin'?"

"Where is what going?"

"This… relationship. If we can even call it that."

"Are you breaking up with me?" I scoffed. I was deeply offended.

"Well, now, no, I wouldn't say that, but were we ever *really* datin'? 'Cause I'm pretty sure I've been nothin' but a place holder these last few weeks."

"What?" I whipped my head in his direction even though I couldn't see him. "Why would you say that?"

He pulled my hand free from the clench I held it in and squeezed. "Look, I don't take any offense. Finn Cade is—well, I been comin' in second fiddle to that guy my whole life. I get it. And you and I don't have much in common. But we're meetin' him and his date tonight, and I just thought, maybe we oughta be honest with each other? I guess I just wanted you to know that I know."

"I don't care about Finn Cade."

"Sweetheart, you do. You know the only time you allow me to kiss you is when he's around, and you've talked about nothin' besides this dinner for three days. And tonight, I pick you up, and you're nervous and combative. It's plain to see. And I see the way he watches you."

"Please don't call me sweetheart, and he does not."

"He does. A lot."

"Well, it doesn't matter. I can't stand him."

He sucked his teeth. Ugh, how annoying. "Well, still, I think it's best if you and me are just friends. Okay? That'll be the best thing."

Sometimes, not being able to see was a small relief because I would never have to see the look of pity on Brock's face, though the sound of it in his voice was just as humiliating.

"You want a beer?" Brock asked when we sat on the cold wooden bench in the entrance to the pedestrian restaurant Evvie had suggested for the group date while we waited for everyone else to arrive. Seriously, anywhere that offered two-for-the-price-of-one entrees and buffalo wing salads was not a restaurant. It was a cafeteria. I slapped myself mentally for the thought. My nerves were making me mean again, and the discomfort I felt in my own skin made me want to throw up.

"No, thank you."

I never found my jeans, so I was dressed in my usual rich-girl clothes, probably sticking out even more than I normally did, like a spoiled sore thumb. And I was mortified after the conversation in Brock's truck. He'd known this whole time that I'd been leading him on. I was embarrassed and ashamed of myself.

Brock sighed. "I'm gettin' a beer." He stood and his knee popped. "Maybe six."

He left me sitting there, nervous and wishing I was anywhere else. We were early, and no one else had arrived yet. There was a foal being born, so Jack and Evvie wouldn't make it, and Kevin and Luuk were running late because Luuk had to take a farm call. Great. That left Finn and this Jules, whoever she was.

Thinking about what she most likely looked like—probably blonde, pale, and perfect, with eyes that actually worked—I slid my pea coat off my shoulders, letting it fall down around me on the bench, thinking I would probably need to have it dry cleaned now, and then hating myself for having another petulant thought.

"You goin' golfin'?" A strange male voice asked as he sat way too close to me. When I smelled his sweaty skin and the alcohol on his breath, my whole body stiffened and I froze. Where was Brock? How long did it take to buy one beer?

On the other side of me, a second male voice said, "She does look like she's goin' golfin', but she's too dressed up for that. You look fine, girl, like a dessert just waitin' for me to take a bite. Those fancy white clothes make your skin look like hot coffee. Lotsa *cream*." *Disgusting*.

"You know it's nighttime, right? Why's she wearin' sunglasses inside at night?" Hadn't they noticed the cane in my hand, like a billy club?

Moron number one moved closer, and his breath washed over my neck like foul-smelling smog while he trailed his finger down my arm. "Maybe she thinks she's too cool for school."

"Excuse me, please don't touch me."

"Aww, and she's so polite. I like your hair. Most guys don't like their girl to have a boy's haircut, but I don't mind." Man one tugged my hair behind my ear. "You're pretty. You here on a date?"

"That's none of your business."

Man two laughed. "She told you! Don't worry, darlin'," he breathed in my other ear, slurring, "you can tell me. I won't let my buddy know."

"Yes, I'm here on a date, and you had better leave me alone. I did not give you permission to touch me, and if you do it again, I'm calling the police."

"Look at me." Man one gripped my arm, pulling me closer so his mouth touched my cheek. "You think you're better than us?"

"I think she does, Pip. She's so high and mighty, she can't even see us from up there."

"I can't see anything. I'm—"

I tried to stand, but he yanked me back down to the bench.

The creepy teasing was gone from man one's tone of voice. Instead, it had been replaced with a threat when he said, "Where you think you're goin'?"

They both laughed, the sound sending chills up my spine, until the door ten feet in front of me was thrown open. Cold air rushed over my body, and the silence in the little vestibule was electric.

The lowest rumble of a voice broke through the uncomfortable lull. It was edged with an eerie calm. "Touch her again, I'll break both your fuckin' necks. Step back. *Now.*"

Oh, Finn. Thank God. But it didn't feel like Finn. He didn't exude his usual bouncy, good-time energy. I'd never heard him sound so intimidating.

The disgusting men mumbled apologies, backing away, and escaped out the door, and then it was just Finn and me.

He stepped toward me. "You okay?"

"I'm fine," I said, standing on shaking legs and gripping my cane so hard, I thought it would break in two. I wanted to reach for him, but I didn't.

"Where's Brock?"

"I don't know. He went to get a beer."

"He just left you here?"

"He didn't *leave* me." I scoffed, pulling my always-available scorn on around me like a superhero's cape. "He simply went to the bar, and I am perfectly capable of taking care of myself. I had the situation under control." I said it, but I knew it was a filthy lie. My heart was still racing and I was nauseous.

The door squeaked open again behind him. "Finn? Everything okay?"

His energy shifted once more when he heard the annoying, chipper female voice, and he said, "Oh, uh, yeah." He cleared his throat and tried to sound like his normal happy self. "Jules, this is Aislinn. Ace, this is Jules Markham."

"Hi, nice to meet you. I love your outfit. What kinda pants are those?"

"You wouldn't know the designer."

"Oh." Jules tried to laugh off my rude remark.

Why had I said that? I wasn't being a brat on purpose—or, well, maybe I was, but I was rattled. And then, with Finn standing so close…

"Well, you look real nice. I wore jeans. Maybe I shoulda dressed up more. Do I look okay, Finn?" she asked, and I just knew she was touching him.

"Uh, yeah, you look… great."

The hostess interrupted us. "Your table is ready, miss."

"Thank you," I clipped and took a deep breath, trying to erase the last hour from my mind and trying to seem more in control than I actually was. Reaching behind me, I bent to find my coat.

"Take my arm," Finn said, and he took my coat from my hand.

"No."

"Jesus, Ace."

Jules giggled awkwardly next to Finn, and I could hear from the direction of her voice that she was looking up at him. Probably in adoration.

"I'll wait for my date, thank you." I tried to yank my coat from his fingers, but he held on.

"You might be waitin' a while. Brock's downin' PBR at the bar like it cures all ails."

Jules laughed again.

"Fine," I said, and I held my hand in the air.

Finn took it, wrapping my fingers around his warm forearm. The muscle flexed and relaxed, and I wanted to rub my face all over the soft hair and wrap his arms around my back. Just my small hand on his arm was enough to slow my racing heart. "G'on ahead, Jules. We'll follow you."

"Right, sure."

While he led me to our table, I straightened my spine, pushing my breasts out, feigning confidence. "I didn't need you to rescue me. Those men were harmless. They wouldn't have done anything in the middle of a restaurant."

"Probably not, but you shouldn't have been left alone."

"I'm perfectly fine on my own. I'm not a child."

"Here we are," the hostess said, and a chair scraped across the floor. "Your server will be right with you."

Finn wrapped his other hand around mine, and he pulled my fingers away from his arm, holding my hand so softly. "Two steps. There's a chair on your right."

Brock joined us silently at the table, and when I was seated comfortably—well, as comfortably as possible, stuck between Finn on my left and a soon-to-be-drunk Brock on my right—Jules spoke.

"So, Aislinn, what do you do? Or, I mean, what do you like to do… for fun?"

"What? Because I'm blind, I can't work?" I rolled my eyes behind my sunglasses. I was right, she was ditsy.

Finn leaned closer to me, whispering, "Aislinn, don't be a dick. This is uncomfortable for her. You don't exactly put people at ease."

I inhaled his breath and gripped my cane tighter beneath the table, then removed my sunglasses. "I've been working at the ranch, learning to run the office. With the new therapy business, they need help. Shonda's been teaching me," I said, and Finn pressed two fingers to the outside of my knee under the table, thanking me for relenting.

I felt the warmth from his skin through my palazzos, and his touch was like a shock. An erotic one. I tried not to let my reaction show on my face, but remembering the dangerous sound of his voice when he entered the restaurant and scared those morons off, my nipples pebbled, and I hoped he didn't notice.

I wondered if he was wearing a cowboy hat. Billie said he had blond hair, and I imagined it flipping up from the edges of a black hat. Why did trying to imagine what that looked like make my knees weak?

Jules said, "Oh, that's cool. Who's Shonda?"

"Ms. Bell," Finn said, relaxing back in his chair. "Jay hired her to get the office organized and runnin' right. She's great. Actually, Jules, if you still wanna bring your class out to the ranch, that's who you'll go through to set it up. Ms. Bell or Aislinn. Aislinn here's a hardass when it comes to our schedule." Finn sounded proud, like I was his twelve-year-old little sister, and Jules giggled awkwardly again.

"Oh, well, it don't have to be an official thing," she said, and I wondered why her country accent annoyed me, but Finn's and the guys' didn't. "I was thinkin' maybe you could just help me."

"Oh, yeah, I mean, I guess."

The silence then between Finn and Jules was palpable, and with a deep breath, she changed the subject. "So, Brock, I haven't seen you in a while. How's your dad?"

"He died."

"Oh, God," she squeaked. "I'm so sorry. Yeah, I think my mom did tell me that."

Thankfully, Kevin's loud voice broke through the

painfully forced and uncomfortable chitchat. "Well, this looks enormously pleasant," he said, sliding a chair out and huffing a breath when he plopped into it across the table from me. I could imagine him slumped in his chair with his legs spread wide and a sarcastic smirk on his face. I had the feeling he was devilishly handsome and he knew it.

Behind me, there were sounds of some kind of commotion near the bar, loud voices, the bartender arguing with someone, and a man slurring his words, then a glass shattered on the floor.

I knew that voice.

Kevin breathed a laugh. "Shit. Is that Theo?"

I turned in my chair. Theo was drunk and making a scene. Shaking my head, I faced forward, but I wanted to go to him. For him to be that drunk? He was in pain.

"I got it," Finn said.

"No, please, let me," Luuk said. "Come, KC. They are already seated. We will drive Theo home."

"Man," Kevin whined, "I wanted a steak."

"Get off of it. You will live."

I was glad it would be Luuk handling Theo. He would be gentle and kind to my brother, I knew. I felt like the world's worst sister, sitting there with my arms crossed, just letting my brother flail and make a fool of himself. But I kept reminding myself I was still angry with him while I listened as Luuk approached him and tried to distract him.

"Good God, man," Theo slurred loudly. "Where did you come from? Heaven?"

Luuk laughed quietly. "*Hallo*, Theo. We have never met, but I believe you know Kevin, and my friend Brady. He's your lawyer here in Wyoming, yes?"

"What's up, man?" Kevin said. "Looks like you're havin' a rough night. C'mon. Let's get you outta here."

"Your brother said you had a boyfriend. Is this that one? I mean, this is the—I mean, oh God. You're both fucking hot. I've never had a threesome, but can we go to your place?"

Oh my God. I covered my face with my hands. Theo would be utterly mortified tomorrow. I had to do something to stop him. I stood, and Finn's chair scraped across the floor when he did too.

"Take my arm," he whispered again. I did, and he led me to Theo, who was falling apart at the bar in a crappy restaurant in the middle of Jackson on a Wednesday night.

"Theo?"

"Aislinn!" he said way too loudly, and his chair scraped and wobbled on the floor. "Whoa. I almost fell on my butt-butt-buttery-butt." He snorted and giggled at his own joke. "This'my sisser."

"*Ja.*" Luuk laughed a little. "We have met."

"Oh, man, I love your accent. What is that? Spanish? Finn! Ugh. You know, God must've been feeling really fucking generous the day he made your family. I know you're not gay, but fuck, what I wouldn't give to—"

"Oh. Nope." Kevin laughed, muffling Theo's drunk musings with a hand over his mouth. "We ain't goin' there. C'mon, rich dude. Where's your keys? Luuk, I'll drive his car and you can follow."

"*Ja.*"

"I don't have a car. I took an Uber, and the driver was hot. Wait." Theo struggled with Kevin, grunting and breathing hard, and Kevin sighed. "Aislinn, I'm sorry. I'm s-so sorry I hurt you. I can't seem to stop hurting you and I-I miss you. Will you please be my sisser again?"

"Theo." I tried not to cry. So hard.

"I wanted to kill that man, Aislinn. He threatened your life. You're my only family. I've been taking care of you forever, and that fucking pissant threatened you. What was I supposed to do? But I-I'm not a murderer. You don't think I am, do you? Please don't hate me anymore."

Tears streamed down my face while Kevin and Luuk maneuvered Theo out of the restaurant. What was I supposed to say to that? Theo had never talked to me like that. I couldn't think of one time he'd shared his feelings with me. He would never have said it if he'd been sober, and he wouldn't remember saying it tomorrow anyway.

"Aislinn, wait," Theo yelled across the restaurant while Kevin steered him toward the door, his shoes dragging and squeaking on the tile floor. "Your mother—I know you. I know you want to find her, but you'll only get hurt. Why do you think I lied?"

"Shit," Kevin said.

The entire restaurant was looking at me. I felt it.

"Wh-what? Theo!"

I stood there shaking, trying to breathe, but I couldn't. It felt like time had stopped.

Did he mean my mother was alive? And he knew? He knew who she was? Did he know where she was? And he'd kept that from me too? Billie had said it *might* be possible she was alive, but Theo had just admitted it was true.

Nothing made sense anymore.

I recognized the bell jingling on the front door when it opened and again when it closed, and then conversation throughout the restaurant resumed when Theo, Kevin, and Luuk were gone.

"C'mon. Let's get some air," Finn said, and he reached for my hand and held it. Not to lead me, but like a best friend would, or a boyfriend. He walked me outside, and the crisp late-fall air stung my face like ice water. "You okay?"

I sucked in a breath. "I—what just happened?"

"Here, sit down. There's a bench behind you." I stepped back and sat, and Finn sat next to me, but he didn't let go of my hand. "Ace, it's pretty obvious Theo's not in a good place. Maybe you shouldn't listen to him. Talk to me. Tell me what you're feelin'."

My mother was alive, and she didn't want to know me. She never had. Now I knew for sure. That reality slammed into me like a kick in my head, and I was ashamed and embarrassed that Finn knew. I wanted to tell him how I felt, but instead, the shame came out.

"I'm *fine*." I stood because my body wanted to wrap around his, and I was afraid it would. "I keep telling you I'm not a child, but you keep treating me that way." I said it, but it was just another lie. I was being my usual bratty self, and I couldn't stop. "I'd like to go home now. Where's Brock?"

"He's drunk. He ain't drivin' you home."

"Yes, he is. He brought me here." Now I was just arguing to argue. Of course I didn't want to get in the car with someone who'd been drinking. Hello! No parents, no life, and no fucking eyes because of a car accident!

Finn sighed. "Well, it's lucky for you that he and Jules just snuck off in the black of night, probably tryin' to avoid the super-fun family drama. Hopefully, Jules will drive Brock. Looks like you're stuck with me tonight, Queen of Sheba."

"She left with him because you were out here with me instead of in there, adoring her like she's been adoring you all night."

"Well, maybe so, but I was tryin' to be a nice guy. Either way, I'm your ride."

I crossed my arms over my chest again. "Fine."

"Fine."

CHAPTER ELEVEN

AISLINN

MY ENTIRE LIFE flashed through my head the whole way back to Cade Ranch: every memory, the sound of my parents' voices, the sound of Theo's when he said, "you'll only get hurt." The images of my family tried to break through the nothingness inside my mind, but they became garbled and blurry before I could grasp them.

Nothing was real and everything was all too real, all at the same time. I hadn't said one word in the truck, and neither had Finn.

"Well, that was a fuckin' disaster," he finally said when we walked into his kitchen. His truck keys clattered on the counter. "I'm gonna call Jack. Maybe we oughta postpone our trip to Montana tomorrow."

"Whatever."

I wanted to hit him. He was acting like Theo's drunk outburst was hard on him, when all it could be considered to him was a minor annoyance. To me, it was life changing, embarrassing, frustrating, maddening, and now I felt so sad. Everything had changed in the last hour.

"It wasn't hard for you. Nothing is ever hard for you. You

live a charmed life. Don't stay here for me. I want you to go. I can't stand you."

"'Scuse me?" He turned, stepping in front of me. His voice was aimed right at my face, and even from his tall height, I felt his stare. "What the hell's wrong with you? Good goddamn, Aislinn. What? What is it you want? I don't have any fuckin' clue what to do with you. Everything I say is wrong. Every move I make. I tried to help you tonight. I was nothin' but kind. I'm always kind to you, and this is what I get for it? What the fuck do you want from me?"

Breath left my mouth in shudders, faster and faster as he became angrier.

I knew exactly what I wanted, but I wouldn't say it. I could never. "I-I want you to leave me alone!" I lied, but I stepped closer to him.

"You ain't foolin' me. You don't know *what* you want."

"Not true. I do know. I'm not a child."

"You keep sayin' that, but all this attitude and bullshit— it's as childish as it gets. I know tonight was hard for you, but damn. I'm fed up, girl. I let you live here, I cook for you, I clean for you. My whole life has been taken over by you. And you know what? I've had enough of it. Good night." He turned, and the air swirled around me, ripe with his annoyance and frustration.

It made me dizzy. It made me want to hit him and push him and kiss him.

Throwing my hand out, I closed my fist around the first thing I touched, which happened to be his forearm below his cuffed sleeve. Digging my nails into his skin, I thought about the threat and the eerie calm in his voice at the restaurant. I wanted that Finn.

I wanted the dangerous Finn, and I knew, to get what I wanted, I would need to be confident.

"What the—?"

"I know what I want," I said when he turned back toward me, trying to pull his arm away, but I held him tighter. I whispered because saying it out loud scared me. "I want you. I want you to make me forget this whole night. This whole year." Making my voice louder, I said, "Make me forget everything."

He laughed at me. "Are you kiddin' me? You treat me like shit on your fancy shoe, and now you want me to… what? Get you off?"

I dropped his arm and squared my shoulders. "Yes."

He was quiet for a moment, and I felt like I was naked in a sea of people. I couldn't read his reaction.

Finally, in a slow and measured voice, he said, "What about your boyfriend? Remember him?"

"He's not my boyfriend. You know he's not. You paraded that woman in front of me tonight on purpose. To make me jealous. Didn't you? What do you think I've been doing?"

He gasped, and suddenly, his big hands were wrapped around my waist, and he pulled me against his body, pressing his hips against my stomach. He was hard, and I smiled.

"You sure?" he asked, his voice that low, slow, sexy rumble. "Make certain it's what you want, girl, 'cause once I start, ain't nothin' stoppin' me." Stepping forward, he ushered me backward until I felt the kitchen counter behind me. He was angry with me, but I knew he wouldn't let me fall.

Raising my face, I felt his warm breath on my lips like the rush of a mysterious wind descending from the top of the tallest mountain, and I wanted desperately to be able to see the anger flash in his eyes. I'd never wished so hard that I could see.

But I *was* certain. I was nervous, but the words hung in the air between us. I couldn't take them back, and I wanted to forget the awful, awkward evening. I didn't want to feel like the rude, needy burden I was. And I didn't want to think for one more minute about Theo, about what he'd said, and about how much pain he was in. And if I thought about my birth mother, I'd scream.

Pressing my hand to Finn's chest, I gripped his soft flannel shirt in my fingers, but I didn't push.

I pulled.

Finn groaned, and then his tongue was in my mouth. His body hard against mine, he lifted me, rubbing his erection between my thighs. And now I was groaning as he set me on the counter and stepped between my legs. Removing my purse strap from my shoulder, he lifted it over my head and set it on the counter, taking my cane from my hand too.

He was practically vibrating with desire, but he stopped. He held my face in his hands, looking at me. I had no clue what he saw or what he might be looking for.

"What? I know you're staring at me. It's not fair. I can't see you."

"Maybe not, but you can *feel* me." He pulled his head back, holding me in place with his hands still, but the heat from his breath dissipated, and he guided my hand to the extremely hard bulge in his jeans. He whispered, "Just this once, just for tonight, can we pretend we don't hate each other?"

I gasped and then moaned when he touched his lips to mine so softly as he guided my legs around his back, holding them there while he pressed into me. He removed my hand and lifted it to his face while he notched his cock exactly where I wanted it, hard against my pussy through our clothes, and all I could think about was what it was going to feel like when he was inside me. With him this close, nothing else mattered.

He was exactly what I needed.

He leaned back and lifted my shirt, then moaned and bent, sucking my bare breast into his mouth. I whimpered and arched my back, pushing further into him, but I liked the way his scruffy five-o'clock shadow felt on the tips of my fingers, so I let them explore, and he leaned into my touch, rubbing his face back and forth in my hand, then he rubbed it against my chest, and I shivered at the sensation. It was drugging.

His tongue was hot and wet, and he flicked my nipple with it, fast like lightning, and it sent zings of pleasure to all kinds of places. Wetness gushed between my legs, and I slid my fingers through his hair, pulling him closer.

He'd worn it up in a stupid man-bun, so I tugged the elastic band out, letting it drop to the floor, and the long strands overflowed my hands.

Oh my God, his hair was like silk on my skin.

Mumbling against my breast, he almost growled, "Take these fuckin' pants off." His breath cooled my bare, wet skin, and my nipples peaked and beaded so fast that they hurt while his thick fingers slipped inside the waistband of my palazzos.

"You're so rude," I said, but I moaned again wantonly, like one of the ridiculous characters in my books.

"Oh yeah? How's this for rude?" Reaching for something next to my leg, he dug through a drawer. "Hold still. Don't move."

Cold metal caressed my stomach, and I flinched a little at the surprise, and then the clipping sound of scissors registered. The scissors clattered and slid away from me on the counter, and then Finn's hands whispered over my skin above my pants. He pulled, and the fabric split, making the loudest ripping noise, and cool air licked my bare thighs, making goosebumps rise everywhere. The ache in my nipples was almost unbearable, and my underwear were soaked clean through.

"I'm going to kill you for that. Those were my favorite, and they cost more money than you've ever had."

Lifting me a little with one arm around my waist, he pulled more, dragging my tattered pants from my body. "Oh yeah? How you gonna kill me? Huh? Gonna complain me to death?"

He set me back on the counter and dropped to his knees, and I swayed, rudderless and lost with him no longer pressed against me.

"You're so fuckin' beautiful like this."

My voice was the smallest wisp of air. "Like what?"

Kneeling between my spread legs, he said, "Messy. Ripped open. Naked."

I groaned and my head fell back. I almost fell backward but caught myself at the last second, planting my hands hard on the waxy, laminate countertop.

He groaned, too, and ripped my bikini briefs away from my body. *Ripped* them. "Open your legs more." He didn't wait for me. With his big heavy hands hot on my thighs, he spread them wide, angled my hips back, and licked from my entrance up to my clit, sucking it into his mouth.

I breathed, "Fuck!" and he groaned.

"You make me cuss," I said, but I moaned and rolled my hips into his face while breath forced its way in and out of my open mouth. It probably sounded very unladylike, but I couldn't focus on it. Not with Finn between my legs, his hair tickling my skin, his wet lips wrapped around my pulsing clit. I squirmed a little because the sensation was overwhelming, and knowing it was Finn touching me there was an intoxicating feeling.

Sliding his hand up my stomach, between my breasts

under my shirt, he reached with his long arm, and his fingers wrapped around my neck, squeezing gently, but the command in them held me in place. My breath caught in my throat, and he squeezed a little. His other hand on my thigh disappeared, then wrapped around my ass, and he pulled me harder against his mouth.

When he had me where he wanted me on the edge of the counter, he pushed a finger inside my desperate, dripping core, dragged it out slowly, and smeared the slick all over my throbbing pussy lips, then lapped it up, the sound of him eating me like a hook in the air, snagging me and dragging me toward some edge. It was right in front of me, and I wanted to fall more than I'd ever wanted anything.

"Jesus, you taste so fuckin' good."

"Finn! Uuungh." Sliding down the counter, unable to hold myself up anymore with three of his fingers inside me now, pumping, and my hips thrusting against his hand, and with his mouth on me, his nasty words all around me, my body gripped those fingers like they belonged there.

I panted and tried not to pass out from the utter pleasure. Not being able to see him, what he was doing, what he would do to me next, was the sexiest, most torrid experience I'd ever had. And his other hand was still wrapped around my throat.

But then he released me. He was still kneeling in front of me, but he backed away, and I swayed from the loss of him. I heard him removing his belt, the hard metal buckle sliding over thick, fat leather, and the sound did something to me. Ripples of need and fervid naked pleasure fluttered then burned in my lower belly. I wanted to feel that leather on my skin.

I'd listened to hundreds of steamy romance audiobooks— the smuttier, the better—so I had some idea about what would make me hot—not that I wasn't already on fire, but I wanted

Finn's belt on my skin so much that my wrists ached for it. And something about me not being able to see his face or his reaction made me feel brazen.

I held my wrists out in front of me, pulse point to pulse point, and Finn froze.

"You—?"

"Do it."

Now he breathed, "Fuck."

Breath seethed out of him. If I hadn't felt it, too, I wouldn't have known it wasn't anger anymore making him shake.

It was want, and the smug satisfaction that he *did* want me rolled through me like wildfire. It blinded me to any insecurity I'd been feeling before.

But he stilled, controlling that shaky breath, and slowly and silently, he wrapped his belt around my wrists, binding them together, tying it somehow, sliding the cool leather strap between them, then snapped the knot into place. It stung my skin, and I moaned.

"Who *are* you?"

I had no clue. I had no idea what I was doing, practically naked in front of him, demanding and begging him, but I thought I would die if he wasn't inside me in the next five seconds.

My heart was beating so fast, and I was writhing on the counter. "Fuck me. Hard," I demanded, begging for him to do to me what I knew he'd done to many women before me, but Finn didn't respond because we heard a truck door slam outside.

I couldn't stop myself from lurching forward when he moved away, cursing, "Shit."

"No, damn it. Don't you dare stop."

"Don't move," he said, leaning away from me and

collecting my discarded clothing, but he came back quickly, grabbed my purse, gripped the belt, and threw my bound wrists over his head. He stood and lifted me into his arms, and then we were moving.

It was so disorienting, and normally, I would've thrown a fit, demanding to be put down. But now, it was the hottest thing I'd ever felt, being whisked away to somewhere secret, bound in Finn's arms, his breath rushing over my face, his heart pounding behind his ribs so close to me. I felt it, and I wanted my body to be the thing that would make it beat faster.

I lifted my face, begging my eyes to see him. They didn't, of course, and then a door slammed, and I was pushed against it.

He dropped my purse and clothing, and I asked, "Where are we?"

"Bedroom."

"Is the light on?" I wasn't sure why I'd asked. I knew it wasn't on, and it didn't matter one bit because I couldn't see him or myself.

"No."

The kitchen door clattered closed, and Evvie called my name, but Finn kissed me hard, and I couldn't answer. She called again, and he tilted his head, plunging his tongue into my mouth, pressing me against the door with his chest and pushing his jeans down, then slid his bare cock between my thighs.

"Finn," I whimpered, but I spread my legs wider.

"I told you to be sure. You changin' your mind?"

"No, but Evvie's out there."

He locked my door. I heard the click of the metal two seconds before Evvie knocked.

"Aislinn? Are you in there?"

In my ear, he whispered, "Answer her."

"Y-yes, Evvie. I'm here."

"Oh." She jiggled the door handle, trying to open it. "Are you okay? Luuk called. He said you saw Theo."

I squeezed my eyes shut, trying to forget.

"I'm here if you want to talk."

Finn whispered again, "Tell her no."

"I'm fine, Evvie."

"Okay, but are you sure? He said you were pretty upset."

"I said I'm fine. Leave me alone. I don't want to talk to you."

"Ahh, there she is," Finn said in my ear. "There's the girl I love to hate."

"Who are *you*?" I whispered back.

He didn't answer. Instead, he yanked my arms over his head and grabbed the belt, pushing my wrists into the door silently. With one hand high above me, he held me there, and I dangled in front of him like a writhing, slithering, oversexed snake.

Something crinkled in front of my face, and I heard paper ripping. Finn spit something from his mouth, then buried his face in my neck, moaning when he rolled a condom over his cock with one hand. His fingers found their way between my legs again, and he pushed two back and forth between my swollen, sopping wet lips.

"Okay," Evvie said, being nice to me even though I'd just yelled at her, "if you're sure. But call me, okay, if you need anything? The truck is here, so I'm sure Finn's home, too, if you need him."

"I'm fine. Go away!"

Finn moaned in my ear, his voice so low, and I imagined a rolling thunderstorm brewing over our heads. He removed his fingers, wrapped my legs around his ass, and rammed his cock inside me.

"Good night," Evvie said, and a few seconds later, we could hear her talking to Jack. The kitchen door thudded shut when they left, and I bit my bottom lip to stop the screams of pleasure trying to rip out of my mouth.

"Did you enjoy that?" Finn rasped in my ear, holding still inside me, biting and licking my neck. His voice shook a little. "Bein' such a brat to just about the nicest person in the world?"

"No."

"No? You sure?" He cupped my breast in his big hand and squeezed, and I groaned.

I panted, trying to respond. "I did it because y-you told me to."

"No, you did it 'cause that's who you are."

"It's *not* who I am."

"Yes, it is." He pulled out and punched back in. How the hell was he holding me up with one hand?

It felt like he was punishing me for being an entitled monster, for demanding things from him I had no right to demand.

But it was more than that.

I wanted to be punished—for the way I'd treated my parents, Theo, all my tutors, the people who'd worked for us, who'd all tried to take care of me, but I'd tormented all of them. Even before the accident, I'd treated all those people as subjects instead of friends. And Louise, who was my friend— or she had tried to be, and she was the only person who'd ever stuck around long enough to care for me because I'd been such an asshole.

I wanted Finn to pull the belt so tight it would cut into my skin. I wanted him to pull my hair and bite me.

And I wanted him to pound his cock so far inside me that I would feel it for days. I would hurt for days. Because I deserved it. How could I not? My mother never wanted me, my whole family was a lie, and I had nothing and no one. And it was all my fault because I was an insufferable bitch.

The belt was cutting off the circulation in my hands, and they ached a little. I tried to flex my fingers, but Finn pushed them harder to the door, thrusting harder inside me, fucking me harder. It hurt. I hadn't had sex since I was sixteen. Well, not with another person. Louise, before she'd been killed, had bought me a dildo. She said I needed a good stiff fuck, and I laughed, thinking about her handing me the box. I'd been so confused, opening it, then she laughed at me when I finally realized what it was and dropped it.

Finn's voice was that taut, edged hum again. "You laughin' at me, woman?"

"Yes," I said because it seemed to turn him on when I was cruel. "Is that the best you can do?" The words came out in this low, husky purr. I hadn't meant them to. I hadn't even known I could make that sound, but when he called me "woman," I felt like one. A powerful one.

He growled, turned, and threw me down to the bed. My stomach flipped, and I felt like I was hurtling through space, but then I landed gracelessly on my back. My arms stretched above me, pulling my muscles, and it hurt, but I didn't tell him.

"Fuck you, Finn."

"Oh, you're about to," he said, and I'd never wanted anything more.

CHAPTER TWELVE

FINN

"YOU WANT me to hurt you, don't you?"

I couldn't understand why that turned me on, but it did. All those times she'd snapped at me, treated me like her butler, all the rude comments and condescension—this was my payback, and I wanted it.

It was deeper than that though. It was about control, but I couldn't think about it. No, I couldn't focus on it with her in front of me, wrists bound together, legs open, breasts heavin'. Fuck my life, she was beautiful. That haughty scowl on her angelic face had been replaced with a look so full of desire, it made my whole body ache.

"Yes."

Unghhh. And that she needed somethin' I could give her? Sexiest fuckin' realization ever.

"Get on your knees," I said, toein' my boots off and pushin' my jeans the rest of the way down my legs. I ripped my flannel off and tore my T-shirt over my head, and she scrambled up on the bed, wobblin' a little since her hands were still bound. "Turn around."

I had no clue where this drill sergeant Finn was comin' from, but there were all kindsa firsts happenin' tonight.

I sat quietly beside her on the bed and untied her wrists. We were both shakin' with nerves and need, but I removed her white slip-on tennis shoes and lifted her shirt over her head, then brought her arms behind her and wrapped 'em with the belt again. Her breasts jiggled with the movement. They were small, but round and perfect, and I wanted 'em in my mouth again.

Her whole body quaked, but she moaned when I pulled the belt into place and tugged. The extra length of leather smacked her ass, makin' the loudest slappin' noise in the quiet room, and she called out a pained but needy cry, and my dick *throbbed*.

Silently, I stood and walked to the end of the bed, climbin' up behind her on my knees while my hands slid down her body, and the sound of my skin on hers turned me on so much that I had to bite the inside of my cheek to keep from comin'.

Yankin' her back to meet my cock, I punched inside her tight body again, and she groaned so loud, fallin' forward, but I still held the belt in one hand so she didn't hit the mattress. I kept her there, in the air, buckin' into her from behind like I was king of the fuckin' rodeo.

It was the hottest, raunchiest, sexiest experience of my whole life.

Moans became gasps the harder I fucked her, and gasps became little cries while I used her body to get back at her for bein' such a brat. I poured all my energy, all my insecurities, doubts, anger, frustration, and angst into fuckin' her. It all loaded up at the base of my dick, like a rocket ready to launch.

She growled like a big ol' bear, and her pussy walls

clamped down on me hard, but she was drenched in need and want, and her body's slick, hot grip on my dick while I thrusted in and out made my eyes go black for a few seconds. I struggled for air and shook 'cause I'd never known sex could feel this good. Each push in and glide out was a pleasure so intense that I could barely think.

Now, I knew what all the fuss was about.

"Harder," she begged, and I obliged. Yankin' her arms back even more, I fucked into that woman like I'd die if I didn't.

It didn't take long then, with her bent over in front of me, her ass slappin' back against me every time I pulled on the belt and punched my hips.

She cried out, and I roared my release to the heavens when I came.

Jesus, God Almighty, it felt so fuckin' good.

When I could catch my breath again enough to speak, I released the belt, and she fell forward, limp like a spaghetti noodle. I pulled out slowly, shiverin' at the loss of her warmth around me, and leaned down to kiss her ass cheeks, rubbin' my hands up and down the sides of her thighs, and she moaned softly, but when I rolled her and removed the leather from her small wrists, intendin' to massage 'em, she sat up.

She was the most beautiful woman I'd ever seen with her hair all messed up and her cheeks flushed pink against her dark skin in the black of the room, the moon comin' in the window the only light for me to see by. She looked wild.

"Did I hurt you too much?"

"No," she said, wrappin' her arms around herself, hidin' her breasts from me and clampin' her legs closed.

I rubbed her shoulders, but she jerked away from my hands. Through clenched teeth, she gritted, "I'm fine."

"What's wrong?"

"Nothing. I said I'm fine. I'm not a baby. You don't need to soothe me."

"That ain't what I'm doin', but that was pretty intense."

"That was nothing. I wasn't a virgin." She huffed, closin' herself off to me.

"No?" I laughed. It wasn't funny, and it wasn't happiness or relief I was feelin', but the laugh slipped past my lips anyway, like a confession. And speakin' of confessions —"Well, till about fifteen minutes ago, I was. So thanks, and thanks for blowin' me off right after. Guess it's true what they say: I'll never forget my first time."

She gasped, and I grabbed my clothes from the floor, threw her door open, and left her sittin' there, naked and fully fucked, just like she'd wanted.

***

"I had sex last night," I said, then chugged half a thermos of hot and delicious coffee.

Jack rolled his eyes. "Uh. Great." It was four in the mornin', and we'd already been drivin' an hour. We still had five hours left to go till we got to the Misty Mountain All Access Barn outside Great Falls, Montana, but I couldn't just sit there silent. I wanted to scream. Dean was asleep in the back seat, curled up and snorin' like a grizzly bear.

"Yeah, so it was my first time."

"Your first time what? Why are we talkin' about this?"

"'Cause I need to talk about it." I pushed my boots against the floorboard, tryin' to stretch my legs 'cause Jack's damn truck was so confinin'. "This truck is so small. I feel like a sardine."

"This truck is huge. You're just a giant."

"Whatever. It was my first time havin' sex."

He nearly drove off the road. "What in the world are you talkin' about?"

"Yep."

"Bullshit."

"Nope. It was."

"So what? You need me to tell you about the birds and the bees or some shit?" He scowled out the windshield. "Wait just a fuckin' minute. How in the fresh hell are you a virgin?"

"Well, technically, I'm not anymore, but I was, I dunno, savin' myself? Man, that sounds ridiculous, but it's the truth."

"I've seen you all over women. You go home with 'em often enough."

"Actually, I haven't gone home with a woman in two years. You're just unobservant. And there's all kindsa things you can do with a woman that don't involve puttin' your dick in a pussy."

"Jesus, Finn."

"Well, what would you have me say? I've done everything under the sun, just never with... penetration."

He groaned, lookin' like he might hurl. "Okay, TMI, brother." He grimaced but then looked over at me. "Savin' yourself for what? This some kinda religious thing?"

"No. When's the last time you saw me go to church? I dunno. I just couldn't picture myself with any of those women, like, married to 'em or in love with 'em."

"Since when do people need to be in love to have sex?"

"I know, but I just didn't feel like it was right. But last night, it felt right. And it was..."

"What?" Jack peeked at me. "Why was last night different?"

"I dunno. This girl—this *woman*—she's different."

"Who is it? Wait, Jules?"

"No, not Jules. Just never you mind. But it was… whew. I tied her up."

Jack choked on his own spit. "Finn, I really don't wanna talk about this with you. If you're feelin' weird about it, talk to Kevin. He's into all sortsa weird shit."

"Why? Because he's gay?" I shook my head and clucked my tongue. "Now look who's insensitive."

"Not 'cause he's gay, 'cause I find rope wherever I turn in the barn in places it shouldn't be, and I kinda sorta walked in on him and Luuk one day. They fuck all over the ranch. Jesus." He turned up the radio, blarin' old Hank Williams's "Hey Good Lookin'".

I turned it down. "Oh. Well, I didn't use rope. I used my belt."

"How the fuck did you go from town virgin to BDSM daddy in one day?"

"How do you know what that is?"

"I'm a man. I've watched porn."

"Oh, right," I said, noddin'. "Well, I'd never done anything like that before. But she—this woman, let's call her Ashley. No! Um, let's call her Camilla." Ashley was too close to Aislinn. "Anyway, she asked me to do it."

"Why do we need to give her a code name? I don't give a shit who you sleep with."

Oh, he'd care. He'd probably stop the truck to beat my ass if he knew I was really talkin' about Ace.

"Anyway, it was hot."

"Yeah. So?"

"So, I mean, is that weird? Like, why would that turn me on? Does that say somethin' weird about me?"

"No, Finn. Good grief. I'm so over this conversation. Talk about somethin' else or just shut the fuck up."

"How do you know? How do you know it ain't weird?"

"Jesus."

"Well?"

"Because it's just not. As long as what you're doin' is consensual, it's fine. Okay? Now can we stop talkin' about it?"

"Nope. Sorry."

"God, you're weird."

"See! You just said I wasn't weird." I chuckled to myself 'cause I was purposely tryin' to egg him on, knowin' how uncomfortable I was makin' him.

"I meant you're weird for always wantin' to talk about your feelin's."

"I was kiddin', but why's that weird? Normal people talk about how they feel. I think it's fucked up that we're so closed off, always afraid to say what's on our minds."

"I talk about how I feel with Evvie. She's the only person I wanna talk about it with."

"You didn't used to."

"No, 'cause I didn't used to have Evvie. Talk to Code Word Camilla about it."

"I can't."

"Why?"

"'Cause she's, um, she's… difficult."

"How?"

"Mmm, she's… I dunno. She's a pain in my ass."

"So then, why do you want her?"

"I don't. I mean, I do, physically, but otherwise, no." I winced on the inside when the words squeezed my stomach, 'cause they were a lie, even though I had no fuckin' clue why I wanted her.

"She on board with that?"

"I think so. She don't like me either."

"Who don't like you?" Dean asked, sittin' up in the back seat, rubbin' sleep from his eyes.

"No one."

"Lemme break it down for you," Jack said. "Finn had sex —for the first fuckin' time—last night with a difficult woman we are ominously callin' Code Word Camilla. He tied her up and he liked it, and he thinks that makes him a pervert."

"Shit, man, if Oly wasn't pregnant, she'd still be tied to our bed. She loves it."

"Oh. So it runs in the family?" I rolled my eyes. "Dean, don't be gross."

"Are you fuckin' kiddin' me?" Jack barked a scoff from the back of his throat. "You been nothin' but gross for the last damn hour!"

Dean stretched behind me, yawned, then said, "Wait. Shut the fuck up. You're a virgin?"

Montana was cold and dreary. It snowed most of the time we were there, but it was kinda fun learnin' new stuff. Most of it I already knew, but there were two therapists there workin' with us, showin' us cues to look for to know when a client was reactin' poorly to their therapy session. Some people couldn't talk or wouldn't, so we'd need to be able to read physical clues to know when to intervene or not to. And we learned about some equipment we could use to make mountin' and dismountin' easier for clients with physical disabilities, and I was excited to get my hands on all of it. I figured Bigsy would let us use him as a guinea pig when we got the equipment for Cade Ranch.

There were a lotta kids runnin' around, and I played with 'em, carryin' 'em on my shoulders while they giggled and squealed. The barn hosted a campout one night for a group of kids, ages eight to twelve, though they didn't actually sleep there. Dean was all into it, too, probably imaginin' his daughters at that age. Jack started a fire that evenin', we roasted marshmallows, and the kiddos soaked up our attention like itty-bitty sponges.

"Are you a real cowboy?" Zoe asked, tuggin' on the ends of my hair. "I didn't know cowboys had long hair."

"He's a hippie cowboy," Dean said, chucklin'.

Zoe skipped over to Dean and crawled into his lap, lookin' up at him, and the smile on his face? Oh boy. Guy was a goner. "What's a hippie?" she asked. She was very affectionate, and Miss Pearl, the camp counselor, told us it was a characteristic of down syndrome. If she wasn't holdin' my hand or Dean's, she was huggin' Jack.

I laughed, watchin' him smile at Zoe. The difference between Jack now and Jack a year ago was night and day. When it was time to work or to ride, he always picked Zoe to be his partner. I took pics with my phone of the two of 'em together, dancin' around the arena or out ridin', and sent 'em to Evvie. She texted back that she was gonna make Jack knock her up the second he got home. Gross, but yeah, I could picture it.

"A hippie's just someone with long hair and stinky clothes who listens to weird music. So, basically, Finn," Dean said, and Zoe howled with laughter.

"My grandma said she was a hippie," Justin said. That kid was smart as a whip. He also had cerebral palsy, and he had the best sense of humor and was always crackin' us up. "She said when it was the nineties, she choked the peace pipe."

Snortin' hot chocolate out my nose, I tried not to laugh but failed, and Justin giggled, pointin' at the mess on my jacket.

"We really are cowboys," I said, "but we don't work with cows, only horses."

"Doesn't that mean you're horseboys?"

"Hm, s'pose you're right, Justin," I said, "but horseboy don't sound quite as cute as cowboy, now does it?"

"You're not cute, you're handsome," Zoe told Dean, and she patted his bearded cheek. "You have mighty muscles and I gonna marry you."

"You are?" he said, laughin' a little. "Well, that's real sweet. You think you could teach me how to make a snow angel like you made yesterday?"

"Yeah! Come on." She jumped down, tuggin' Dean behind her, and Jack and all the kids and their aides wandered out to the lawn in front of the ranch house to flop around in the snow.

I stayed behind. A twelve-year-old boy, Matthew, sat alone in his wheelchair, lookin' down at his hands in his lap. He and his daddy had been in a car accident over a year ago, and he'd lost the use of his legs. His mama said he'd been havin' a real hard go of it. His daddy hadn't made it, and Matty had been strugglin' with survivor's guilt. Plus, he just really missed his ol' man.

"Matty, would you like to make a snow angel?" Miss Pearl asked. "Finn, would you mind carrying him? I'd rather not risk getting his chair stuck in the snow."

"No, snow angels are stupid," he said, crossin' his arms.

Miss Pearl sighed, a look of heartbreak settlin' on her face. Noddin' for her to join the others, I waited till she was far enough away that she couldn't hear us.

"Snow angels aren't stupid. They're fun," I said, ploppin' down on a log next to Matty's chair.

"Oh yeah? What do you know about it? You're a horseboy."

"Maybe so, but we got plenty of snow in Wyoming, and I personally make it a habit to do at least five snow angels every day."

"You're a liar."

"I'm just jokin' with you, man. Just tryin' to have fun."

"Yeah, it's a real hoot, making fun of the crippled kid."

"I ain't makin' fun of you. I was tryin' to entertain you."

"Well, the joke's on you. You need working arms and legs to make snow angels. Can you tell me which one of those things is missing, or are you too stupid for that?"

"You're right. I am stupid. I can't read."

Matty scoffed. "Yeah, right."

"I ain't lyin'. Technically, I know *how* to read, but when I look at words on a page, they jump and flip around in my mind, and I can't understand what they mean. I get real frustrated."

"So?"

"So, I was just thinkin' that maybe you and me have a little somethin' in common."

"Being illiterate is different than being a paraplegic."

I tried not to be offended. "Oh yeah, that's for sure, but still, I have a disability like you do, but I don't let that stop me from havin' fun."

"Okay then, genius, how exactly would you propose I make a goddamn snow angel?"

"Well, I am a genius 'cause I got two ideas."

Finally, Matty looked up.

"My first idea is that maybe we change our perception of what a snow angel is s'posed to look like." I scrunched my fingers in the air, imitatin' quotations. "Who says a snow angel has to have arms and legs? I bet real angels come in all shapes and sizes."

"There's no such thing as 'real angels.'"

"No? How do you know?"

He looked down again. "I just do. Besides, everyone will make fun of mine."

"Hmm. Yeah, that's hard. I get that. I got made fun of a lot when I was your age."

"You did?" He looked in my eyes, searchin' to make sure I wasn't lyin' just to make him feel better.

"Oh yeah. I wasn't always the debonair gentleman you see before you now."

Matty snorted.

"Seriously, though, I always held up the rest of the class since it took me so much longer to read and write. And I'd get so frustrated, so my attention would wander. The teacher was always mad at me, and the kids got annoyed if we had to stay after class or skip recess 'cause of me."

"So, what'd you do?"

I smirked. "Welp"—I popped my lips—"I have many *other* skills, so I used those."

"What other skills?"

"I'm resourceful. And I'm good with people. And I play a pretty mean guitar."

"Okay, but how did that help you not get made fun of?"

"I dunno. I guess it made me quicker and sharper. You know? I learned how to do other things better and faster than the other kids. Besides, name one guitar player that don't get plenty of love from the ladies, and I'll shave my head." Bumpin' my shoulder against his, I winked when he looked at me, wigglin' my eyebrows, but he dropped his eyes again.

"Anyway, my point is, since I'm not good at readin', when I need to figure out what somethin' says, like instructions or somethin', I look it up online. There's usually a video I can watch. I learn much better that way."

"You want me to Google 'how does a paraplegic kid make a snow angel?'"

"No. I want you to think outside the box. That's what I do."

"That's dumb." He looked up. "How do you do that?"

"C'mon, I'll show you. Ooo, and I just had a third idea. Instead of a snow angel, let's make a snow alien. That'll be way outside the box." I grinned, and Matty shook his head but then rolled his eyes and smiled.

I carried him out to the field, and we lay down in the snow head to head. I used my legs, and he used his arms, and we made a really tall, two-headed alien snow angel with four arms, then we instigated a snowball fight, and Matty used me as a shield, naturally, and since Dean was such a good shot, I was soakin' wet and loaded with welts by the time the kids went home.

CHAPTER THIRTEEN

AISLINN

"THE GUYS WILL BE BACK TOMORROW TOO," Jay said, "and damn, I'll be glad for it. Even with Isaac helpin' me and Kev, I've never worked so hard in my life. We have got to find some more ranch hands."

"It's just making your muscles musclier. I approve," Billie said through Jay's speakerphone.

Jay, Shonda, and I were in the office, getting ready to close down for the day.

"I miss you so much, Jonathan. I can't wait to see you."

"I miss you too. Tomorrow can't come soon enough."

"My first Thanksgiving with my new family," Billie said. "There will be pumpkin pie and whipped cream, right? You're making pumpkin pie?"

Jay laughed. "Uh, no, you don't want me to make it. But Finn'll make it for you."

"Okay, good."

Jay made kissing noises into his phone and ducked out of the office, and Shonda groaned.

"Good Lord, those two are so bad. How can you live with them?" She laughed.

"Yeah, it gets pretty old pretty fast," I said, "but it's cool too. Billie was so different before she and Jay got together."

"Really? How so?"

"She was always funny and caring, but she was closed off. She put on a big front to everyone, you know, so we wouldn't see her softer side. I guess she still does that, but not with Jay. And not with me. She's my best friend."

"Well, I'm glad you have someone in your life like her. I know I never have to worry about you if she's around."

"Why would you have to worry about me?"

"Oh, I just meant, she's a great friend, that's all. I had a friend like that once. It was nice to know she had my back no matter what."

"What happened to her?"

"Oh, she... Well, she met a man."

"So? She stopped being your friend because she found a boyfriend? That doesn't sound like a great friend to me."

"She didn't do it on purpose, and there were other factors." Shonda sighed across the room. "The snow is so pretty. I wish you could see it. It's really fine, and it's glittering as it falls."

I didn't need to see it. I felt it on my face every time I was outside. I tasted it on my tongue and listened to the beautiful silence that came with every snowfall. What are your plans for Thanksgiving? Did I tell you Theo's coming here? I didn't invite him. Jay did." Now I sighed.

"Oh, I, well... I'm going back to Nevada. Didn't I tell you that?"

"No."

"I'm sure I did. You must've forgotten. That's what I'm doing. My... my sister is there."

"You have a sister? That's nice. Will you have a big dinner together?"

"Yes. I do have a sister, and we'll probably have a turkey. And a ham. And all the sides. You know. Big family thing." She sounded so chipper, but why did I get the feeling she was lying to me?

"You never talk about her."

"No? Oh, well, she's… sick, and I guess I don't really like to think about it."

"What's wrong with her?"

"She's… mentally ill."

"Oh. I'm so sorry." That was vague, but maybe she was just embarrassed to say it. Any kind of mental illness was still treated with a lot of shame and disdain in the US.

Grabbing my hand, she said, "I'm just glad you won't be alone. I know you said the holidays haven't been the same since your parents died. But this year, you'll get the big family affair. That'll be fun, huh?" She patted my cheeks and held my face between her hands.

Sometimes, Shonda made me a little uncomfortable. She was nice, always nice and kind, and she was always helpful, but I'd had enough mother drama in my life, and I wasn't looking for more, but that was how she treated me. Like she was my mother. I felt bad for her because she didn't have any children, but this was the first time I was hearing about a sister.

She seemed lonely, and because of that, I felt like maybe she focused a little too hard on my life.

"When do you leave for Nevada? Are you driving or flying?" I backed away, searching with my hands for the file folders I knew were on the table, tidying up for the night.

"Oh, I'll just drive, probably leave tomorrow after we're done here. This was a last-minute arrangement."

"Shonda, if your plans don't work out, you can always

spend Thanksgiving here. I know the Cades would love to have you."

It wasn't my place to invite her, but I knew they wouldn't mind. And everyone kept telling me how much food there would be with Finn and Evvie cooking, and Daisy and Oly's mom would be bringing food too. And apparently Phil Beasley, the weird old lady who lived on the mountain, would be bringing so many desserts, we'd have whole pies left over to take to the women and children's shelter in Jackson the next day.

I had purposely been blocking Finn from my mind, but now, thinking about him coming home, spending Thanksgiving with him and Theo, my stomach twisted into a knot. Until Billie's house was ready, I'd still be stuck with him.

Or more like, he'd still be stuck with me.

I hadn't told Billie about having sex with Finn yet, and it was killing me. But I was afraid it would change the dynamic between us, or between his brothers and me, and I didn't think I could handle that. I was learning to depend on myself with their help, and they were all so accepting of me. I didn't want to screw that up.

A virgin? He expected me to believe that? Please. But why would he lie? And how did he know how to make me come like that if he was a virgin? I was so confused.

And I—oh my God, I wanted more. I was practically drooling just thinking about it—the pain in my wrists when he held me up against the door. When he held me in the air and fucked into my body like… I didn't know! It was desperate and so hot. The sounds he made, the sounds our bodies made slapping together… I couldn't get the red-hot image out of my head, and I ground my teeth and bit back a moan.

I couldn't even listen to my smut books anymore. None of

the hunky, alpha wolf-shifters compared to Finn. Not one! Great. Now I would have to start listening to autobiographies or instructional manuals because any romance book I tried to listen to just made me think about Finn, about when his leather belt slapped my—

"Aislinn?"

I squeaked, "What?" and dropped the folders.

"You okay, sweetie? You seem distracted."

"Oh, sorry," I stuttered and picked up the files, then turned to walk them to the "in progress" folder basket. "I was just thinking I'd like to contribute to the dinner menu, too, but I don't cook."

"Oh, well, I can help you with that. Would you like to come to my house tonight? We can run to the grocery store on the way. I've got a bunch of recipes I haven't made in years, but they're all people pleasers."

"Really? You'd do that for me? Don't you have something else you'd rather do tonight?"

"Oh, no, I was just planning to watch TV or maybe check out that wolf book you told me about."

I groaned. "I don't want to talk about that book."

Shonda and I strolled through the grocery, my hand resting lightly on her arm as she guided me, and it was kind of fun. I ignored the thoughts spinning around in my head about Finn and just relaxed. She seemed to be at ease around me too. We were friends and it was nice. Since my mother passed, I hadn't had any other black women in my life, and it felt good to acknowledge that part of myself.

I hadn't yet told Shonda about how my parents had died, but I talked a little about them as we strolled through the store. I didn't talk about the accident or what I'd gone through, just about my parents in general. Memories from when I was little. Memories of Theo and all the trouble I'd gotten us into because I never listened and always did the opposite of what my parents wanted, like the time I'd gotten us lost in New York City when we'd gone as a family when my father had had a big meeting there.

I was seven and Theo had been ten or eleven. I wanted an ice cream cone, and I'd seen a shop down the road. We were waiting on a bench outside of a jeweler—my father had insisted on taking my mother in when she'd swooned over some necklace or bracelet she'd seen in the window. As a mixed-race couple, my parents had gotten a lot of looks and rude comments, and my father said he wanted to cover my mother in jewels just to shut them up.

Theo hadn't wanted to disobey our parents, but I'd talked him into it, or, well, I'd forced him into it when I marched away. He followed because he was afraid I'd get lost or kidnapped. He was my protector even then. We did get lost because, after we had our cones, I'd walked away. Just to do it. I wanted to see how far I could get before our parents caught up to us. But all those tall buildings looked the same to us back then. After we'd turned a corner and I'd wandered into a candy store, when we came back out, neither of us had any idea where we were.

I thought about only myself back then too.

Finally, after walking for an hour, getting even more lost and crying and blaming Theo, I sat on the sidewalk and wailed. Theo flagged down a police officer, and he took us to the nearest station to wait for our parents. And when they showed up, they were furious with Theo. They blamed him, too, but he never tattled on me.

Shonda assured me that I was just a child back then, and

that I should be nicer to myself now, that it hadn't been my fault. She did that a lot. Made excuses for me. She seemed protective of me.

When we arrived at her house, she led me inside, and I wandered around, exploring her simple and sparsely decorated space. I was nosy and felt my way through the few knickknacks and things on her bookshelf, on her counters, and the small table behind her couch.

"Who are these pictures of?" I asked, lifting a picture frame and feeling the glass, like I could see the person in the photo with my fingers.

"Oh, that's my sister, and the others are pictures of me with her and our parents."

"Where did you grow up, Shonda? You've never said."

"Didn't I?" she asked, taking the photo from my hands. She touched my arm, and I let her lead me into her kitchen. "Here, sit down at the table. I'm just going to get the ingredients ready. We can prepare the casserole, and then you can keep it in the refrigerator until Thursday. It'll keep."

"Okay, thank you. No, you've never said where you're from."

"Oh, well, I grew up in Waltham. In Massachusetts."

"Waltham? That's Boston. You lived in Boston? Why didn't you ever say?"

"I guess I thought I had."

"That's crazy. We were neighbors."

"Not neighbors exactly. Waltham is no Beacon Hill."

"Close enough. You could've been friends with my parents."

"Mm, oh, yes, maybe." She took a deep breath. "Okay, ready? Let's cook."

There hadn't really been any cooking involved. We mixed together cans of sweet corn and creamed corn, sour cream, melted butter, and boxes of corn bread mix. That was it. Honestly, corn bread casserole sounded disgusting, but Shonda assured me it would be a hit.

She was quieter then, and she barely let me help, taking over for me when I couldn't get the can opener to work properly, stirring the mixture for me when she said I needed to scrape the edges of the bowl. Finally, sitting at the table, I gave up and let her finish.

It hadn't taken long, and she drove me back to the ranch.

"Jay should be here, Shonda. Is the Jeep here? You don't need to come in. I'm sure you'd like to get to bed. He can help me with the food."

"It's no problem," she said and her car door creaked open. Okay. It really wasn't necessary, but whatever. When she opened my door, she lifted the heavy glass dish from my lap. "So, you'll cook it in the oven at 350 degrees for about forty minutes, then take it out and sprinkle shredded cheddar cheese on top. Cook it for another fifteen minutes, and voila. Cornbread casserole."

"Okay."

"Maybe I should just cook it for you. I could drop it off and then leave to go to my sister's."

"Shonda, that's ridiculous. It's one casserole. I think I can manage. Don't worry." I said all this, but inside, I was seething. Just one more person who treated me like a child. If she didn't think I could figure out how to slide a dish into the oven or stir corn slop, how could she rely on me every day in the office?

"I don't want you to burn yourself."

"I'll be fine. Thank you. I'm sure everyone will love your dish."

"Okay. If you're sure." She handed the dish back to me,

then took it away again. "You can't hold this and use your cane. I'll walk you in."

"Fine."

We walked into the house and she made herself busy, scurrying about the kitchen. I had no idea what she could be doing since placing the casserole in the refrigerator should only have taken thirty seconds, but I could hear her milling around. Was she cleaning?

"Thank you, Shonda. I'm going to bed."

"Okay, yes, I'm sure you're tired." She moved toward the door, and I extended my cane and headed toward my bedroom. "Oh, here, let me help you—"

"Shonda! I'm fine. Thank you. Good night."

"Oh. Okay. Good night."

"Everything okay, ladies?" Jay asked, walking in from the front porch. He must've been working late in the arena. He brought the cold air in with him, and it smelled like a snowstorm was heading our way, that crisp, clean, quiet smell.

"Yes," I said. "Shonda was just leaving."

"Good night to you both," she said, and she left.

"You okay, Ace? You look weird," Jay said, closing the door behind Shonda.

"I'm okay, Jay, thank you."

"Did I hear you yell at Sho?"

"Yes, I guess I did. She was babying me, and I kind of snapped."

"Oh, well, I'm sure she knows you didn't mean it."

"Right. Have you talked to Billie? I kind of need to talk to her."

"Not since earlier. She's deep in a search tonight. Why, somethin' wrong? You can talk to me, if you want."

Really? Would you like to hear all about how your

brother fucked me up against my bedroom door? "No, thank you. It's girl stuff."

"Okay," he said. "I'm gonna take a shower and head to bed. I've got a long day tomorrow before I have to pick Billie up at the airport, and if the barn's in tatters when Jack gets home, he'll kill me. You wanna come with me to pick her up?"

"No, thank you. You two will probably spend an hour kissing in the car, and I don't think I want to listen."

He laughed. "Good call. Okay, night then."

"Good night."

Just as I heard the bathroom door click closed upstairs and the shower turn on, the house phone rang.

I called up the stairs for Jay, but he didn't hear me, so I walked back to the kitchen to answer. "Cade Ranch."

"Aislinn?"

"Finn?"

"Yeah, um, is Jay around? I wanna talk to him, but he ain't answerin' his cell."

"He's in the shower."

"Oh. Okay… Well, how are you?"

"I'm fine." *And I'm freaking out! I loved what you did to me, but I don't know why, and I want you to do it again. I miss you. But I hate you. But I really miss you. But I don't want you to be another person who leaves me, and I don't want to make you mad anymore. Do you miss me?*

"'Course you are. How am I?" He laughed, but it was bitter. "Oh, well, I'm so glad you asked. I'm fan-fuckin'-tastic. See you tomorrow," he snapped, and he hung up.

"Oly?" I whispered into my cell phone because I didn't want to take the chance that Jay would hear me.

"Yeah? Aislinn?"

"Yes. Um, I need your help."

"Okay? With what?"

"I need you to look something up for me, and I need you to help me find some books."

"Oh, sure, I can do that. Why you whisperin'?"

I snapped, "I'm not." I was embarrassed about what I wanted her to do, but it would take too long if I did it myself.

She laughed. "Oookay. What kinda books?"

"You're a doctor, right?"

"I'm a veterinarian. There's a big difference. Why?"

"Well, can we just pretend there's such a thing as patient confidentiality with veterinarians?"

"Aislinn, if you wanna tell me somethin', you don't have to worry. I won't tell anyone else. What is it?"

"W-what do you know about… about bondage? During sex. And can you find me some smutty bondage audiobooks? I need you to read me the reviews. Make sure they have lots of good ones. And an HEA."

"Uh-h-h, um, a what?"

"A happily-ever-after ending."

"Who the eff is this?! Did Finn put you up to this?"

Oh, he put me up to it all right.

CHAPTER FOURTEEN

AISLINN

OLY HELPED me find the books I wanted. We were on the phone for over an hour while she read me the titles and descriptions, describing the book covers to me. We compared reviews, and I ended up with some wildly popular bondage books that had been made into movies. The plot was kind of boring, but the bondage scenes were hot. The first book didn't really help me understand myself any better than I had the day before though. It was more about a guy who had been abused and used women to ease his pain because they looked like his dead mother. I gave up on that book.

But before she had to get off the phone because she was having something called Braxton Hicks contractions, Oly found me a women's fiction book by a new author, and it sounded promising. It was about a young woman around my age who was trying to find herself. She discovered that she enjoyed light bondage play with her boyfriend. The story was her journey through discovering what she did and didn't like. Her boyfriend broke up with her because he was threatened by her curiosity, of course, so she set out to find herself in other places.

Oh my God, it was so hot.

The next night, Jay had gone to get Billie at the airport, Shonda had left for her sister's, and Finn and his brothers were on their way home from Montana. There was a big storm roaring outside, and Jay had set a fire for me before he left, so I was in the living room alone, sprawled out on the couch, chilling and listening to my book.

I'd been listening to it every spare moment I could since I bought it the night before, so I was well into the story, and already, I could imagine a whole host of things that turned me on. And I could really imagine them when I pictured doing them with Finn. I'd masturbated twice already. I waited until Jay left, of course. I wasn't gross.

I was about to do it again during a particularly smutty scene involving blindfolds and oral sex with the woman's ankles tied to her wrists—*Oh my God!*—when the kitchen door was thrown open.

"Hello?! Is anyone here?"

When I heard Oly's voice, I jumped up and almost fell on my face, but I caught myself with my hands on the arm of the couch.

"Aislinn? Billie?"

Ugh. Great. Did anyone ever mind their own business around this place?

"Hello!" Oly called.

When she came closer to the living room, I said, "I'm kind of busy, Oly." I really didn't want to stop listening to my book.

"Aislinn, oh, thank God. Look, I don't have time for your attitude. I helped you, and now, you're gonna help me. The babies are comin', and it's a hundred year storm out there! Dean's somewhere between here and Montana, I can't get ahold of Luuk or my parents, and I can't get through to 911."

I backed away from her voice because the sudden panic made me dizzy. "Call Evvie."

"I did! No calls are going through." She moaned loudly, and the sound came from the floor. "Oh my God."

"Use the house phone. Why are you on the floor?"

"Because this fucking hurts! There are two babies trying to exit my body at the same time, Aislinn. The phone lines are dead. The house phone won't work. Damn thing is about as useful as a spoon in a ten-foot pile of hay."

"What do you want me to do? I don't know anything about delivering babies." My heart was beating so fast, and the pit in my stomach made me want to throw up. She was scaring the shit out of me.

"Aislinn, you have to do it. There's no one else. *Please.*" She whimpered and panted in pain. "Please. I know it's scary, but I'll talk you through it."

"You don't want me, Oly. You know you don't. Can't you drive to Jack and Evvie's house? It's less than a mile away, and she's probably there."

She cried out, "Aislinn!" and my heart stopped. There was so much pain in that cry.

"Oly?"

"Please," she begged, " I need your help."

"O-okay."

"Okay." She sighed in relief. "Good. First"—she exhaled through her lips, two deep and even breaths—"I need you to find some towels. Several. And then you need to scrub your hands and put gloves on. I think there's a box under the kitchen sink. They're for deliverin' foals, but they'll do."

"Okay," I said, but I just stood there. I was paralyzed with fear. How could she ask me to do this? I couldn't do it! I'd mess up. If I couldn't see the babies, how could I get them out of her body?

What if I hurt her? What if I hurt *them*?

"Aislinn, please!"

"Right. I'm going." Searching behind me for my cane on the coffee table, I found it and clutched it in my hand. The cold handle was familiar, and it gave me a little bit more confidence. Extending it, I moved toward the stairs.

"Oh!" Oly groaned so loudly and I froze.

"What? What's wrong?"

"It *hurts*. Go, Aislinn. Hurry. They're comin'."

I ran to the stairs. I knew there were a bunch of obstacles in my way, but I didn't have time to be afraid of falling or of getting hurt. There were actual lives on the line.

Amazingly, I didn't trip over anything until my toes collided with the first step, and I fell forward, dropping my cane. But I used the position, crawling up the stairs quickly, patting the wood with my hands, feeling for the top stair, until I reached it.

"Oly! Where are the towels? Is there a closet?" It occurred to me that I should've known where the towels were. I'd been living in this house for over two months! But like always, I'd allowed everyone else to do everything for me. To wait on me.

I was furious with myself. If I hadn't acted like such a princess, I'd already know where the goddamned towels were.

"Yes! All the way at the end of the hall. Walk straight till you find it. Middle shelf."

"Okay. Oh, God."

Fumbling and stumbling down the hall, I used the wall to guide me. I passed three doors and then bumped into a skinny door at the end. When I yanked it open, things clattered to the floor all around me. I didn't know what any of it was, but it didn't matter. Reaching forward, swiping my hands out in front of me, I felt for the harsh, terry-cloth feel of inexpensive towels. I found them and tried to slow my breathing, tried to stop my hands from shaking so I could count.

There were only four towels. Was that enough? I grabbed them and turned, terrified of falling down the stairs, but I couldn't go slow. Damn, my cane was somewhere at the bottom. I clutched the towels to my chest with one arm and used the other to feel out in front of me until I hit another door, but it was open.

Instantly, I knew it was Finn's room. I was so thankful for his slovenly ways. I remembered when Billie had told me that Finn's room smelled, but it smelled good to me. It smelled like healthy, sexy man.

Oh my God, Aislinn, what is the matter with you?

But from the scent, I knew where I was. There were only five steps to the stairs from Finn's bedroom door. I knew because I counted his footsteps every time he left his bedroom at night, hoping he'd come to mine.

It was heart-palpitatingly terrifying, but I pulled off my socks so I could feel better with my feet and inched forward, taking larger steps then I normally did since Finn's feet were probably twice the size of mine, until my big toe dipped over the first step, and then, because walking would take too long, I lowered myself to my butt and slid down the stairs like a child. But it worked.

When I hit the bottom stair, my feet firmly planted on the living room floor, I kicked around until my cane clattered beside me. I grabbed it and stood, racing back to find Oly now halfway between the living room and the kitchen.

"I have the towels," I said when I could hear her quiet but rapid breathing beside me.

"Okay, oh God," she panted, "we need somethin' to cut the umbilical cords."

"Scissors! I know where they are." Of course I did because I remembered when Finn had used them to cut the pants off my body.

"Oh my God, Aislinn."

"What?" I found the counter and ripped the drawer next to the sink open. It came all the way out, clattering to the floor, and all of its contents spilled around my feet. But when I bent to dig through the mess, the scissors were on top of a pile of other utensils. Thank God for small favors. I gripped them hard and turned on my knees. "Oly?"

She whimpered, but her voice had moved again.

"Where did you go? Oly?"

"Oh!" she cried. "I-I'm here. I'm on the floor five feet away from you. Oh, it hurts so much!"

"Breathe. Just breathe. Did you take those classes?" I asked, angling my body in the direction of her voice. "You know, like in the movies?"

"Lamaze?"

"Yes."

"I did, but it's so hard to focus. It feels like my stomach is bein' ripped open!"

"Focus on me. Focus on the sound of my voice. You can do it. I'm going to keep talking, probably about stupid stuff, but just listen to my voice, okay?"

"I can't! I can't do this. I need Dean," she cried, groaning again in pain.

"I know. He's coming, Oly. He'll do anything to get to you. You know he will. But while he's fighting to get to you, we have to fight too. We don't have a choice. The babies are coming and they need you. Okay? Focus on my voice."

Reaching up and behind me, I patted the counter for the towels until I located them, then I crawled across the floor, pushing them in front of me until I bumped into her leg. I set the scissors beside her foot and kneeled next to her. "I'm going to make two little nests with the towels for the babies. I'm sorry. I don't want to put them on the floor, but I can't risk dropping them if I try to carry them to the couch."

"It's okay. They'll be okay."

"No. It's not okay," I said, trying really hard not to cry and freak out. My voice was a lump in my throat. "I don't ever want them to feel like they were discarded or unwanted. But I don't know what else to do."

Through her panting, she vowed, "They will *never* feel that way. We'll make sure of it. You can help me." She laughed through her tears. "Auntie Ace?"

I smiled, nodding, tears running down my cheeks in rivers, and right then, I realized the vow in my voice too. "Yeah."

Oly let out a guttural groan. "Oh God. I think it might be time."

"Okay."

"I'm gonna guide your hands, and I need you to tell me what you feel."

She grabbed my hands, pulling them between her legs, and we felt with our fingers, until they came to a hard rounded protrusion. There was no time to feel awkward or weird about touching her. I just had to do it.

"Oh my God. I feel the head!"

"Ohh. I have to push."

"Okay. Don't be scared. I'm here. I won't let her fall."

Oly strained and pushed, and when she stopped breathing, pushing harder, I reminded her to take a breath. The baby came further and further out, until I could feel her face, her tiny nose, eyes, and lips.

"Her head is all the way out."

"Is she facin' down?"

"Yes."

"Oh, thank God."

She panted through her contractions, and I kept talking. I told her to think about Dean when he finally arrived and how happy he'd be to hold his children. I told her about my bondage book, and in the adrenaline-fueled sisterhood fest, I told her about having sex with Finn. I couldn't see her reaction, but it seemed to occupy her attention for a few minutes, and then she blurted, "Wait just a hot minute! You wanted bondage books for Finn? I mean, who's corruptin' who here?"

But we counted and breathed and counted and breathed.

Then she screamed.

"Oly? What? Tell me what to do!"

"I think it's her shoulders. Oh, it hurts! They're too wide!"

She bumped my hands, reaching between her legs, but I couldn't tell what she was doing.

"Oly?"

She grunted and moaned, whimpering and hissing and making all kinds of noises. None of them sounded good.

"Oly, please talk to me. I can hear you breathing, but what's happening?"

Her voice shook when she asked, "Are you holdin' her head?"

"Yes. I have her."

She growled and strained, then pulled her hands away and pushed with all her strength.

"Pull, Aislinn. Gently."

I did, and suddenly, there was a tiny human in my hands.

Oly cried out and collapsed back onto the floor.

"What now?" There was no sound. *Oh no.*

"Aislinn, she's not breathin'. Cut the cord an inch from

her body, then hold her upside down. You need to smack her back."

"What!"

"It sounds awful, but do it. She's not *breathing*!"

Cradling the baby in one arm, I felt for the scissors next to me and found them, then opened them.

"Wait. Here," Oly said, "give her to me."

"Right. Good thinking." I set the scissors on the floor, then handed the baby to her, and she cried, "Oh, my baby. *Please* breathe. Now, Aislinn, cut between my fingers."

When I could feel two of Oly's fingers, I gripped the scissors hard and angled them in what I hoped was the right direction. I was terrified, and my hands were shaking so much.

"Yes! Right there. Don't worry about hurtin' her. I won't let you. Just cut."

I did, then let the scissors fall to the floor and whisked that baby into my arms so fast. Without once thinking about dropping her, I held her tiny ankles between my fingers, dangling her upside down, and patted her back, then smacked it over and over.

Finally, the baby wailed her first breath, and I sobbed.

And Oly cried and growled. "Oh, God. I have to do that again?"

"What's her name?" I asked, wiping the tiny, shrieking baby with a towel, tucking it around her and counting carefully. "She's so soft. She has ten fingers and ten toes. She's breathing well." I hadn't needed to say it; the baby still cried her tiny but powerful cry.

Oly sobbed in relief. "Her name is Fiona."

"Hello, Fiona," I whispered, kissing her little forehead and cradling her to my chest. "Welcome to the world. Your mommy and daddy love you, and so do I."

"Ace, put her in her nest. It's time again. Sara's comin'. What in the ever-lovin' fuck is happenin'? I thought first births were supposed to be slow!"

I laughed at Oly's cursing. She rarely did it. "It's okay. We can do this." Placing Fiona so carefully on a towel on the floor, I made sure she was tucked tight like a burrito while she screamed her raspy newborn cry, then turned my attention back to Oly.

The wind howled outside, the house creaked, and I saw nothing but darkness, but my confidence was growing with Fiona next to me, still wailing, but she was breathing. She was alive.

"Oh no!"

"What? Oly, what is it?"

"The power's out. There's no light."

I laughed. "What's your point?"

"Wh—oh."

"I can't promise we won't freeze to death, but I just delivered one baby in the dark. Let's go for two."

CHAPTER FIFTEEN

FINN

MY BROTHER RACED up the snow-covered lane, flashin' the truck's headlights and honkin' the horn. I wasn't sure what good he thought that would do, but he was frantic, tryin' to get to Oly, so I didn't make a fuss.

She'd called and left a message on Dean's cell, yellin' into the phone, tellin' him the babies were comin' and she was stuck in a snowstorm. We'd already been on our way back to Wisper, but Jack had stopped the truck on the side of the highway 'cause Dean was freakin' out when he couldn't get ahold of her or get through to Doc Whitley or Luuk—no one was answerin' their phones—and Dean practically threw Jack out the door so he could drive. Jack climbed into the back seat of his own truck and kept quiet.

When we finally made it to the ranch, after racin' through a whiteout blizzard, nearly slidin' into two ditches, and through panic, anxiety, and a weird cryin' spell that I planned to *never* let Dean live down, we parked next to Oly's still-runnin' SUV with the driver's-side door wide open and about a foot of snow on the seat. The ambulance was a mile behind us, but even through the ragin' storm, we could hear it and see the lights off in the distance.

Dean and Jack jumped out and left our truck runnin', too, so I switched 'em both off and closed the doors, then made my way inside.

When I got there and found the baby party with a flashlight, Dean was on his knees in front of an exhausted and sweatin' Oly. She was propped up with cushions from the couch on the hard kitchen floor, she and Dean each holdin' a tiny baby in their arms, with tears streamin' down both their faces. There were candles glowin' on the dinner table and one by Oly's head, and she smiled, lookin' at Dean and then back down at the other bundle in her arms. Dean leaned down to kiss her, and they were lost in each other's eyes.

The whole thing truly was a sight to behold.

Jack stood next to Dean, starin' down at the babies with a look of utter bewilderment on his face, and Aislinn sat next to Oly on the floor, shakin' from head to toe, but smilin' and lookin' proud while the baby girls wailed.

"Everybody okay?" I asked, inchin' my way toward Ace, the snow from my boots leavin' melted puddles behind me. The kitchen looked like a small tornado had ripped through it. There were drawers on the floor, towels everywhere, and a box of foalin' gloves strewn all over the place, litterin' the floor like huge condoms after a frat party.

"We're okay, Finn," Oly said. "The babies came a little early, but they're okay."

"Ace?" I asked when she just sat there.

"I did that," she whispered. "I delivered two babies."

"Yeah, you did?" Steppin' around Dean, who was still silent, sittin' in reverence, still starin' down at his daughters, I lifted Ace into my arms and carried her to the bathroom. Her hands and my "F#ck, Sorry Ma" T-shirt she wore were covered in blood and goop.

Turnin' on the faucet, warm water poured out, and I guided Ace's shakin' hands under the flow. "Here, lemme help you."

She took an enormous breath when we heard the paramedics enter the kitchen.

"Everybody's okay," I said, caressin' her cheek with the backs of my fingers. "You did good."

She threw her arms around me and clutched me to her body with wet hands. "Oh my God, Finn."

I whispered, "Thank you."

"For what?"

"For deliverin' my nieces."

Breathin' a laugh, she said, "They're my nieces too. I'm Auntie Ace. Fiona and I are besties for life."

"Fiona?"

"Yeah, Fiona and Sara."

"My baby sister's name was Fiona, and Ma's name was Sara." I chuckled and looked up at the ceilin', hopin' Ma could see the smile on my face and that she could see the babies. "They're perfect." I hugged her tighter. "I'm sorry for bein' a dick on the phone last night. You didn't deserve that."

"Yes, I did. I'm the dick. I've been nothing but a dick. I've been here for months, and I've taken advantage of all of you, expecting to be taken care of when I could have been learning to take care of myself. *I'm* sorry."

Jack knocked on the bathroom door and peeked in. "Aislinn? You okay?"

"Yes, I'm okay."

He pushed the door all the way open, then pulled Ace gently from my arms and enveloped her in a hug so tight, I didn't think she could breathe. "Thank you."

"What in the name of hot Hades balls happened here?"

I snorted and laughed at the surprise in Billie's voice when she and Jay arrived, and I looked out at the dumbfounded expression on her face. Jack released Aislinn, and he laughed too.

"The babies came?" Jay asked, lookin' so excited when he tried to see around Dean while the paramedics lifted Oly up onto a stretcher.

"The babies came," I confirmed. "Ace delivered 'em right there on the kitchen floor."

"Ew," Billie said. "But cool. Ace, you okay?" Never mind that Oly was bein' carried out by paramedics after just pushin' two bowlin' balls from her body.

"I'm okay," Ace said, and a whole bunch of different beams of light from Dean's and the paramedic's flashlights illuminated her face, flashin' over her skin like strobe lights. It was the weirdest thing. She was lookin' up at me, eyes wide, like she could see me.

"I'm going to be okay," she said, and then she went limp, and I caught her in my arms before she melted down to the floor. "Does anyone have a piña colada? I think I need a drink."

Teton County closed its roads till they could clear 'em, so we couldn't go to the hospital to see Fiona and Sara or the new mama and daddy till mornin'. Billie and Jay had gone up to their room and were currently fuckin' each other's brains out since they'd been apart for so long.

I'd come downstairs to avoid the bangin' and shoutin', and I watched Aislinn sleep in her bed for a few minutes. She'd downed two shots of the Gentleman's Jack Tennessee

Whiskey we'd been savin' for openin' day of The Cade Ranch EveryBody Rides Barn, then she stumbled into bed.

I'd lied to Jack. I did like Aislinn. I mean, yeah, she could be a real pain, and sometimes I wanted to throttle her—which oddly turned me on—but she'd just performed a fuckin' miracle for my family. She was shaken, but man, that woman radiated pride tonight, and it was so sexy.

Finally, I let her alone and sank down to the couch, hopin' for a few hour's sleep before I had to get up to start cookin' for Thanksgivin'. I closed my eyes and breathed, relaxin' back and proppin' my legs up on the coffee table. I was just about zonked out when I heard Ace's sleepy voice.

"Finn?"

"Shit," I whispered, almost jumpin' and knockin' the coffee table over with my big feet.

She stood at the end of the couch, clutchin' the bottom of her sleep shirt in one hand and her cane in the other. Her legs were silky bare brown temptations, and I licked my lips.

"Sorry," she whispered. "I didn't mean to startle you. Is the power back on?"

"Yeah. It kicked back on after you went to bed. How'd you know it was me?"

"I told you, you breathe loudly." She wrapped her arms around her chest, shiverin'. "It's so cold in here."

"Here, come sit down. I'll light another fire. I think the heat's just takin' a while to build back up after bein' out for so long. It's only, like, thirteen degrees outside. Pretty crazy weather for November."

She made her way around the arm of the couch and sat, but she was still shiverin', so I pushed the coffee table outta her way. "C'mon. Come sit down by the fire." Loadin' a firestarter log into the fireplace, I lit it, then pulled her down to the floor next to me. "Wait. Stay here. I'll be right back."

We didn't have a blow-up mattress anymore since Tony had decided it was a squeak toy, so I pulled the mattress off her bed and dragged it out to the livin' room, layin' it in front of the fire, and when she climbed up, I covered her with as many blankets as I could find. Crawlin' in behind her, I wrapped my whole body around hers under the covers, hopin' to transfer my body's heat into hers.

"Why do you do that?" she asked when we were settled.

"Do what?"

"Touch me like that? Two fingertips."

"Oh. I didn't realize I was doin' it. I dunno. I'm a tactile kinda person, I guess."

"Do you do that with everyone?"

I thought about it for a minute. "Nope. Just you. Sorry, does it bug you like everything else about me does?"

She shook her head against my chest. "No, it doesn't bother me, it's just unusual."

"My family wasn't much for huggin' or showin' physical affection after our mama left, but I could see that was hard on my brothers. Ma was here, but my brothers had all started to pull away already. I don't think Jack allowed anyone to touch him till Evvie showed up last year. Anyway, I didn't like that. Everybody needs to be touched, you know? So, I did it in small ways. I guess I just wanted my brothers to know I was there for 'em."

"You touch your brothers' thighs?" she asked, gigglin'.

"No," I said, laughin' a little, "'course not, but I hug 'em or touch 'em in small ways."

"What about you?" she asked, burrowin' back against me. I was hard against her ass, but it wasn't like that. Well, it was. I couldn't lie, it was—I wanted to bury my cock so far up that ass—but that wasn't the vibe I was gettin' from her.

"Whatcha mean?"

"Who touched you?"

"Oh. Well, Ma did. She was always huggin' me, and Jay and I are pretty close. He's the baby, so he was real young when our mama left. He wasn't as fucked up by it as Jack, Dean, and Kev were."

"What about you? Were you 'fucked up' by it?"

I chuckled under my breath. Man, I loved it when she cursed. It sounded so wrong comin' outta her pristine mouth, but fuck, it was hot. "I s'pose I was a little. I was young, too, but I've always been pretty good at redirectin' my energy. I had to be. I had a lot of it. So, I put it into workin' the ranch, cookin' for everybody, makin' 'em laugh, and, later, playin' music."

"You cooked and worked the ranch when you were a little boy?"

"Well, yeah. My dad was pretty strict. I was always tall and big for my age, so I think I started workin' the horses when I was seven or eight, maybe. And somebody had to cook. Ma was always bringin' us stuff to eat, but she worked, and my dad could be a real shit. He didn't like people to treat him like he was charity. So Ma taught me how to cook so my dad wouldn't get mad. And that was a good thing. With our pops livin' with us, there were seven men in one house. I needed to know how to cook *big* amounts of food."

"But why didn't your dad cook?"

"I'll be real frank, Ace. My dad was a motherfuckin' asshole. His heart was broken when our mama left—if he ever had one—and he thought that gave him the right to treat everybody around him like shit. He had no interest in bein' a single parent.

"But my brothers were there for me. We looked after each other, and I wanted to find ways to help. I wasn't ever any good in school, so I directed my energies elsewhere."

I was quiet for a minute, and I realized that normally, this kinda conversation would have me pacin'. It wasn't often that I talked about my childhood or my issues with readin', but this was the second time in the last week. "What about your parents?"

"Oh, my parents were… great." She laughed a little, and the soft sound in the dark was perfection. "It's funny, I hated them growing up. They were overbearing and overprotective. And after the accident, I was so angry at them for leaving me. I guess I was heartbroken too. But now, even though I know they lied and they weren't perfect, I see how they loved me. I miss them so much."

"I'm sorry," I said, and I kissed her neck. She shivered, and I nuzzled my nose in her hair, inhalin' and drownin' in her beachy scent. She always smelled like coconut and suntan lotion. "What was that like? After the accident?" I felt kinda bad askin' 'cause I was sure it was probably torture for her to remember losin' her parents and her sight, but I was dyin' to know her.

She side-stepped the subject. "What did you mean about not liking school? Why didn't you like it?"

"School was never my thing, that's all."

"You had to like something about it. What about all the good books? *Where the Red Fern Grows*, *Of Mice and Men*, *The Great Gatsby*. God, I loved literature class."

"Nope. Never read 'em."

"None of them? I thought everyone read *Where the Red Fern Grows*. Isn't that a prerequisite to becoming a high school student? Like, they think they need to torture you a little before you leave middle school."

"Nope."

"Oh, come on, you've read *Lord of the Flies*, right? *The Outsiders*?"

"Nope. Seen the movies though."

"Oh, well, what did you like to read? I bet you liked *The Adventures of Huckleberry Finn*." She snorted the cutest laugh.

"Nope. I don't—I ain't much of a reader. I like movies."

"Oh, I love to read. When I first lost my sight, I was so depressed because I knew I'd never read another book. But there are tons of audiobooks." She fidgeted a little, wigglin' her ass against my cock. "Actually, I was listening to one earlier, before Oly showed up."

"Oh yeah? What book was that?" I whispered, curiosity burnin' a hole right through the tip of my tongue 'cause whatever she was thinkin' about was turnin' her into a puddle of wanton goo in my arms.

"It's called *Her*."

"And what's this book about, pray tell?" I begged, slowly rockin' into her ass with a sudden need inside me I didn't think I'd survive.

"Finn?"

I breathed, "Yeah?"

"Will you… will you wrap your hand around my throat like you did before and"—she dropped her voice to a whisper —"and fuck me with your fingers?"

Sweet Jesus, I almost choked on plain old air.

But I got on board *real* fuckin' quick. Slidin' my hand so slowly down her soft abdomen, bunchin' her nightshirt up in my hand while I moved lower, I didn't say anything. I pushed under her lacy panties with my fingers, slidin' 'em between her hot thighs, and she spread 'em open for me.

She groaned so loud when I coated my fingers in the liquid proof that she wanted me, that she didn't hate me, and I almost came in my sweats. She rocked her body against my hand slow, lazy-like, and I slid my other arm under her head, extendin' it out beneath her, and I bent it, bringin' my hand up to her throat.

I was careful, makin' sure I could feel her chest expandin' with breath, but I flexed my fingers. My hand was so big on her tiny neck that, with another inch or two, I coulda touched my thumb to my index finger around the back.

She sighed a moan and closed her eyes. There was no sound between us except the slowly growin' fire, the cracklin' of the splittin' wood, and our breath gettin' heavier with each pass of my fingers between her legs.

I wanted to make her come like I'd never wanted anything ever before in my life.

I slid two fingers inside her, feelin' that soaked, petal-soft skin, and she gasped and fucked my hand harder. Shimmyin' her panties down her thighs a little, she reached between us, found my cock, and pushed under my sweatpants, graspin' me tight.

A strangled moan escaped my lips when she pulled my dick out and guided me between her ass cheeks, clenchin' it between 'em.

I didn't have a condom, but we didn't need it. With her ridin' herself to ecstasy on my hand, my other hand squeezed tight around her throat, and with my cock nestled against her ass, I rocked into her when she rolled against my fingers, and soon, it was an erotic dance.

Our breath echoed around the room. I couldn't even hear the storm anymore, especially not when she whimpered when the heel of my hand pressed against her clit. *Oh, yeah.* That was it. With every slide in and out, I pressed hard against that swollen little nub, and she vibrated with pleasure.

Her breathin' became quicker the faster I fucked myself against her ass, and she squeezed her legs around my wrist, so

I applied more pressure to her throat, and she opened her eyes.

I wished so bad she could see me right then 'cause the vision I was lookin' at was pure unadulterated beauty, and I wanted her to know what I saw. I wanted to reflect it back at her through my eyes.

That wasn't gonna happen, though, but there were other ways for me to show her how beautiful she was.

Pushin' another finger into her, I squeezed harder, and her breathin' became shallower, so I pressed my thumb against her jaw, guidin' her face back toward mine, and I buried my whole hand inside her body when I buried my tongue in her mouth.

She came so hard, every muscle strained, and her ass cheeks strangled my cock, and that was it for me. She cried out, squeezin' the fuck outta my fingers, and I came all over her back while I kissed her like I'd never kissed anyone—like her breath was the only air I needed and my lips and tongue belonged to her.

CHAPTER SIXTEEN

AISLINN

THANKSGIVING STARTED OUT REALLY FUN.

I woke in the morning, still on the mattress in front of the fire, but Finn was already up, already cooking in the kitchen.

After what we'd done the night before, and after he'd washed and kissed every inch of my body in the shower, I wanted to be close to him, and I got the chance all morning. I helped him cook and prepare for dinner, and he flirted with me every chance he got, grabbing my ass, hugging me, showing me with his hands how to peel carrots and set the table, rubbing his body against mine while he did it. It was adorable. I wasn't exactly good at cooking, but he didn't care.

As always, his easy mood set the tone for the day, and I reveled in it, letting it lift me up, letting it wash away the last ten years of memories full of hotels, being stuck with Theo in boring business meetings, and Thanksgiving dinners in empty restaurants.

When the snow had been cleared from the roads, the Cades took turns driving to the hospital in Jackson to see Dean and Oly and the babies, so people were in and out all day while Finn and I cooked. When someone would come into the kitchen, he'd pull away from me, like we were a secret. I supposed we were. His family was in business with my brother, and everyone knew how protective Theo could be of me. Finn didn't want to jeopardize the opportunity my brother's money was affording his family, and I couldn't blame him.

I wasn't sure how that made me feel, but I pushed those thoughts aside because I also couldn't keep my hands off him.

I wanted more. More of that feeling he'd given me last night when he'd made me come in front of the fire. He had played my body just like I'd imagined, like I was his guitar, my skin the strings, and he'd played them expertly. He knew what to do, knew how to make me feel alive. So, had he lied about being a virgin? I didn't ask him because we were getting along, and I wanted that feeling again.

I was addicted to the way he made me feel, addicted to the rush when he commanded my body. I still couldn't believe I'd had the courage to ask him to do it, but after helping deliver the twins, I was on a high. I was so proud of myself, and I felt like I could do anything. Nothing could stop me from having what I wanted.

Not my blindness, not my insecurity, not my naivety about sex, about the world. I felt like anything and everything was within my reach.

Finn was in my reach.

"There's no one here," I purred, wrapping my arms around his chest from behind while he stirred berries on the stove for a sauce he was making for his homemade New York-style cheesecake. I loved the soft feel of his T-shirt, the silky fabric the only barrier between me and his body. I traced the lines of his abs and pectoral muscles with my hands, and his nipples hardened.

"No, there ain't," he said, and his big hand covered mine, his skin whispering naughty secrets over mine in the quiet kitchen. I could hear the smile in his voice. "Were you just pointin' that out as a general FYI, or was there a reason for your observation?"

Releasing him and stepping to his left, I patted the countertop, looking for the container of strawberries I knew was there.

"Whoa, Ace! Careful." He grabbed my hand and pulled it against his stomach. "You almost touched the stove."

The warmth from his skin under the T-shirt traveled up my arm, and a moan threatened to escape my throat. "I was looking for strawberries."

He turned, facing me. "They're right here. Want one?" Suddenly, a plump, seedy berry was pushed past my closed lips, and I opened them. I licked the strawberry, then bit down and juice overflowed my mouth, running down my chin.

"Good God, girl." He swooped down to kiss me, his tongue dueling with mine to steal my strawberry. He licked it into his mouth and licked my chin, chuckling and chewing, scratching his unshaven stubble against my face, and I wondered what color the shiver-inducing coarse hair was while he stepped into me, ushering me back against the counter.

"The observation was an invitation," I said, batting my eyelashes in his direction.

Gasping lightly, he kissed me again, but it quickly turned from silly and playful to hot and desperate. His big, tall body loomed over me like a threat, but it was a threat I wouldn't run from.

His hands on either side of me clutched the countertop, and I placed my hands over his, then guided one between my legs and the other up to the back of my head. Threading my fingers through his, I flexed them, tangling them in my hair and pulling.

He took the hint and pulled harder. My head fell back, and he growled into my mouth when he kissed me deeper. I dropped my hand, letting him control the pulling, and lifted my skirt high above my hips so I could feel his hard cock through his jeans against my stomach while his fingers slid between my legs, in and out between my wet thighs.

Working his mouth, sucking and kissing down from my ear to my neck, when he got to my collarbone, he froze, his head lifted, and he looked at me. I didn't need to see to know; I felt his gaze on my skin like it was made of pure burning energy.

"Good sweet goddamn. Is that a thong?" He turned me just a little, inspecting my ass, I hoped.

"Yes. I wore it for you." I lifted my skirt higher. "Tell me what it looks like."

"It looks like my dreams made flesh." Dropping to his knees, he nuzzled my belly, inhaling and peppering kisses everywhere until his hot mouth landed on the lightly covered mound of hair above where his fingers were still stroking me.

"They're white. Snow white. And the lace is see through. I can see your black hair through the tiny holes, and it's makin' my mouth water." He licked the fabric, and his wet breath heated my skin, making my clit tingle. "This little string," he said, pushing a finger underneath the stretchy strap, "is so fuckin' sexy against your skin. The way you fill this thing out should be illegal, it's so goddamn hot."

"Shit," he said when we heard the sizzle from his sauce as

it spilled over the sides of the pan, "the berries are boilin' over. Ah, who gives a fuck. We can eat cheesecake without berry sauce." Clicking the stove off and removing the pan from the heat, it thunked on the counter, and then he was standing and pulling me by my hand.

My skirt fell into place, and I followed him. "Where are we going?"

"Secret spot," he said, and my breath hitched at the memory of him ramming his cock into me while he held me against my bedroom door.

We hadn't gone far, but he turned, pulling my body against his, pushing me back against a wall or a door and dropping back down to his knees. He pushed my skirt up, burying his head underneath, and he sucked my thong into his mouth, capturing my skin and pubic hair and sucking on it.

I cried out, and he reached up to cover my mouth with his hand.

"Fuck. Turn around." Dropping his hand, he gripped my hips and whipped me around to face the wall, then slid his fingers between my thighs again, and I whimpered and shuddered when he thrust them past my thong and into my body. "Step back and bend forward."

I did what he ordered, holding myself up with my hands planted hard on the wall, waiting in the black silence for what he would do next. When he did nothing, I bent further, opening my legs wider, begging for him to touch me or lick or something. Need so strong gathered in my belly, in the core of me.

I whined and whimpered, "Finn, please."

His big hands covered my ass cheeks, and so slowly, he dragged them down, dipping his thumbs between my soaked thighs, then down my legs and back up. Spreading me open then, he blew on the wet flesh and I jumped.

"Finn, please! Do something. Lick, suck, pound—I don't care. Just do *something*."

He chuckled, then shoved his face between my legs, licking my ass, my pussy, my thighs. Everything. Everything!

"Yes! Everything. Finn, please, everything!"

"God, your cunt's glistenin', you're so wet."

I scoffed at his dirty words, but they made me wetter.

"You kiddin' me? You want me to choke you and pull your hair, but you don't want me to talk dirty?" Pulling away, he stroked one finger slowly through the wet mess between my legs. "Tough shit, little girl." He stood, and I could feel him unbuckling his belt and pushing his jeans down. That sound of metal sliding over leather again made it even worse. "'Cause I'm about to fuck you so hard, you're gonna be cursin' and beggin' for more."

With his hand on my arm, he squeezed hard, tugging me around to face him, then shoved something into my hand. "Put it on me." A condom.

"I can't. I can't see your… your cock."

He pulled his shirt off, and I felt the heat from his chest between us. "Was that hard for you to say out loud? Say it again."

"Cock?"

"Yes. Tell me how much you love it and wrap my cock in that condom before I fuck you bare."

"I can't see what I'm doing. I don't know where it is."

In a whisper, he drawled, "You know where it should be. Find it."

I moaned at his reminder of the day I rode Sammy, the day I felt that power and freedom, and I embraced it, sliding down the wall and kneeling at his feet.

He gasped and gripped my hair in his fingers, and the

sound of his voice coming down from his tall height was intoxicating. "Fuck, Ace."

I could feel his heat and smell his musky scent in front of my face, so I tilted my head up so he could see me, and I reached forward, feeling for his cock. It bumped against my lips, hard and pulsing, and I pushed up on my knees and took the whole thing in my mouth in one swallow, and he pulled my hair hard.

I moaned around him, he choked out a breath, and his legs began to shake.

"Ace!" he whispered. "Oh fuck, Ace. No. I'll come. Oh God. If you don't stop doin' that, I'm gonna come in your mouth."

I groaned at the image he'd created in my head: a current of his hot cum sliding down my throat while he thrusted his cock in and out, my lips surrounding it, the obscene noises from the suction my tongue would make against his sensitive skin. I wanted him to come in my mouth so much that I shook too.

"That's not what I meant for you to do."

I moaned, mumbling, "Yes."

"Ace, no."

Nodding, my forehead butted against his lower abdomen, stretched and straining, the muscles rippling with pleasure every time I sucked.

"No," he breathed, but he rocked his body into me, pulling his cock in and out, slowly fucking my mouth. "Ohh," he moaned. "You're really good at that."

I was a little proud of myself. I'd listened to enough cock-sucking smut to be a well-read expert, but I'd never experienced it. And now that I was doing it, it was way better than in my books. His skin was so soft, and it moved back and forth along his hard shaft with every stroke of my tongue. He smelled so good, his sweat and skin salty and heady. Distinctly male.

I sucked harder, delivering the head of his cock to the back of my throat, and he growled and yanked my head back by my hair. With my neck stretched taut, he fucked into my mouth in earnest now, and I swallowed every few seconds, loving the sound of his shuddering breaths in the dark, the sound of his control threatening to snap each time. Reaching behind him, I scratched my nails down his back and dug them into his ass, and he cursed and clenched.

When he was moaning and fucking faster, I released him, letting him fall from my mouth with a pop of my lips.

"You did not just do that."

"Do what?" I asked innocently, feeling power surge through my body in heated waves.

Growling, he dropped to the floor, patting around, searching for the condom, but I still held it in my hand.

"Looking for this?" I asked, holding it up in front of him.

In two seconds, it was ripped open and securely fastened onto his cock, and then he was lifting me from the floor into his lap, and *I* was securely fastened onto his cock. Not even bothering to take off my thong, he just screwed around it. His jeans were still bunched low around his hips, and the buttons pinched my skin when his body pounded into mine.

Using his grip on my hair to hold me in place, he reached between us to rub circles over my clit, which was thoroughly wet and coated in liquid need, and with every hard push into my body with his, I was knocked back against the wall—it sounded like someone was knocking on a door.

His breath was shallow, and I felt every shuddering exhale in his chest. He was overpowering me with his hand pulling my hair and his big body taking over mine, but I smiled because I was in control of him. I was the one making him frantic and gasp for air. My body did that.

I did that. I made him crazy.

"Wipe that smile off your face, girl. You think you got some kinda control over me? You don't—"

I laughed, a husky, low-throated sound, when I lifted my shirt and pushed my breasts together, rubbing them against his chest, the hair there tickling my hard-as-ice nipples, and he choked on a growl, pumping into me harder, rubbing my clit faster and faster.

But all my taunting came to a screeching halt when he lowered his head to kiss me. He fucked into my mouth with his tongue, wiping the smile off my face himself, punching up into my body so hard that I had to release my breasts so I could hold onto his shoulders, so that I didn't fall off him.

Oh God, just the sound of his breath was enough to make me come, so loud around me, forcing its way into my mouth. It was powerful and needy and sexy.

But we both froze when a car door slammed outside.

"Ace, come. Come now." He drilled into me, pushing me against the wall again, lifting me higher with his thrusts. "I can't... Oh God, I can't hold back anymore."

He pinched my clit and bit my shoulder, pulling my head back so far that the muscles in my throat seized, and I couldn't get a breath.

It was so hot. I squeaked and came around his cock while my whole body locked in place, and millions of colors burst and flashed behind my useless eyes.

He groaned and growled, and the sound vibrated through my whole body. "Fu... ughh!"

"Jay'll be in in a minute. He's checking on the horses. Man, it's so freakin' cold outside. What were you guys doing back there?" Billie asked when she came home from the hospital, stomping her boots on the rug by the kitchen door as Finn and I stumbled out of the back hallway. He held my hand until Billie spoke, then he let go.

"Nothin'," Finn said. "I was just showin' Ace where we keep the extra canned goods."

She snorted. "How stupid do you think I am?"

I tried to steer the conversation to a safer subject. "How are the babies? How's Oly?"

"Fine. Change the subject, but you'll tell me later." She plopped into a dining chair, and her bag thudded on the kitchen table. "The twins are good. Little Fiona's got some lungs on her. Kid wailed the whole time we were there. Is that all babies do? Cry?" She scoffed.

"Oly's good too. I think she's sore, but she's happy. And Dean? Oh my God." She barked a loud laugh. "I've never seen anything like it. That guy looks like he's on drugs, just staring at the babies with the dumbest smile on his face, and then Oly asked him to change Sara's diaper, and he panicked!" She laughed harder. "You should've seen it. The look on his face? Sheer terror. That big ol' Marine brought down by a poopy diaper!

"Anyway, they're going home tonight around six, so Oly's mom said we can take some food over later."

"Good. I'm glad they're doing well."

"You didn't happen to take a picture of my brother's dumb face, did ya?" Finn asked.

"Well, as a matter of fact." Billie stood and walked over to us. "Here, look."

Finn snorted and slapped his thigh. "Oh, man, look at that

moron. He looks like somebody just shoved somethin' up his ass!"

They both laughed, and I turned away, walking to my bedroom, feeling my way without my cane. I couldn't even remember where I'd left it, but I didn't need it inside the house anymore.

When I closed my bedroom door, I backed to the bed and sank down, letting the mattress support me. I cared about Oly and the twins. About Dean. About Billie and Jay. Everyone.

And Finn.

But I realized, when Billie showed Finn the picture, I wasn't part of their family. I never would be. I was still just Theo's sister. They didn't treat me like that, but I was still just the blind girl. The person relying on and depending upon the Cade family. They were taking care of me because of my brother and because I was disabled.

And that meant that Finn had probably just taken pity on me.

He was indulging my fantasies to keep me happy. Well, happier. But it wouldn't go anywhere. It couldn't. He'd lied. He hadn't really been a virgin. Why would he give that up? For me? No.

A sickening feeling and embarrassment flooded my body when I realized he'd only said that to me to make me feel better about what we'd done. He'd been placating me, babying me, and I hadn't even realized it.

And what did it matter anyway? I would never be right for him. I was sure he knew that. How could he not? All he had to do was look at me, at my prissy clothes and my blind eyes.

I would never be what he wanted. I would never be like Billie or Jules or Oly.

"Ace?" Billie knocked on my door and opened it quietly.

"Yes?"

"Can I come in? What're you doing sitting in the dark?"

I sighed. "Yes, Billie, you can come in. Since when do you ask permission? And it's always dark to me. I don't need light."

She flipped it on anyway, and I blinked, little sparks dancing in my mind like they always did.

"What's wrong? Your face changed in the kitchen. When you came out of the back hallway with Finn when I walked in, you were glowing. But then, when I showed him the picture of Dean—"

"Nothing's wrong. You're part of their family. I'm not. I was just excusing myself."

"Ace, what's this about? You're part of my family. You're the best friend I've ever had. You're my sister, and you know I don't take that lightly."

"I know." Billie had lost her only sister to suicide, and I knew she held our friendship in the highest regard. We were like sisters.

"Ace? Talk to me."

"I slept with Finn."

"I knew it!"

"Shh, Billie."

"Well, so? How was it?"

"It was… Both times were amazing."

"Both times? Ace, you slut." She laughed.

"Maybe I am a slut."

"I was kidding. Why would you say that?"

"Because Finn only slept with me because of my brother. I mean, he's a man, so sure, he got something out of it, too, but he didn't sleep with me because he wants something with me. He slept with me to keep me happy. To try to keep the peace between his family and mine."

"Did he say that?"

"Of course not, but I know it's true. Aren't you the one telling me all the time how beautiful he is? How every woman wants him? Why would he want me, Billie? Why? What do I have to give?"

"Ace," Billie whispered, sitting next to me on the bed, wrapping her arm around my shoulders.

"No, Billie. I know I'm right. As soon as I realized it, it clicked."

"I think you're wrong. Finn isn't like that. He's a genuine person. He wouldn't do that to you. But even if it were true, how would that make you a slut? I'm sorry. I was joking. I shouldn't have said that. I just meant it like how we call each other our bitch. Like, 'you're my best bitch.'"

"I knew what you meant, Billie. But I… I asked him to do things to me—no, I demanded—things I've never done before, and I don't think he knew how to deny me. I think he was just giving in to my whims. And that makes me a slut because I would've done anything to be with him, but I know he was only with me to, I don't know, to keep the peace. But it didn't matter to me, because I wanted him."

"I don't understand where this is coming from. I think everyone is aware that you're your own woman. You've come a long way in the last few months. Before you came here, did you ever think you could live without Theo? Did you ever think you'd manage an office, ride a horse again, or get drunk at a bar?"

"No," I admitted, "but I'm still dependent on people. Not Theo anymore, but you and Evvie. Shonda, Jack, Jay… I'll never be like you."

"What does that mean? Why would you want to be like me? I love who you are."

"I know you do, but I meant, I'll never be that woman.

The woman that a man can't stop thinking about. The one he can't keep his hands off of. And I'll never fit in here. There's nothing I have to offer, other than my bad attitude and dirty laundry for them to do."

"Ace—"

"It's okay, Billie. I guess I'm realizing all of this and I'm accepting it. I'm blind. I'm disabled." I sighed, feeling the weight and the truth of my own words. "He'll never want me, Billie. Not like that."

"I think you're wrong again, Ace. I think he already does." She sighed. "But what did you mean you 'did things you'd never done before?'"

"Nothing. I'm not very experienced when it comes to sex, so I haven't done a lot of things."

"Like?"

I couldn't tell her about my sudden need for depravity. What if she didn't understand? It would just be one more thing to set me apart.

"Like blow jobs. I'd never given one before."

"Oh. Well, did you like it? Was he gentle with you? Did he reciprocate?" Billie demanded. "I'll kick his ass if he didn't."

I laughed a little. "No, he did. He's..." My head swam with memories of how I'd felt when I was with Finn. When he was inside me, when he was giving me what I wanted— what I needed. "He's... God, Billie, he's fucking magnificent."

She laughed. "I'm not surprised. But so are you, even if you're inexperienced. You're a strong woman. I'm sure he's just as hung up on you as you are on him."

"I'm *not* hung up on him."

"Oh, come on. It's me. You can be honest. You like him."

"Actually, no. I don't." I said the words, but they burned

leaving my mouth. They were so untrue. But telling her would mean admitting it, which would also mean that the truth would have the power to hurt me. "He doesn't like me either. But I like his body, and I like the way he makes my body feel. I like that he makes me come, and I like his muscles. I like his body. It's really that simple."

CHAPTER SEVENTEEN

FINN

THE REST OF THANKSGIVIN' was fine, but Ace was different with me after sex in the back hallway. She'd withdrawn. I didn't get a chance to ask her about it 'cause everyone was there for dinner by the time she and Billie had come outta her bedroom.

I pulled the bird outta the oven, whipped up some mashed taters, doused 'em in gravy, and, only when I set 'em on the table, realized Ace couldn't eat 'em. *Dang.* I quickly scooped some outta the bowl that hadn't been touched by the delicious turkey juice, and I made a plate for her.

Ace's cornbread casserole was delicious, and I'd made veggie stuffin' for her. I even cooked up some weird vegetarian bullshit called nutloaf, but it was actually kinda tasty. Jay looked it up for me online, and Ace seemed to like it—she all but licked her plate—but she didn't say anything. Didn't thank me. Not that I was diggin' for compliments or gratitude, but I thought she might've said somethin'.

After I ate the oddly satisfyin' nutloaf 'cause Kev dared me, the jokes were unendin'. "How's that nut taste in your mouth, brother? Is it salty or sweet? Luuk's taste like—" That earned him a punch to his kidney from his boyfriend, groans from Jack, Jay, and Carey, and Evvie smacked the back of his head when she walked behind him. Billie laughed, though, and Kevin kept on. "Luuk, will you feed me your nutloaf tonight? But don't put any mushrooms in it 'cause I don't wanna trip balls when I'm—"

"*Houd je kop, Kevin, of ik sla je hoofd en je lul,*" which was later translated for me as, "Shut your mouth, Kevin, or I'll punch your head and your dick."

But the best joke, and the only one that was actually funny, came from Phil, our somewhat-of-an-adopted aunt who only seemed to come down from her house on the mountain when we had large amounts of food to offer. "Pass me Finn's dickloaf, please. I've been thinkin' about goin' meatless."

I laughed so hard when she said it with a straight face, I fell outta my chair, clutchin' my stomach and tryin' not to pee my pants.

Ace didn't laugh, and she spent the rest of the evenin' with Evvie or Billie and Jay, and when I tried to talk to her, she'd listen, but she was quiet, and then she'd wander back to whatever conversation was closest. Her brother had shown up for dinner, and it was awkward between 'em. It was just plain weird between Theo and everyone else 'cause of the drunken come-ons he'd made toward us all at the restaurant. I was kinda surprised he remembered, but he apologized up and down.

He also tried talkin' to Aislinn, but she wasn't havin' it. She wanted nothin' to do with him. I didn't think they'd talked about what he'd said that night, the thing he'd blurted about her birth mama bein' alive, and I wasn't sure if Ace would ever hear him out.

He left my house like a puppy with his tail between his

legs, and Ace went to her bedroom then. I tried checkin' on her, but she was asleep or pretendin' to be. She didn't answer when I knocked on the door.

I was stupid confused. But I still had a lotta work to do cleanin' up and boxin' up leftovers. Oh, and it was common knowledge that I saved the turkey carcass to make turkey soup. The week after Thanksgivin' was always my favorite 'cause I ate it for just about every meal. Turkey broth and hot sauce cooked with the leftover meat, sweet corn, tomatoes, rice, onions, mushrooms, green peppers…

"Night, Finn."

"Oh, night, Billie," I said, turnin' to smile at her when she and Jay interrupted my turkey daydreams as I washed the last of the dishes. "You have a good Thanksgivin'?"

"Yeah. Thanks for the pumpkin pie. It was so good. Don't you dare throw the leftovers away. I'm eating that for breakfast."

"Wouldn't dream of it. Hey, is Ace okay? She—I dunno. She was different tonight."

"Yeah, I noticed. I think maybe Theo being here was hard for her. She still won't listen to what I found about her birth mother, and I think she might be kinda freaked out by what Theo said when you guys went to dinner."

I wiped my hands on a dish rag and pulled a chair out at the table. Sittin', I asked, "What'd you find?"

Billie sat too. "I mean, it's nothing concrete, but I've been digging through this woman's whole life. I even went to Boston to follow up on some leads. Her name was Monique Washington. She only worked for Ace's dad's company for a summer, and then she got pregnant, and by the next summer, there was no mention of her anywhere." With her elbows on the table, she steepled her fingers together. She reminded me of a detective from some old 1970s show.

"Her family filed a missing person's report, and Ace's dad was questioned by police—an anonymous source had reported that he'd knocked her up—but by then, Burroughs had enough money that he could afford good lawyers, so any involvement he had with her was quickly covered up and/or disposed of, besides Ace." Billie shrugged. "But there are no company documents, no personal references, and only one measly missing person's report. And her family didn't follow up on that report.

"Monique's parents died a long time ago, but she had a sister who also worked at Burroughs Financial, but that lady disappeared too. But I found something on this sister. Her name was Regina, and she was friends with Ace and Theo's mom. I found a blurry picture of them together from some society group in Boston before Ace was born. They did charity work together.

"This Regina had money. Her husband was some big tycoon like Ace's dad, but he died of a heart attack around the same time Ace was born. And then both women just dropped right off the face of the earth. I've searched and searched, but I can't find any communication between Ace's adopted mom, Monique, or Regina after Ace was born." Billie shook her head in frustration. "There are official birth and adoption records for Ace—her birth mom's name wasn't hidden—but then she just ceases to exist.

"When I found out what Theo said at the restaurant, I started poring through his shit again. I haven't found anything yet, so I don't know how he knows she's alive—*if* she is— and I tried talking to him, but he blew me off. Told me to mind my own business."

Sittin' back in her chair, she placed her hands flat on the table. "But did I listen?" She snorted. "Uh, nope. Ace *is* my business. So I've set up some facial recognition searches on everybody. We'll see what pops up."

"Ace just needs time to process," Jay said, standin' behind Billie, runnin' his fingers through her hair. "She'll come around. It's a pretty big deal, findin' out you aren't who you always thought and that your parent is alive but never wanted to know you. Give her time, Billie."

"Yeah, I know. I will. But I want to be able to tell her definitively when she's ready, you know? Is her mom alive or not? I won't give up till I know for sure."

"Alright, well, you good, Finn?" Jay asked, pullin' on Billie's shoulders. "I got a date with my fiancée and some movie called *Christmas with the Kranks*."

"Yeah, I'm good," I said. "That's a good one. Classic Tim Allen. Night, guys. Happy Thanksgivin'."

Life went back to normal, but Ace didn't come around over the long weekend. She seemed sad, and she was her old, haughty self. I knew I hadn't done anything wrong, so I went back to work. But I was a little sad, too, 'cause I thought we'd connected. I mean, yeah, it was sex, but I'd told her I didn't go around doin' that with just anybody. Didn't she know she was special to me? But maybe I wasn't special to her.

"Mornin', Shonda," I said, walkin' into the office early come Monday mornin'. "How was your Thanksgivin'?"

"Oh, good morning, Finn. It was fine. Good, yeah."

"I'm glad. Uh, these papers were just delivered by a courier. I dunno what they are, but Jay and Jack aren't here, so..." I handed the big orange envelope to her, and she looked at it.

"Okay. Um, it's probably best if we leave it for Jay."

"Yeah, but uh, the courier said it's time sensitive, so can you just open it and tell me what it says? Then I'll call Jay and let him know."

"Oh. Sure. Do you have a headache or something?"

"No."

"Okay." She looked at me in confusion. "Why can't you read it?"

"I don't—I ain't the best reader, 'specially when it comes to official crap like that."

Shonda blinked, understandin' dawnin' on her slowly. She searched my face, lookin' for any clue that I was lyin', that I wasn't really a twenty-eight-year-old idiot. When she didn't find one, she nodded. "Okay, sure, Finn. Of course. Um"—she opened the envelope and pulled the papers out—"it's just a contract from the company that we're going to be buying some equipment from. There's a few items Jay isn't sure we'll need, so we're going to rent them from this company until we know. This is basically a rental contract. It's not really that time sensitive. You can just put it on Jay's desk."

"Oh, good. Okay, thanks." I took the papers from her and turned, intendin' to do just that, but Shonda stopped me.

"Finn?"

A little embarrassed, I didn't turn around. "Yeah?"

"I could help you. I mean, i-if you wanted. I used to volunteer, working with at-risk youth, teaching them how to read, helping them get their GEDs."

"I don't need a GED. I have a high school diploma."

"That's good, but if you... if you'd like to get better at—"

"Nope, I'm good, Shonda. Thanks."

"Finn?" Ace's voice behind me in the barn warmed me. Man, I loved the sound of it.

"Yeah?" I turned slowly, lettin' her beautiful face and the memories of what we'd done together wash over me like a warm (and slightly kinky) hug.

"I'd like to ride again. Will you help me, please?"

"'Course I will. C'mon. A ride sounds good, but let's bundle up first. Still pretty cold out."

When we were decked out in down coats and thermal underclothes, we set out. Ace rode Sammy and I rode Gertie across the snow-covered fields. She seemed much more confident than she had that day in the paddock, though the snow changed Sammy's gait, so she was still a little wobbly. And she was cold, snuggled up behind her thick coat and scarf. The sky was gray and overcast behind the misty mountains, and it looked like a black-and-white paintin', except for the red of the scarf she wore. It was bright Christmas red, and images of her tied to my bed with the scarf were turnin' me on so much that I was havin' a hard time stayin' in my saddle.

She grew more comfortable the longer we rode, trustin' Sammy, and I could tell he trusted her too. Her body was relaxed once we got into the rhythm, and we rode a while in silence, but we went slow, just to ride. We weren't in a hurry.

Finally, I couldn't stop the question. "What happened on Thanksgivin' after…?"

"Nothing."

"Ace, your whole demeanor changed, and you barely spoke to me all weekend. I thought we were past all that. What's goin' on?"

"I said it was nothing."

"Yeah, you did, but you're lyin'."

She huffed a breath, and it turned to steam in the bitter cold. "How dare you? I am not."

I sighed. There she was—Ms. Aislinn Burroughs. *Here we go again.* "Okay. Whatever you say." I clicked my tongue, nudgin' Gertie into a trot, and Sammy followed with a gasp from Ace. "You said you wanted to ride, so let's ride."

I took off. I knew it was mean, but she was givin' me whiplash with all her back and forth. I heard her callin' my name behind me, but I kept goin' till I realized she'd pulled Sammy to a dead stop and was perched on his back with her arms crossed over her chest and a scowl on her face, her steamy breaths comin' faster now.

"Dammit. C'mon, Gertie." Headin' back to her, I snuggled into my own coat, pullin' the zipper up tight 'cause I was fuckin' freezin'. "What's wrong now?"

"Why would you leave me like that?"

"I didn't leave you, but you're—"

"What?"

"Aislinn, I'm puttin' my heart out on the line here, and you keep stompin' on it. How long you expect me to keep it up? This is the last time I'll ask you why."

"Your heart? And why what?"

"Yeah. My heart. And why do you keep pushin' me away? You think I go around havin' sex with every beautiful woman I meet?"

She sat straighter, squarin' her shoulders, and she closed her eyes. "Yes. I do."

"I told you. I was honest with you."

"No. You lied. You weren't a virgin. You just said that to make me—"

"Make you what?"

"You said that because you thought I needed to believe it. You're just like everyone else. You baby me."

My eyebrows hit the sky. "I *baby* you? When my cock's down your throat, is that what you call babyin'? Tyin' you up with my belt and fuckin' into you like—that's *babyin'*?" I shook my head, scoffin'. "You got some balls on you, girl. I thought you'd changed. I thought you'd grown up a little. I thought I was gettin' to know the real you. But you don't wanna grow up, do you? You wanna stay in your pampered little bubble. Well, more power to ya. I won't stand in your way." Grabbin' Sammy's reins, I tied 'em to Gertie's and headed for home.

"What are you doing?" she demanded when Sammy followed Gertie and me.

"Goin' home. I got work to do."

"I'm not done riding. Let me go. I'll come back when I'm ready."

"You just screeched at me when you thought I'd left. Now you *want* me to leave?" I clicked my tongue. "That ain't happenin'. C'mon, Sammy."

"No!" Ace swung her leg over and slid down Sammy's side into the snow, but she didn't land right and she fell on her butt.

"Goddammit, why you gotta be like this?"

"Go home, Finn. Just leave me here. I don't need you."

"You don't need me? You don't need anyone, do you?" I said, towerin' over her, still atop Gertie. "Except you do. I hate to break this to you, Ace, but you're disabled. Whether you look it, whether you like it or not, you are. But guess what? So's everybody else at one point or another. We all need help sometimes. You ain't that special."

She crossed her arms over her chest again, feelin' monumentally sorry for herself, I was sure. "What do *you* need help with? You're not disabled. You're not blind. You're perfect and everyone knows it. Why don't you go find Jules and have her suck your dick? She's probably better at it since she can see it!"

I jumped off Gertie and stomped toward Ace. "God, what is the matter with you? Don't you get it? I don't want her. I don't want anyone else. For some god-awful reason, I want you. But you're just so determined to make me change my mind, aren't you?" I stepped back, crossin' my arms over my chest too. "Know what I think?"

"I don't care."

"Yes, you do, and I think you want me to hate you so you'll feel better about hatin' yourself. Well, mission almost accomplished. And fuck you. I need help just like everybody else. In fact, I just asked for help this mornin'.

"I can't read, Aislinn. I have dyslexia and probably a whole host of other issues, ADHD—I don't fuckin' know. When I look at letters on a page, they make no sense to me. They move and I can't understand 'em. It ain't the same as bein' blind, and I know you've been through hell, but are you really gonna stand there and compare my shortcomin's to yours?

"You're so wrapped up in your self-pity, you can't even see straight. Well, I'm done. I've tried over and over. I wanted to fall in love with you—maybe I already did—but it don't matter, does it? 'Cause you don't love yourself. Now, get up. Get back on that goddamn horse, or I'll throw you over."

CHAPTER EIGHTEEN

AISLINN

"WHAT'S THIS ABOUT, ACE?" Billie asked through a yawn. "Why are we driving to Idaho at six in the morning? I haven't even had coffee yet."

"We're going to pick up a dog."

"A dog? Uhh… Are you sure that's a good—"

"I already asked Jack, and he said it was fine. The dog is one of the animals from that old woman's farm. Remember from a few months ago? She passed away, and the animals were all alone until some Good Samaritan saw Surely from the highway. She was wasting away to skin and bones."

"Vaguely."

"Surely's lonely, so Finn and I thought if we could find her friend, it might cheer her up." I shrugged. "Well, Finn thought that. It was his idea."

"Okay, but why's it so urgent? We could've waited till Saturday."

"I'm *so* sorry, Billie," I complained. "Did I put a kink in your schedule or something?"

"No, Ace. It's fine. I was just curious. What the hell crawled up your ass today?"

"I'm sorry." I sighed. "I didn't mean to snap at you. I had an… argument with Finn, and I just thought, maybe the dog would be a good apology. He was trying to figure out where the dog might've gone, and I wanted to help him. And I want to help Surely. Thank you for driving me."

"A dogology?" Billie snorted and laughed at her own joke, and I smiled, but I wasn't in the mood to laugh. "C'mon, Ace. Start talking. What's going on with you?"

My whole body slumped in my seat, and I groaned when I said, "I messed up. I was scared and feeling insecure, and I think I've finally pushed Finn away for good. You were right. He's genuine and honest, and I think I'm in love with him."

"I won't say I told you so, but I *so* told you so."

That did make me laugh. "Thanks."

"How'd you mess up?"

"I snapped at him, too, and I told him to go find someone who isn't blind. I told him I didn't need him, and I basically said, 'My problems are worse than yours.'"

"Hm. Sounds like you were being a douche."

"Thank you for pointing that out, Billie. Yes, a total douche."

"You're welcome. But I think this can be fixed. Ace, you don't see what I see. That man's eyes are always on you. No matter what you're doing or who else is in the room, he's watching you with stars in his eyes like a cartoon. You rattle him like no one else can."

"He rattles me too. He rocks me to my soul, but that's the thing. Until very recently, I didn't know my own soul. You know?"

"What do you mean? You know who you are."

"I think I do now, but I didn't. You kept telling me I was this great person, but I didn't actually agree with you. I've spent the last ten years hating myself and feeling sorry for myself because I can't see. Everything I was before is gone. The person I was before is gone, but I'm realizing that it's a good thing. It's not the person I am now that I don't like.

"Now, I'm smart, I'm independent, I'm kind and even funny sometimes. I love helping animals and people, and I want to work and try to make a difference in the world. I couldn't say that before. Before, I just wanted everything handed to me. I thought I deserved it because of what I went through. But now, I want the world, but I want to *earn* it. I want to earn Finn. I want to be worthy of him. He's such a good man. He's everything I've ever wanted to be."

"Well, after that proclamation, mission accomplished. You are worthy, and you're gonna get your man. I'll kick his ass if he doesn't forgive you."

"Thanks, Billie." I reached across the seat, holding my hand in the air until she grabbed it, and I squeezed. "I love you. Do you know that? You're the best friend I've ever had, and I want you to know that you make me a better person just by being in my life."

"Ditto, sister." She squeezed back, then cleared her throat quietly, maybe a little teary-eyed, but she'd never say so. "So, what's this dog's name? What kind of dog is it?"

"Her name's Pepper. She's an older mixed-breed, and the shelter in Idaho was going to euthanize her, but I did a little fast talking, and they said if I came to get her today, I could have her. I called Luuk and Kevin, and they're keeping Tony at their house tonight so Pepper can settle in. Then, tomorrow, we'll introduce them. I can't wait to hear Surely's reaction."

"Wait, Tony and Pepper? Like—"

I smiled. "Yep, exactly like the movie. It's one of Finn's favorites. He's gonna love her."

Standing in Finn's bedroom doorway, I whispered into the darkness, "Finn?"

Billie and I hadn't gotten back to the ranch until eight thirty at night, and Finn was already in his room by then. Now, it was two thirty in the morning, but I couldn't sleep. I hadn't slept much at all since Thanksgiving. I'd heard him tossing and turning, so I thought he was awake, too, and I couldn't wait until morning to talk to him.

Pepper went before me and jumped onto his bed.

"What? What the f—? Whose dog is this?"

Taking the first step into his room—the first time I'd ever actually been in it—I tripped over something on the floor, and suddenly, I wasn't standing up anymore. I was on my butt, my legs sprawled out in front of me.

"Ace? Shit." I heard him moving, his bed springs squeaking, and then he was standing over me. Pepper jumped down and sat beside me, nudging me and trying to help me up. "What're you doin'? Seriously, where did this dog come from?"

"That was less graceful than I planned. I'm sorry. This is Pepper." I patted the floor, trying to feel around me in the dark. I had no idea where I was in his room, but it wasn't disorienting because he was right there. I always felt safe when he was near. Pepper nudged my hand and I scratched her head. "Remember, you wanted to find the animals from Surely's farm? Pepper is one of them. The other animals were already adopted, but Billie helped me track her down."

"She did?" he asked with the usual happy sound in his voice, but then he sighed, and I knew he was remembering how mad he was at me. "It's the middle of the night. What do you need? I can't see you."

"No, but you can *feel* me," I said, imitating him, trying to remind him of the connection between us before I'd pulled away. Before I'd ruined everything he'd been trying to give me.

"Cut it out. I ain't interested in doin' this with you." He switched the light on. "I'm tired."

"What's going on?" Billie asked, opening her bedroom door, her feet padding toward Finn's room. "Ace? What the hell? What'd you do to her, Finn?"

"Shit, people. I'm naked here!" Finn yanked the blanket or the sheet from his bed and covered himself. I felt the air move when he wrapped it around his hips. "What do you mean, 'What did you do?' You kiddin' me? I didn't do nothin'."

"Guys?"

Great, Jay was awake too. The entire house now knew I'd snuck into Finn's room.

Billie stepped forward. "Here, Ace, let me help you."

On unsteady legs, I pushed myself up, and Pepper leaned against me. "No, thank you, Billie. Please go back to bed. I want to talk to Finn. I'm sorry I woke you up. Will you take Pepper with you?"

"Sure, but you're okay?"

"Yes, I promise I'm fine."

"Fine." I could tell she was eyeing Finn. I could feel it. She was ready to kick his ass like she'd promised.

"Please, Billie. Finn didn't do anything. I snuck up here, and I tripped and I'm embarrassed. Go back to bed."

"All right. Good night."

Billie called Pepper, and when the door shut behind them, I took a step toward Finn but tripped over something else. Thankfully, I caught myself before falling again. "What is all over your floor?"

"Well, I wasn't expectin' company. Besides, you sneak up

here like a thief in the night, and now you're complainin' about the state of the room you broke into?"

I laughed at the incredulity in his voice. "You're right. I'm sorry."

He sighed again, and this time it was a full-body sigh. "Here. I gotcha." He lifted me over the mountain of mess on his floor, holding me to his chest, and he sat on the bed. "What's goin' on? Can't you sleep?"

Maneuvering myself so I was straddling him, my legs on either side of his, my chest touching his and feeling his expand with breath, I reached up, searching for his face with my hands. I found it and held it, rubbing my fingers over his jaw. "No, I can't sleep. My mind's racing in circles." I took a deep breath, trying to gather any courage I could find.

I was head over heels in love with him, and I was terrified to tell him. There was still a chance he didn't want me, but I had to take the risk.

"I'm sorry, Finn. I owe you a thousand apologies. But I don't understand why you want to be with me. And I don't understand why—*how*—you were a virgin before we slept together. And I don't understand why you gave that up for me. It doesn't make sense. Why would you do that? If you waited this long, it had to be important to you, so why?"

"Why's it so hard to believe?" he asked, his voice and his breath whispering over my face. Sitting in his lap, facing him, I was almost as tall as him.

"Because you're Finn Cade. Since I got here, all I've heard is how beautiful you are. You're sexy, you're confident, you're a panty melter."

Laughing, he said, "I'm a what?"

"Tell me women don't fall at your feet wherever you go."

"Aislinn, yeah, I get a lotta offers for sex. I am good lookin'. I can't deny it." He chuckled. "But meaningless sex don't interest me. You ain't so bad yourself. What's the difference? You want people to like you because you're the most beautiful woman on the planet? Or do you want 'em to like you 'cause you're you? 'Cause you're kind and smart. You're courageous and funny and sexy."

"You think I'm all those things?"

"No." He touched a finger to my bottom lip, then dropped his hands to wrap low around my hips. "I know you are. You act like a brat, but I know better. You're scared, but that don't make you different. It just makes you like everybody else."

"Oh."

"'Oh'? What's that mean?"

Shrugging, I said, "I guess I've spent a lot of time feeling sorry for myself, but you're right that everyone goes through hard things. Mine might've been harder at first than most, but you're also right that I'm no different on the inside than anyone else."

"That ain't what I meant. You are different on the inside, but that's a good thing. I can't imagine what you went through, wakin' up to blackness and your parents bein' gone. But don't you see how strong it made you? If you could get through that, you can get through anything. You're made of steel, Superwoman."

"I didn't wake up to blackness."

"What?"

"I mean, I'm blind, yes, completely, but I can still see colors sometimes, if the light is bright enough. It was blackness and nothingness in my mind." I squeezed my eyes shut, remembering. "I was devastated when Theo told me our parents were both dead. I was sixteen, and I couldn't imagine how I was supposed to live without them, you know? They wouldn't be there for anything: graduation, college, my wedding. But then I realized that I probably wouldn't have those things anyway. I thought losing my sight was the end of my life too.

"I acted like it was. I punished everyone around me for it. I was the perfect spoiled princess, and all of that was gone in an instant, and I made the decision that I was ruined. But do you know, now I'm starting to think that maybe everything happened the way it was supposed to. Like it was fate or something because I never would've met you if it hadn't. I never would've met Billie. I'd still be a rotten princess in her lonely castle."

I laughed a little. "Okay, so maybe I still am, but I'm trying to climb down. And I'm not ruined. There's nothing wrong with me, and I like who I am. I'm just different than a lot of people. But I never would have seen you. I never would've allowed myself to know you because I only surrounded myself with fake and ingenuine people, people who could feed my ego and worship me.

"You don't do that, and I-I love that. Finn, I love that. I love you."

When he didn't respond, the only sound or movement his thumbs rubbing my hips, I went on, "And I still see in my dreams. I see my parents' faces, Theo's. I remember horses and flowers and cute boys." I smiled. "I wish I would've seen your face before the accident. I wish I could dream it. But I dream of you in other ways."

"You dream about me?" he whispered, and he nuzzled his cheek to mine.

I inhaled, breathing him in, letting him fill me up, and I realized right then how lucky I was. All those women came on to him, they wanted him, and they flirted with him, I was sure, but I was allowed to *know* him. I was being honored with the privilege of knowing who Finn was on the *inside* and with the privilege of letting him truly know me, even the mean and ugly parts I'd always thought no one could love.

"Yes. All the time. I hear your voice in my dreams and your guitar, I smell you, and I feel you. Your kindness for everyone, for me even when I don't deserve it, especially then. The way you lift your brothers up every day, and they don't even know. I dream about the happiness inside you because wherever you go, it spills out. I chase it in my dreams because I want it. I want to feel the way you do. I want to laugh at things like you do. I want the freedom you have. To be silly. To live. To… love.

"But I also dream about sexy Finn," I said, blushing a little, even though it was ridiculous because he'd seen me in all kinds of precarious and depraved situations.

"Who's that now?"

"You know. Mad Finn. Dangerous Finn. The Finn who… who fucks me hard, who pulls my hair and chokes me."

"Ace, they aren't two different guys. Happy Finn is Mad Finn. There doesn't have to be a difference. I can be whoever I want, whenever I want. So can you. You don't have to be poor tortured Miss Aislinn Burroughs, except when you feel that way. But you can be her and be happy at the same time. That's bein' human, baby."

"Baby?"

"Mmm, yeah, baby. And FYI, anytime you wanna be sexy dominatrix Ace or submissive Ace, you just let me know. I will not complain." He lifted me into his arms and stood, then laid me on the bed. "But right now, I just want you to be Ace."

"You didn't answer my question. Why were you a virgin? Why did you wait?" He inhaled a breath to speak, but I held up my finger. "And how the hell do you know how to do all the things you've done to me if you were a virgin?"

He laughed, lifting my legs one at a time, and he pulled my pajama pants down, following the fabric with his lips, placing quick, soft kisses on my skin. "I waited 'cause none of them women were you. They weren't right for me. All they cared about was what was on the outside, but I wanted someone who liked all the weird shit inside me."

"But I didn't like you. In fact, I wanted to kick you in the balls up until yesterday."

He chuckled, a low, sexy rumble, that faraway thunderstorm in his voice again. "Yeah, well, you keep tellin' yourself that, but I know the truth. You wanted to kick my balls 'cause you were mad at yourself. You can't help how much you want me, and it pisses you off.

"And just 'cause I hadn't had sex doesn't mean I didn't do *other* things." Climbing over me, he whispered, "But I wanted my first time—the first time I shared my body with a woman, the first time my body was inside hers, the first time I came inside her—I wanted to love that woman. And I wanted her to know she was special to me, that she owned me, body and soul.

"But I've done this," he rasped, licking up my leg. He went straight to the apex of my thighs, spreading them and licking deep between them. "And I've done this," he whispered, dipping his finger beneath my underwear, playing in the wetness there, smearing it all around, then dragging his finger up and underneath my shirt between my breasts, covering my body with my own arousal. He followed the line with his tongue, pushing my shirt up to my neck.

My breath was the barest hint of sound because the desire in my body was overwhelming. "Finn?"

"Yeah?"

I tried not to moan when I asked, "Why didn't you tell me you have a hard time reading?"

He froze with his head between my breasts, his hair tickling them. "You know why. I was embarrassed. It ain't somethin' I'm real proud of."

"Can I tell you a secret?"

"I'm dyin' to know." He flicked my nipple with his tongue, then sucked it into his mouth, and I almost forgot what I wanted to say.

"I can't read either."

"Right, but you used to."

"I did. I read a lot. But now, I use special apps and technology that help me. You know that little voice on my phone you hear any time I use it?"

"Yeah, the really annoyin' one who interrupts all the time?"

"Yes. That's Voice Over. It's a special feature for the visually impaired. Every smartphone has a version of it. It reads everything on my phone's screen for me. And I use other apps when I'm online. If you need help reading something, you could use them too. I can show you. I can teach you something for once."

"Oh yeah? You'll be my teacher? I never liked teachers, I gotta warn ya." Moving above my shirt, he rubbed his cock between my legs, and it was already wet at the tip with cum, the damp heat soaking his bedsheet still wrapped around his hips, trailing up my inner thigh, making me shiver, and I tried to pull him closer.

Smiling and taunting him, I arched one eyebrow and purred, "You've *never* had a teacher like me."

"Ms. Burroughs? Strict, sexy Ms. Burroughs." He groaned.

"Yes."

"You gonna boss me around?" Slipping his tongue in my mouth, I gasped and sucked on it, pulling him further inside.

I was drowning in his kiss, his lips and tongue so soft and wet, and he pumped his hips, rubbing against me slowly, driving me crazy, and already, I needed to come. I couldn't stop my body from responding to his. I bent my knees, cradling him with my legs, begging him with my body, trying to fit the head of his cock between my pussy lips, trying to make him rub my clit.

My hands found their way to his shoulders and reached and rubbed his bare skin. But I remembered falling into his messy room and said, "Yes, and my first command is: Clean. Your. Room! Oh my God, Finn. It's a disaster in here. What did I trip over? Was that a pile of cowboy hats?"

He laughed. "Yes. It was a very strategically placed pile of clothin'. You kicked it so now I won't be able to find my clothes, and I'll have to walk around naked. It's gonna be all your fault." He kneeled above me. "I'm gonna start now." The sheet fell away, and his body was bared to me, free for me to touch and feel however much I wanted.

But I pulled my hands away. "Wait," I said.

"What?"

"Well, first, thank you for forgiving me for being such a jerk."

"I didn't say I forgive you," he said, and the bed was jostled when he stood. I lay there unmoving, listening to the sounds of him removing my shirt when the silky fabric rustled over my skin, and imagining the hard part of him so ready to be inside the soft part of me. I reached out, feeling the empty air, trying to find his cock. He stepped forward, placing it in my reach, and I wrapped my hand around it and squeezed.

"Oh no? Well, this hard nutloaf tells me otherwise."

He snorted. "Sorry to break it to you, but my nutloaf's

always hard around you, whether I'm mad at you, happy with you, or in love with you."

"You're in love with me?"

"Yes."

"I'm in love with you too."

"Good." He slid my underwear down my legs, kissing and scraping his teeth gently over my muscles as he went.

"But Finn?"

"Shit. There's already conditions on your love? You know you talk a lot?"

I smiled, but what I needed to say was important. "I think we need to keep this to ourselves."

"Yeah. Your brother…"

"You don't know him well, but he's not himself. I'm afraid of what he'll do if he finds out. We've never been here before, you know? I've changed so much just in the last month alone, but he hasn't. Or maybe he has, but I don't think he knows how to handle what's happened."

"Maybe you need to talk to him."

"I know. I will."

"And Billie's got some info for you about your birth mama. I think you need to hear her out."

"I know that too." I heard a condom packet tear, and anticipation surged through my body like fire in a dry forest. It was hot and heady, and it swelled in my heart.

"What're you afraid of?" he asked, hovering above me, finally notching his cock where I wanted him, between my legs, and I opened them wider.

"I don't—I'm not sure. Like, what if she really is alive? Then what does that say about me? Why wouldn't she want me? But I'm starting to realize that that's not it. Because my parents *did* want me. They gave me everything. They did everything they could to make me happy. So I was good enough. You know?"

"Ace, you are good enough. You're way better than good."

"I think you're right," I said, and I realized finally that it was what I'd spent years trying to make everyone believe. But now, *I* believed it. "And so are you."

"Hell yeah," he preened. "That ain't nothin' new. Everybody knows that."

"Don't joke. I'm being serious. You're good enough. Even if you don't read well. Even if you feel like all people see when they look at you is this pretty face." I held his face in my hands, feeling the shape of his jaw, his lips. I ran my finger along the bridge of his nose, over his bushy eyebrows, trying to imagine the color. "I know the truth. You're so much more than that."

His voice was the only sound in the world when he whispered, "Thank you."

"You're everything, Finn, and I love you."

Moaning, he exhaled, and he pushed into my body so slowly. "You gonna shut up now so I can make love to you?"

"Yes."

He did. Slowly and languidly, he moved in and out of my body, drugging me with his, making me see all kinds of beautiful things. He made me see my family, my future with him. Waking up with him wrapped around me every morning. Loving him and playing with him every day. After ten years of being blind, I finally saw myself, who I was, who I wanted to be, and who I knew I could be.

And all of those women, strong and weak, damaged and blind or not—all of me belonged to him.

Could a person die of too much sex? Too much happiness? If they could, I was in trouble. We made love every single chance we got. In the old truck, in the arena office after Shonda had gone home. In the shower. Who needed a bed? Though we slept in mine because he still hadn't cleaned his room.

Billie and Jay knew Finn and I were together, and Billie had told me it made Jay nervous, but neither of them said anything. I thought Billie might've threatened to never have sex with Jay again if he said anything to Jack.

And I thought Shonda might've had some clue, because she made all kinds of disapproving noises when we were all three in the same room together. I had no idea why she would care, but she seemed to, though she never said anything.

No one said a word, and I was drowning in satisfied bliss until Finn and I had fallen asleep in the barn after having sex so hot that I was embarrassed in my dreams that night. We'd tried to make it up to the house after working late one night, but we were just too impatient. He played my body again like his guitar, and I couldn't wait one more minute to have him, so he'd made love to me in the little room above the barn with my wrists tied to my ankles, just like in my book.

But when we woke in the morning, that core-clenching bliss disappeared like smoke.

"What the fuck is going on here?" *Theo? Why is Theo in my bedroom?*

"Finn. Fucking. Cade. Wake the fuck up," Jack bellowed. "I'm gonna kill him this time. I swear to God. Dean, you better stop me." The voices slurred together in my head, and I was sure I was still dreaming.

I opened my eyes but saw nothing, of course. Finn and I were still nestled up together, his hand cupping my bare breast possessively.

He stiffened behind me, and I rubbed my ass against him, trying to nuzzle back into the dream I'd been having about him kissing my neck as we rode Gertie together through the wide open Wyoming fields. In my dream, I could see the grassy hills and valleys, and they were breathtaking.

I smiled when I felt his erection between my ass cheeks. Maybe we could sneak another session in before work. I wanted to blindfold him so he could experience sex the way I did.

"Um, Ace," he whispered in my ear, "you might wanna wake up."

"What time is it?" I mumbled, yawning.

"How dare you take advantage of my sister! I'll kill you!"

Theo's voice filled up the room, and all of a sudden, I was bouncing on the mattress, realizing instantly where I was. It was not my bedroom, and we were not alone. I sat up, patting around to find a blanket and yanking it up over my breasts when Finn let go because Theo struck him, knocking me onto my side as he charged.

"Theo? What are you doing here? What's going on?"

"You were supposed to be taking care of her, not fucking her!"

"Calm down, man," Finn said, but his voice came from the floor.

"Theo! Get out of here!"

My brother laughed, but there was no humor in his voice. "I thought you were hurt. We couldn't find you, and I was worried, but you were up here the whole time, doing God know what with... Aislinn, get up *now*. Get dressed. We're leaving."

"No!"

Theo gripped my arm hard, and then Finn's voice was moving next to the bed.

"Now, that ain't necessary, Theo," he said, but Theo dropped my arm, and all I could hear were the sounds of him attacking Finn.

"How dare you? You had no right! She's a child. She's innocent."

They fell back to the floor, and I followed the commotion, leaning over, trying to understand what was happening.

There were all kinds of scuffling noises, Finn grunted, and then Kevin's voice rang out from across the room, yelling at Theo to let go. Theo was beating Finn. Or trying to.

"Theo, stop it! I'm not a child. I'm twenty-seven years old, and I am far from innocent." I reached out, searching for Theo, and when I found him, I pulled on his arm, but he threw it back and hit me.

Gasping, I fell backward, almost falling off the bed on the other side. My jaw and lip throbbed, and something warm and wet trickled down my chin. Touching it tentatively, I pulled my hand away, stunned, feeling the viscous blood between my fingers.

Everyone stilled. Everything stopped. I begged my eyes to see. Was Finn okay? Who was in the room? I was naked and bleeding. I felt my eyes racing all around, and I wanted to reach for Finn. I wanted him to hold me so I could ground myself, so I could find my bearings.

"You hit her," Finn said in a low, deep voice, Mad Finn coming out to play.

"Oh God. Aislinn, I'm sorry. I'm so sorry! Are you okay? Are you—"

"No! Don't you touch me!" I shrieked when Theo grabbed my wrist, the Mad Ace coming out in me too. I launched myself at him, punching air but also landing blows on what I hoped was his face or his stomach or anything that would hurt. I felt wild and crazed, but it felt good.

"Aislinn!" Shonda pulled me off of Theo, crawling in front of me on the mattress, creating a barrier between my brother and me, and I fought and struggled with her, trying to get to him. I knew he was going to try to take Finn away from me, and that realization and the rage that came with it, topped onto the rage I still felt from learning that he'd hid so much more from me—it all took over, and I couldn't stop myself from pummeling him.

"That's enough," Jack thundered, and the room grew still in an instant.

Great, so how many people were in the room with us? The blanket had pooled around my hips, and I was naked in front of everyone. Shonda hugged me, covering me with her sweater.

"You may be in charge of our fate," Jack said to Theo, "but *nobody* lays hands on a woman. Not in my house."

"It was an accident. I didn't mean to do it. Aislinn, I'm so sorry!" Theo called out while Jack dragged him across the room, the heels of his shoes squeaking across the floor, and he mumbled into his hands, "Fuck. What am I doing? I'm so sorry."

They left the little room above the barn, Jack leading Theo down the stairs and Theo pleading to be forgiven.

I touched my lip again and hissed at the pain.

"Ace, you okay?" Finn asked, picking himself up. I heard the zip of his jean's zipper and the rustle of his shirt when he pulled it on, but his feet were still bare. They padded on the floor, and then the bed dipped a little when he sat next to me.

"I'm fine, I think. I'm sorry."

"What are you apolo—"

"You have nothing to be sorry for," Shonda interrupted Finn. "Come on. Come with me. We'll get you cleaned up."

"Shonda, I got this," Finn said, but then Jack barked up the stairs.

"Finn! Get your ass down here now!"

"Go. Go deal with your brother. I'll take care of Aislinn."

"It's fine, Finn. I'm fine. I just need to get dressed. Go. I'll be there in a few minutes. I'll talk to Theo."

"'Kay." He kissed my forehead. "You sure you're okay?"

"It's just a little cut."

Kissing the edge of my lip, he swiped the blood away with his thumb. "I love you. Don't worry. We'll work this out."

When Finn had left the room, Shonda clicked her tongue, and I wasn't sure if it was in disapproval of Finn telling me he loved me or of the whole situation in general. "Come, dear, I'll help you. We'll clean that cut," she said, her voice a tone I'd never heard before. It was low and weird, and she gripped the back of my arm.

CHAPTER NINETEEN

FINN

My breath came out in hard puffs against the really fuckin' cold air in the arena while Jack scolded me like a kid and my brothers all glared at me. He'd dragged Theo from the barn, I assumed so Aislinn wouldn't hear him tell me I couldn't have her. It was the reason we'd tried to keep things a secret, poorly executed secret though it was, but Theo had gone for a drive. He was probably tryin' to calm down.

"You can't, Finn," Jay said. "You know you can't. This has gone too far."

"Can't what? And it didn't seem to bother you yesterday, Jay."

"You knew?" Jack speared Jay with a look, then swung back to me. "What if she gets hurt?"

I laughed in disbelief. "She's already hurt, and it wasn't me who did it! And what if she hurts me? Ever think of that?"

"Finn."

"What, Jack? What're you tryin' to say?"

"It was her you were talkin' about," Dean said, standin'

behind me, "wasn't it? In the truck on the way up to Montana? Code Word Camilla?"

"Yeah, well, maybe."

"I thought you said you didn't like her."

I winced.

"You're sure actin' like you like her," Jack said.

"Maybe I lied about that, or maybe I just hadn't figured it out yet."

"Finn! You cannot fall in love with her." Jack paced in front of me for once. "Goddammit, I warned you. I told you to stay away from her. This is all gonna end in disaster, and it won't just be your tender fuckin' heart on the line. It's our whole business. It's our livelihoods!" He stopped and looked at me, shakin' his head. "Finn, please don't do this."

"Don't do what? What am I doin'?"

"You're about to piss away a whole year's worth of work and goodwill with Theo. We've already got two guys signed up for the veteran program. How do you think we're gonna pull that shit off if Theo rescinds his money?"

"Jack, she's an adult. He can't control her. She makes her own decisions."

He tossed his arms in the air. "I know you ain't that stupid. I don't know what fucked up dynamic they have between 'em, but obviously, Theo hasn't gotten that memo. The guy's clearly not in a good place, but there's nothin' we can do about that. The only thing we can do is try not to piss him off further."

"Yeah? And what if this was Evvie? Would you be able to walk away? Just like that?"

"Now, I love Evvie, Finn," Jack said, cockin' his head to the side. He was doubtin' me. "Do you love Aislinn? Are you willin' to lose *everything* for her?"

"Yeah. I do." I said it, but the weight of the last twenty

years lookin' after my brothers, workin' this ranch, tryin' to help my family—it settled on my chest like a hundred pounds of horse shit. How could I fuck it up now, just when everything was comin' together? Was that what was happenin'? Did I have to choose between my brothers and Ace?

I couldn't live with myself if I flushed my brothers' dreams down the drain. How could I do that to 'em?

But I couldn't walk away from Ace. No way.

I stood tall and declared, "I do. I love her. I don't wanna fuck this up, Jack. I don't wanna ruin our plans, but I've waited my whole life for her. I ain't goin' down without a fight." I knew my brothers would have my back.

Jack sighed and dropped his head into his hands. "Finn. What have you done? You're bein' so selfish."

"Selfish?" Or maybe they wouldn't.

"Yeah, selfish," he said. "Why're you doin' this? You can have anyone else in the world. Why does it have to be her? Why now? This is serious. She isn't someone you can play with, Finn, like everything else you do."

Oh, now I was mad.

"*Fuck* you, Jack." Aislinn was right. Mad Finn reared his ugly head. "Somebody had to be the fuckin' voice of reason around here. Y'all were fallin' apart. This ranch was dyin' a slow death. You—oh, King Jack—were becomin' mute, Dean went off the fuckin' deep end, Kev wanted to kill himself, and Jay couldn't find his fuckin' balls. So, I did it. I joked. I laughed. I cooked. I was tryin' to keep y'all from losin' your shit! So fuck each and every one of you. Selfish? 'Cause I found someone to love?

"And let's not even talk about Dad. That motherfucker was abusive. Verbally, physically. He beat the shit out of Kev on a pretty regular basis for no good goddamn reason at all. 'Cause he was lonely, or he hated the world. Maybe he hated us. I dunno. But if I kept him laughin', he didn't do that shit so much. So, y'all are fuckin' welcome."

"Finn—"

"No. Eat shit, Jack. I'm done talkin' about this," I said, turnin' to storm dramatically from the arena, but I bumped right into Theo.

"Where is she?" he demanded, steppin' right up to me, starin' up at me with clear hatred in his eyes, glarin' daggers right into mine. "Where's my sister?"

Jay's phone rang and he denied the call, but as soon as he did, it rang again. It rang and rang till he answered it.

"She's probably up at the house," Kev said. "Shonda was helpin' her."

Theo shook his head, squarin' his shoulders with his hands on his hips. "She's not in the house. Where is she?"

"Billie," Jay whispered into his phone while I stared samurai swords right back at Theo. "It's not a good time. We got a bit of a situation right now. I'll call you back in a few minutes."

"If this is some Romeo and Juliet bullshit," Theo spat, "you can cut the crap right now. You are not in love with my sister. You can't have her. She's not for sale."

"'Scuse me? What did you just say?" Theo backed up when I advanced on him. I couldn't stop the threat in my voice. "I don't give a fuck who you are. I don't care about your fuckin' money, and right now I barely care that you're her brother. Do not *ever* talk about her like that again. You hear me?" I crowded him against a stall door, and he shrank away from the tone of my voice.

Somebody was yellin' my name, but I couldn't be bothered.

"I don't know what the fuck is goin' on with y—"

"Finn!" Jay stuffed himself between Theo and me, tryin'

to push us apart. "Shut up for a minute. Would you listen to me?"

"What, Jay? Goddammit. What?"

"Billie's on the phone. Shonda is, um"—Jay cleared his throat, looking up at me and back down to Theo—"she's Aislinn's biological aunt."

In unison, five voices said, "What the fuck?"

"There is no one here," Luuk said through Kevin's speakerphone. He'd already been in Jackson for a farm call, so he drove to the address we had on file for Shonda, but no one was there. Ace wasn't in the house, she wasn't in the office, and Shonda's car was gone. Tony and Pepper were runnin' circles around where it had been parked just an hour ago. "I'll wait, shall I, in case they come here? Maybe they are on the way."

"Yeah, Luuk," Kev said. "Thanks, babe. I'll call back if she shows up."

"*Ja.* Okay."

"Okay," Billie said through Jay's speakerphone. "I'm not kidding, you guys. It's her. She's way older and she's done something to her face—I don't know, a nose job or something weird, or maybe she just aged *really* badly—but I'm looking at a picture of Shonda from twenty-eight years ago with Ace and Theo's parents at some big fundraiser in Boston. And you're never gonna believe me, but I just got a hit on Monique Washington—Ace's birth mother. She is alive. And guess who she just visited in prison?"

Theo's voice was small when he said, "No. She's sick. She doesn't leave her—"

"You know what, Theo, I'm gonna kindly ask you to shut

the fuck up," Billie said. "You could've saved us all the trouble, you could've saved me a shit-load of time, and you could've saved your sister a whole *truck-load* of heartache. But you didn't. If I could bitchslap you through the phone, I would."

"Who did she visit in prison?" Kev asked, confused.

"Blake Ormand," Billie said. "Remember the douchebag who beat the shit out of Jay?"

"Did you know about Shonda?" Jay asked Theo, and I swore I could hear a little bit of the respect in Jay's voice die.

"No. I swear I didn't. I knew Monique had family, and maybe I kind of remember a sister? I'm not sure. But no, I didn't know she had anything to do with this."

"What *did* you know?" I said, steppin' up, towerin' over him again.

"Finn, back off," Jack said.

I turned to pace the aisle. What in the ever-lovin'-fuck was goin' on? Where was Ace? Why would she leave? Did she leave, or did Shonda take her somewhere? And why would Shonda lie about who she was? If Billie was right, Shonda's real name was Regina.

"I'm so confused, Billie," I said. "Where is Ace?"

"I suspect Shonda thinks she's trying to protect Ace. Her sister is indeed sick. She has schizophrenia, and she's been sick for a long time. Once I saw her on the prison video feed, I was able to find all kinds of evidence that she's alive, though Shonda tried hard to hide her identity. She struggles with severe mental illness, and Shonda put her in this home, like a nursing home, but I think, a few months ago, when Theo took off and Jay and I raced across the fucking desert to find him—I think it was Monique on the other end of the phone call Blake Ormand made the night Jay got beat to shit.

"I don't know how," Billie said, "but I think Shonda

figured that out, that her sister was involved somehow with Blake, and she tried to intervene. And then she came here. I think she took this job so she could be close to Ace. I don't know how she found her but… Damn it. I should've known. I should've run a background check on her when Jay told me she applied for the job, but she was a nice old lady."

"Fuck. What have I done?" Theo ran his hands through his hair, and I lost it.

"That's right, you moron," I said, and it felt good to put the idiot in his place. "This is all your fault. All you had to do was be honest with Ace. Why couldn't you do that?" I stomped over to him and pushed him, and he tripped backward, landin' on his ass in an empty stall. "You've been too busy treatin' her like she's a piece of property and drinkin' yourself into oblivion that you didn't notice what was right in front of your face. You're drunk right now, aren't you? It's what, nine in the fuckin' mornin'?

"If anything happens to her," I promised, "I'll kill you."

CHAPTER TWENTY

AISLINN

"SHONDA? What's going on? Why won't you talk to me? I know Theo was upset, but he wouldn't hurt me. Not on purpose. He didn't mean to hit me. It was an accident, although he did mean to hit Finn. That's an issue. I don't know what's wrong with him. I don't know how to talk to him." I waited in the blackness in her car for her to say something, anything, as the tires sped faster and faster away from Finn and Theo. I touched the crusted blood covering the cut on my lip and winced. The side of my face was a little swollen and sore.

On our way up to the house so I could clean up before going back to the barn to hash things out with Theo, Shonda had shoved me into her backseat and taken off. And now she wasn't talking, and I was growing more and more nervous. "Where are we going?" When she didn't answer again, I screamed her name, "Shonda!"

"Please, Aislinn," she said, her voice a nervous pleading. "Please be quiet. I can't think."

"Think? Think about what? Where are we going? Why did you take me? Why don't you want me to be at the ranch?

Please"—tears streamed down my face because she was scaring the shit out of me—"please tell me what's going on."

"You're just like her, you know. You get mad and then you cry." She laughed. "I remember when she was—"

"Who! Who are you talking about? I'm just like who?"

"Actually, you're like them both. Both of your mothers. Monique and Elizabeth."

"What? You knew my—but… how?"

She grabbed my hand over the seat, and I tried to pull it away, but she held on.

"Shonda, please, you're scaring me."

"I'm sorry. I don't mean to." She sighed and released my hand. "Your real mother is my little sister. Her name is Monique, and she's sick. And years ago, the woman who adopted you, Elizabeth Burroughs, was my very best friend."

I gasped, realization settling in my stomach like a lead weight. "She was the friend you told me about? The one who dumped you for a man?"

"Yes. I had to choose between them, Monique and Elizabeth. I'd worked for your father's company from the very beginning. I was the first employee he and his partner hired— my husband got me the job because he was friends with your father, and he'd invested in the company—and Elizabeth and I quickly became friends. I used to babysit Theo for her when he was just a little thing. I doubt he remembers—but this is all because of your father's partner."

"You're talking about David Ormand?"

"Yes. He was a bad man, Aislinn. And your father was very successful. He was lucky in business, and he was fast making a name for himself. Ormand was jealous, I think. So when I got my sister a job there one summer, he figured out how weak-minded she was, and he… he took advantage of her. He manipulated her, and ultimately, he controlled her.

"Monique had always struggled with depression and mental illness. We learned later that she had schizophrenia, but back then we had no idea. She was sleeping with Ormand, and he convinced her to seduce your father. She was very beautiful and young, and she would have done anything to please David. She thought she was in love with him, and he convinced her that he loved her too.

"Your father made a mistake, but when he figured out she was pregnant, he did the right thing. He tried, anyway. But by the time you were born, David Ormand had moved on. He and your father had gone their separate ways, and he didn't want anything to do with my sister anymore. But she followed him and begged him to come back to her. She threatened to out their affair, and Ormand tried to kill her. He drugged her. When she came to in the hospital, Ormand's wife was there. She threatened Monique and convinced her to leave, to never go back to Boston. But during that hospital stay, we also learned about her schizophrenia diagnosis."

It was so weird listening to her, like she was talking about a movie or book she'd read, not my life. Not my mother. I wanted to go back to the ranch, but I wanted to know about my mother more, so I sat back in the seat and listened.

"Our parents were old and ill-equipped to deal with such an illness, and my husband had just died. I was alone and Monique was alone. I chose to go with her. I chose to hide her from Ormand. I never would have bothered you, but your mother knew about Monique's illness. She knew to look out for the signs, but when she died, I worried she'd never told Theo. Schizophrenia usually presents in young adulthood, and I didn't think he knew.

"I made a home for my sister and I in northern Nevada. I took care of her for years, and there were never any issues. Her medications were working, and I started to live my life again. I worked, I made friends. Things felt like they could be normal again. And I was checking in on you. You'd been through so much, but you were okay. Theo was taking care of you. You didn't need anything.

"But everything changed this past summer. Monique's medications stopped working, and I had to put her in a home, and then David Ormand's son found her. I don't know how, but he did. And I think you know the rest."

"Blake Ormand. The man who threatened my life? He hurt my brother. He hurt Jay."

"Yes. I didn't know he was blackmailing Theo. I never imagined his father would share his vendetta with his son. David Ormand died when Blake was a young teenager, but he must've put the thought in Blake's head. He searched for a long time for my sister—he wanted to hold the evidence of your father's affair over Theo's head for money. He wanted to hold all of your brother's cards.

"And that night—the night Billie and Jay caught up to Blake—I walked into my sister's room, and I heard them on the phone. I heard him threatening you.

"I left my sister that night. I chose you that night, and I've chosen you every day since. I'm sorry I lied to you. I'm sorry I lied about who I was. But I've been stuck in my sister's sickness for so long, and I was afraid for you."

"Shonda, I'm not sick. I don't know anything about schizophrenia, but besides being blind, there's nothing wrong with me." I remembered her fussing over me all the time, babying me, always asking me how I was feeling. "That's why you worry about me, isn't it?"

"Yes."

"You could have just asked me. You're right, I was fine. Theo was taking care of me, but I was alone. I could've used an aunt in my life. Why didn't you say something?"

"I didn't think you'd listen. I didn't think Theo would. My family has caused so much trouble for yours. I guess I was scared to be rejected, and I was scared, if I were, no one would be looking out for you." She reached back to hold my hand again. "You're my only family, Aislinn."

"Shonda. Take me back. Please."

"I can't. Before everyone freaked out this morning, I got a call from the facility my sister was in. She's not there anymore, and I don't know where she is. And I'm worried she'll do something stupid. I don't know what she'll do, and I don't know if this Blake thing is over. He's in jail, but what if he's still looking for you? What if he was working with some-one? What if he's convinced Monique to hurt you like his father did? No. We can't risk it."

"My friends will look out for me, Shonda. The Cades. Theo will. We can call the sheriff. He'll help us. He's a really nice man. And Finn. Shonda, Finn loves me and I love him. He won't let anything happen to me."

"Aislinn, don't be so naive. He's a charmer, but he's just like every other man. He'll lie to you. He'll manipulate you. You can't depend on him."

"I can depend on myself, and I trust my judgement enough to know that Finn is a good man."

She didn't say anything for a few minutes, like maybe she was debating with herself. It was the first time she'd even listened to a word I'd said, so I didn't interrupt her. I counted the rotation of the tires on the road beneath me and waited, but finally, she said, "No. He can't even read. You need to listen to me. Elizabeth was the same way, swayed by love, but your father cheated on her with the first woman he could. And because of him, my whole life was ruined. I won't let you do that to yourself."

Fear rushed through my body, and the feeling made me

sick to my stomach. "You're wrong. Finn's not like that. He wouldn't do that to me."

"Oh, Aislinn, you don't know. You can't see him. You don't understand."

I kept trying to reason with her, but I was starting to wonder if she could hear reason at all anymore. "Shonda, take me back now. You're wrong. Do you think, because I'm blind, I can't tell what kind of man he is? Is this really about you trying to protect me, or is it about you protecting yourself?"

"Maybe I am protecting myself too. Why shouldn't I? But you are my priority."

"So, what are we going to do? Where can we go? We're safer back at the ranch."

"No. We need to be off the grid. We need to hide."

"From who? For how long? You know Billie won't stop looking for me."

"Yes. I know. We'll need a different car. This one doesn't have GPS, but Billie will find a way, I'm sure."

"Shonda, Theo will freak out—he'll hire mercenaries or something. You don't know him. We have to go back."

"No!"

I hadn't wanted to fall asleep, but I begged and pleaded until my voice gave out, and so did my hope as the distance between my family and I grew, and eventually, Shonda's silence, the quiet sounds in the car, and the miles passing beneath my feet lulled me to sleep.

When I woke, it was to Shonda trying to pull me from her car.

"We're here, Aislinn. Come on, sweetheart. I'm sure you need to use the restroom. I know I do."

"No. Take me back, Shonda," I said, bracing my hands on the freezing metal of the open car door.

"I can't do that."

"Is it night?"

"Not quite. It's just after six, but it's already dark out," she said, wrapping her arm around my waist, trying to pull me with her.

"We've been driving for hours."

"I stopped for gas once—this car gets good gas mileage—but you were out."

"Where are we?"

She took a deep breath, looking around when she answered, her voice following the movement. "We're in the mountains. It's nice here. It reminds me of the ranch. You'll like it."

"I won't. I want to go back."

She didn't answer, and I knew she wasn't listening, and I knew it didn't matter what I said. She'd made up her mind. She'd decided she could take better care of me than I could of myself. She thought she could keep me safe and Theo couldn't.

Finn couldn't.

"She'd never remember, but this is where I brought Monique when we first ran, after you were born. She still cried for you every night. She didn't want to let you go, Aislinn, but she was deep into her sickness, and she didn't have control. I knew the Burroughs family would take good care of you. Elizabeth and I had become such good friends. She was angry with your father, but she was ridiculously in love with him. She forgave him." She laughed. "He was a charmer, just like Finn. Do you remember?"

"Yes, *Shonda*, I remember my father."

Turning back to me, she tsked her tongue. "I know you're angry with me, but it's for the best. You'll understand that. You'll be okay. Come on. Let's get inside. I'll start a fire. Your teeth are chattering."

"Yes, because you kidnapped me without a coat."

"I didn't kidnap you, Aislinn."

"What would you call it then?" I asked when she let go of my waist and pulled me by my arm. There were no sounds around us. No traffic, no people, no buildings. The sounds of the forest were barely recognizable. The crunch of the snow was all I heard as I followed her on wobbly legs. What choice did I have?

The cabin she'd brought me to was small, only one room with a small kitchen and a tiny bathroom off of that. There was a small shower stall, but we didn't have running water. Shonda said there was a loft above the kitchen, but I didn't go up there. Who knew how long the place had been abandoned, and I was not about to go snuggling into a pile of spiders or raccoon feces no matter how tired I was and how much space I wanted from my aunt.

There was a small loveseat in the living room and an old, creaky reclining chair, so I sat on the loveseat and listened while she milled around, "tidying up and making it comfortable." She lit a fire in the fireplace, and I could already feel the heat filling up the small cabin.

The anger inside me grew and grew, and I didn't know what to do with it. I was utterly stuck. I had no resources, no options, no phone, and no coat. How did she think we would survive in the mountains without coats? Without water? Without my cane!

"You look just like her, you know?" she said when she settled in the chair. She'd lit a gas lantern, and I could hear the tiny flame crackling on a table between us. "Like my sister. Your mother."

"I don't care." And I realized I didn't. I didn't care that my mother was alive. I didn't care that she'd never been a part of my life. I didn't care at all. It no longer mattered to me.

I already had a family.

Laughing a little, she said, "That's exactly what Monique would say."

And that was when it clicked. That was what this was about. Some misguided attempt to go back. To relive her life with her sister. She wanted me to believe she was being noble, that this was all about keeping me safe, but it wasn't. It was about Shonda, about her being alone in the world, and she wanted me to make that better for her.

"If you don't take me back, you're going to jail, Shonda. Don't you care? Who will take care of your sister then?"

"I've given up on her. I tried so hard for so long to protect her. To keep her happy." Shifting in her chair, she said, "Let's get some sleep. Everything will look better in the morning."

"Nothing will 'look' better to me, Shonda."

***

I didn't sleep. I spent the entire night racking my brain, trying to think of the right thing to say to convince her to take me back to the ranch. When that proved fruitless, I felt my way around the cabin. Kidnapping must've been hard work because I bumped into countless things, made so much noise, but she never woke.

I went through every drawer I could find, every box, every hole. I found weapons, a dull knife and other pointy objects I could've used against her, but what good would that do me? If I stabbed her, I'd be stuck here even more alone.

And I didn't want to hurt her. She was desperate and acting foolishly, but she thought she was protecting me. When my searches amounted to nothing much more than a butter knife and cuts and scrapes all over my hands, I gave up, sinking back down onto the smelly, disgusting, dead leaf-covered couch.

It was a dark place in my mind. No stimulus to keep it occupied. I replayed memories of being with Finn over and over. Memories of Theo surfaced too. Memories of the last ten years.

I'd been so angry with him, but when I really thought about it, Theo had done the best he could. I hadn't been a willing participant in my own life, and he'd tried as hard as he could have. He had no life because of me. The only relationship he'd had was with our driver, an employee. He didn't go out, he didn't date. He'd given up everything for me.

It was me who'd lost my sight the day our parents died, but I'd blinded us both with my petulance, with my unwillingness to even try to live. It was no wonder he'd lied to me. I couldn't blame him for not telling me the truth. I'd been in no place to hear it.

And now, Theo was suffering because of me. He was going through something alone, grieving and flailing at the loss of our sad life, such as it was, and I was doing nothing but making things worse.

Well, I was done with that. When I made it back to him, I would beg *his* forgiveness, and things would be different.

Jay and Shonda had trained me in the office, and I was good at it. I did well with organizing things and keeping up with repeated tasks. I was good on the phone, and I was really good at keeping the guys on track, keeping them on a schedule. I laughed out loud when it occurred to me that I could've been helping Theo with our family's business this whole time.

"What? Aislinn? What time is it?" Shonda asked, waking, moving the chair when she stretched.

"I don't know."

"Oh. Right, I'm sorry, sweetheart. Of course you don't. Um, it's"—she paused, looking at a watch or a… phone? It was definitely a phone; I heard the telltale click of the screen coming to life. All I had to do was get that phone. "It's six in the morning. How did you sleep?"

"Fine."

"Are you hungry? There's no food here, but I grabbed a few things at the gas station last night. We'll need to gather more firewood, and we'll have to make a run into town for supplies. We need water."

"Yes, I'm hungry," I said, using the conversation to distract her while I tried to make a plan. But how was I going to get the phone? I had no clue, but I would just have to wait for the right opportunity. "How are we going to take a shower? There's no running water."

"Well, we won't. We'll just have to do the best we can with bottled water." She sat next to me on the little couch and held my hand. "It won't be forever. Just until I can be sure we're safe."

"And how will you know that? We have no internet, do we? I didn't find a TV or even a radio."

"Oh, Aislinn, look at your hands," she said, turning my hands over with hers, her dry skin sliding over mine. "What have you been doing all night?"

"I'm going to be honest with you, Shonda. I was looking for anything I could use to… to escape or threaten you with. I don't know. I don't know what I was looking for. But it doesn't matter because I didn't find anything. You have me here at your mercy. I can't leave. I can't do anything, not without your help. So I'm begging you, please, please take me back. I will do everything in my power to keep you safe. I won't let them arrest you, and I'll help you. Billie can find your sister. She'll find any threat against us. And if I ask them to, my friends will protect you too. *Please*, auntie, take me home?" I begged, hoping the endearment would convince her. It didn't.

"Come on, let's get going. It's winter. The days aren't long, and we have a lot of work to do to make this place habitable. There's a small convenience store at the bottom of the mountain. We'll go there for food and supplies."

Waiting in the car while Shonda "shopped," misery was quickly taking over. She wouldn't be moved. She was determined to keep me with her no matter what I said. I'd already stopped asking for her to take me back. It was a waste of my voice. And every time she refused, the darkness grew darker.

She was in the store for a long time, and I could've run. I could have simply opened my door and walked away. But where would I go? The store was in the middle of nowhere. I heard one measly car race by on the highway the whole time I sat there. There were no buildings, no people, and Shonda had threatened that if I said anything to the store clerk, she would just take me somewhere else.

Reclining my seat, I closed my eyes and breathed. I was so tired, but I wasn't afraid of Shonda. She wouldn't hurt me physically. That gave me a little comfort, and I turned onto my side, tucking my hands under my bruised cheek, and tried to rest.

The seatbelt was digging into my butt, and I reached around to—

It wasn't the seatbelt. It was her phone! It must've fallen out of her pocket when she'd helped me into the car. I'd been sitting on it this whole time.

I sat up. *Umm, okay.* I had no way to know if it was an iPhone or not. "Siri, turn on Voice Over."

Nothing happened. Damn it. Maybe it was an Android phone. What was the name of the android setting for— "Okay Google. Turn on TalkBack."

"Turning on TalkBack."

Oh! Oh my God. I had to hurry. I had no idea what a freaking Android screen even looked like, but I tapped my way over it, listening to the description of each app until I landed on text messages. But there weren't any. I knew Shonda had texted with Jay, and maybe even Jack, but her text messages were empty, and when I searched for Jay's phone number, it wasn't there. She must've deleted their numbers, or maybe this was a new phone. But my phone was still back at the ranch, so my plan was to text myself and hope to God that Billie was monitoring my number.

But what could I say that would help Finn and Billie find me?

8 hours away. Cabin. Mountains. Cold.

"Okay, Google, send message," I said, and when the phone replied, "Message sent," I deleted the evidence from her phone.

It was all I could think of, and then I heard Shonda behind the car, opening the trunk.

"Okay Google. Turn TalkBack off."

"Turning TalkBack off."

Thank you, Google. Oh, thank you! Reaching behind me

as discreetly as I could, I dropped her phone to the floor in the back seat and waited.

"You okay, sweetie? Not too cold?" she asked when she was back in the driver's seat.

"I'm fine, Shonda. I'm going to be fine."

CHAPTER TWENTY-ONE

FINN

THEO, that rich, drunk douchebag, was on the phone, pacin' my kitchen, barkin' orders at all kindsa people, yellin' at whoever it was to get to work, to start searchin'. But where were they gonna search? We had nothin' to go on. Billie hadn't found the car yet. We had no idea where Shonda would go. Aislinn didn't have her phone. She didn't even have her cane. She was defenseless.

No. That wasn't true. She had her fight and her spirit, and she was smart. She would get back to me. I knew she could.

Man. *I* felt defenseless. I felt completely helpless. I didn't think Shonda would hurt her, but we had no idea what kind of a mind she was in. Why? Why would she take Ace? Why wouldn't she just fess up? We'd welcomed her into our family. She had to know we'd hear her out. If she really did wanna protect Ace, she had to know we'd help her. So why would she run?

The thought of never seein' Ace again was… unbearable. I was in love with her. I'd said it to her, but now, I knew. I knew it in my bones. For so long, I'd wondered what it would feel like, and now, it was obvious. I'd do anything for her. I would give anything for her.

I would kill for her. And I wanted to. Theo's face was close, and I wanted to rearrange it.

Goddammit, I couldn't just stand here, doin' nothin'.

"I'm goin' out there." The flutter of movement in the kitchen came to a standstill. Everyone was lookin' at me. Even Theo. "I gotta do *somethin'*," I said.

He nodded. "Me too. I'll go with you."

But Jack stopped us at the door. "Where, Finn? Where you gonna go?"

"I dunno, but this is fuckin' torture. I can't just stand here. Every minute, every second is takin' her further away from me, Jack. She's scared and she's alone."

Placin' his hand on my shoulder, he squeezed. "I remember. I know how you feel, how scared you are. I'm sorry I yelled at you, brother. I shoulda believed in you. Thank you for lookin' out for us. Thanks for bein' who you are. I don't know what I'd do without you, so please, don't go out there half cocked. Let's wait for Billie. She'll find somethin'."

A phone dinged right then, and an annoyin' electronic voice said, "Text message."

"Billie, that was Ace's—" I whipped back around to see Billie holdin' Ace's white iPhone in her hand.

She looked up, smilin' at me with a little bit of that patented "Billie sass" in her eyes. She wiggled her eyebrows. "Smart girl, our Ace," she said.

***

Once Billie had a radius, we had options.

"Okay, *obvi* the location tracking has been turned off on Shonda's phone, and with a little more time, I can get around that, unless she's ditched it since Ace texted. But 'eight hours and cold' leads me to think they're in Idaho. Following the highways, eight hours straight north would put them in Montana, right at the Canadian border, but that's flat land up there if they stayed on the highway. No mountains. But if they'd gone northwest, that would put them in Idaho or Washington. It could be Oregon too. Just give me some time to find the car. It's gotta show up on some road camera somewhere."

"Finn?"

I turned when Evvie grabbed my hand and squeezed. "Yeah?"

"You need to eat something. Theo, you too. Come on, sit down."

Lettin' her lead me, I sat at the table, and my whole body slumped in the chair. Theo's reaction was similar. "Here, I thawed out some of your favorite turkey soup. We're all out of dickloaf." She winked and placed a bowl and a slice of buttered wheat bread in front of each of us. "I'll get you some milk."

Swallowin' a spoonful, I tried to smile at her, then closed my eyes, lettin' the spicy broth warm me from the inside out.

"I'm sorry," Theo said, and I opened 'em again to find him lookin' at me. "She's not a child. I know that, but it's just been the two of us for so long. I might have seemed like someone who knew what he was doing, but I didn't." He sighed. "I don't."

"You went through a lot," I admitted, tryin' hard to still hold on to the hate I'd felt for him but failin' 'cause I knew he was hurtin'.

"We did. I can't even describe to you what it was like after the accident. She stopped living. She wouldn't bathe, she wouldn't eat. She gave up. I had to live for us both, and I threw myself into school and then work because it was the only way I knew to keep going."

"I don't think she faults you for that."

"No, but I put her in this box. You know? Even I saw her as damaged. Disabled. Helpless. If I hadn't, maybe it wouldn't have taken so long for her to come back to life."

"Maybe," I said, and Evvie set two glasses of milk between Theo and me on the table.

"*You* brought her back to life. You and Billie and this ranch. You all did what I couldn't." He watched me, considerin' me. "Do you really love her?"

"I do."

"And you think you can give her a life? A good one?"

"I know I can. We can give each other a good life. I ain't rich, but I got so much more than money. I got family."

I looked around at that family, at Billie and Jay scourin' the internet, at Evvie doin' dishes at the sink and Jack dryin' 'em next to her. Dean was on the phone with some old military buddy, tryin' to figure a way to find the woman I loved, and Kev and Luuk were outside takin' care of the ranch and horses so we could all focus on findin' Ace. Even Carey was helpin', though he couldn't do much since Ace wasn't in Wyoming, but he was tryin', callin' all his friends, gettin' the word out.

I looked back at Theo. "So do you, you know? I got the best fuckin' family in the world, and Ace is part of that family, so that makes you a part of it too."

He smiled a little and nodded, then jumped in his chair when Billie banged her fist at the other end of the table.

"Idaho! I was right. They're in Idaho!"

Bein' rich sure did come in handy.

Anybody else woulda needed to wait on the FBI to start searchin' since Ace was across state lines, but not Theo. His endless amounts of money bought him instant access to higher law enforcement. It also bought him a team of hard-ass renegades, like super soldier robots, there to do whatever he wanted 'em to.

Billie had tracked Ace and Shonda to the Payette National Forest in Idaho, and there were three helicopters sittin' on my front lawn, revvin' up, gettin' ready to take us to find the woman I loved.

Theo and the super soldiers had relented and allowed Dean and me to come along, and I waved to my family on the porch as we took to the air, slippin' a pair of headphones over my ears, listenin' to chatter between the pilots and Dean. A little part of me registered how cool it was to see my brother in his old Marine element. He fit right in with the super soldiers, knew all their lingo, and probably could've flown the damn helicopter himself, but it was somethin' I'd have to file away for later. I couldn't think about anything but Ace.

The men were talkin' about a town called McCann, Idaho. The FBI would be meetin' us there, and they'd set up a search center when we arrived.

The Payette National Forest was big, nearly two and a half million acres, and it was winter and covered in snow, but everyone had hopes that the snow might help us. We had all kinds of tech and equipment, and we hoped we'd be able to see chimney smoke or packed snow from car tires, but if we couldn't, Theo's robots had some kinda high-fallutin' binoculars that could see through walls and shit. And Shonda's car was a pretty mediocre sedan, but it was navy blue, and it would stand out against all that snow.

It took a few hours to get to where we thought Ace was,

and I leaned back, slowed my breathin', and fixed an image of her in front of my eyes. My nerves and the feelin' of dread I felt tried trippin' me up, but I stuffed 'em down. If Ace was fightin'—and I knew she was 'cause she'd found a way to contact us, and 'cause stubborn was just who she was—then I'd fight too.

When we got to McCann, everything felt so big. The town was small, but the mountains were huge, and findin' Ace in those wild and wide peaks and valleys seemed impossible. I spent the rest of the day pacin' a hole in the floor of the local bar Theo had rented out for us. It was the only place in town big enough to accommodate us all.

The walls were covered in maps and images of different houses and cabins, and pictures of Ace and Shonda. We had one photo of Monique Washington, but it was old, and it was amazin' how much Ace looked like her. Nobody hung that picture up since we knew she wasn't with Ace 'cause Billie'd just seen her on a camera in a prison in Boston.

We had a steady stream of townspeople comin' by to see what all the fuss was about, but so far, no one had recognized Ace or Shonda from their pictures. But the locals were in on it now, so I knew there'd be some kinda phone tree initiated. Small towns were like that. Everyone would be lookin' for Ace, and that only meant we'd find her faster.

It had to. We had to.

I had to find her.

"Son, you wanna sit down here a spell?" an old man asked, pullin' out a chair at a small table when he noticed me zippin' back and forth across the tile floor. He was the janitor, outfitted with brooms and dusters, and he looked tired and flustered with all of us comin' in, makin' a big ol' mess for him to clean, but he looked kind. "Name's Horace," he said, holdin' out his hand for me to shake.

"Finn." I shook the hand he offered and tried to smile. "No, sir. Thank you, but I can't sit."

"Well, I'm not sure pacin' is accomplishin' anything."

"No, it probably ain't, but I gotta do somethin'."

"This woman they're lookin' for, she your girl?"

"Yeah, she is." She was. She was mine.

"I heard them soldiers talkin'. She's blind?"

"She is."

"Hm." He sat in the chair he'd intended for me. "She's a looker. Who's the woman that took her?"

"She's her aunt. They, uh, they were estranged, I guess you could say."

"This about money?"

"No, sir. I dunno what it's about, to be honest. But no, I don't think it's money."

"You know, I lived here my whole life. Grew up on the Nez Reservation north of here."

"Yeah?" I didn't wanna be rude, but I was havin' a hard time payin' attention to what he was sayin'. My mind just didn't wanna focus on anything but Ace. I resumed my pacin' 'cause my legs just wouldn't stay still.

"Yeah. I work here in town now, but I used to clean all them homes up on the mountain for the rich people. I did some handy work, too, choppin' wood, fixin' roofs, things like that, but I'm too old and creaky for that stuff nowadays."

"Mmhm."

"Well, it's just occurrin' to me that I remember a black lady, two black ladies, actually, who stayed at a cabin up on the peak. It's been, oh, I dunno, at least twenty-five years ago now. Somethin' like that."

I stopped on a dime, piercin' his eyes with mine.

"Your girl—she kinda looks like one of them ladies. My memory ain't what—"

"Does she look like this woman?" Grabbin' the picture of Monique Washington from a folder on a table behind me, I tried not to rip it when I stuffed it into his hands. He held it out in front of him, blinkin' and squintin' his eyes.

"Yeah. That's her. That's the one I remember."

"Theo!"

CHAPTER TWENTY-TWO

AISLINN

"AISLINN? Come in, honey. It's cold out there, and you're letting all the heat from the fire escape."

"I don't care," I said, leaning in the open cabin doorway. I wished I could see the stars. The night was still. It was utter darkness in front of me, but it was one of those crisp, cold winter nights and it felt clear. I knew the stars had to be out.

"Don't you want to eat? The ramen's getting cold."

"I'm not eating that sludge, Shonda."

"I'm sorry. I wasn't thinking about you being a vegetarian when I was shopping at the gas station, but it's all processed anyway. There probably isn't real chicken in it. Just have a little. You'll sleep better if you eat."

"No. I'll eat when I go home."

"Aislinn, it's time you face facts. For the time being, this is your home. I'm not taking you back. You aren't safe there. You're not safe with Finn. And what has Theo done for you lately, besides hit you and almost get you killed? Admit it, you're safer with me. And we're family. You don't have to worry. I have money. My husband left me a fortune when he died, and I've been smart about it over the years."

I shook my head. "That's what you think I care about? Money? I couldn't give a shit, Shonda. Leave me alone." Hope was dwindling quickly. I had no idea if Billie had gotten my message. And even if she had, was it enough? Could they find me?

Would I ever be with them again?

With Finn? I was enough for him, good enough, kind enough, and now, I'd never see him again. Tears were threatening, and a lump felt stuck in my throat, but I wouldn't cry. I wouldn't let Shonda know how scared I was. She didn't deserve to know me.

I wanted to scream. After spending ten years playing the helpless disabled girl, it was cruelly ironic that now I was helpless, when everything inside me wanted to be strong.

Could I make it if I snuck away? Or would I just be eaten by a bear or trip over a fallen tree and break my leg then freeze to death?

"Now, Aislinn, stop that. I won't let you push me away. We're in this together. We have to depend on each other."

Laughing bitterly into the quiet night, I listened to my voice echo out between the trees, but I stopped when I heard something else. It was like a fluttering. I tuned Shonda out and listened harder, but the sound had gone. It was probably just a car off in the distance, but once again, I reminded myself, there was no way for me to find it. I didn't even know where the main highway was, and it was at least a few miles on a dirt road to get to it.

I'd found a wooden walking stick when we returned from the store earlier. It had been standing against the wall next to the cabin's front door, so now I clutched it in my hands. I wanted to hit Shonda with it, but she was right. I would have to eat at some point, and it would be better if I didn't kill her so she could cook for me. The stove in the kitchen didn't work, so she was using a portable gas stove, and I didn't have the first clue how to operate it. I'd never been camping.

Turning back inside the open door, I sighed. "What else did you buy at the store? Peanut butter? Bread? Is there anything to eat that doesn't have dead animal parts in it?"

She opened her mouth to answer—I heard her sharp intake of air—but then the cabin was flooded with light, and sparks and flashes danced in front of my eyes. The fluttering sound was loud now, really loud, and it wasn't a fluttering.

It was a helicopter!

The spinning rotator things made an unmistakable sound. I'd heard them in every stupid military movie Theo had ever subjected me to.

Shonda gasped, and I spun, gripping my walking stick so hard, I thought my hands would have to be surgically removed. I used it like a cane, feeling for the stairs to lead me off the porch, and when I was standing firmly in a freezing foot of snow, I screamed, "Finn!"

I knew he would find me. I knew, when he realized I was gone, Dangerous Finn would come to find me. He had gotten my text.

Dropping to my knees, I waited for him. I didn't want to get my head chopped off by walking into the helicopter blades, but I heard them when the helicopter landed in front of me, the trees all around me swaying and whipping in its wind. Leaves and sticks hit my face, and I covered it with my hands.

"Aislinn, no!" Shonda tried to pull me backward. She shoved her arms between mine and clutched at my stomach, trying to lift me, trying to pull me with her, and I kicked and yelled and fought, swinging my arms, trying to hit her.

I remembered the stick I'd dropped, and I dug through the heavy, wet snow with my feet, desperately searching for it.

When I found it, I pulled away from her. She wouldn't let go, but I was able to lean far enough away from her to reach it.

Clasping it in my hand, I yanked my arm back, and she released me when the stick made contact with her face. I fell forward, and then warm arms were lifting me.

"I got you," he said.

Finn.

"I've got you, Ace, and I won't ever let you go again."

<hr>

"I'm so sorry, Aislinn. Can you ever forgive me?"

Theo was on his knees in front of me in a grounded helicopter somewhere in the middle of Idaho, squeezing my freezing hands, begging my forgiveness.

We were alone, and I was sitting in a seat, warming up while my brother's men dealt with Shonda and the local Sheriff. Finn was waiting outside for me, and I couldn't wait to be wrapped up in his arms again.

But this conversation with Theo was important.

"I have already," I said, reaching out to touch his face. "It's me who should be begging forgiveness. I am so sorry, Theo. For the last ten years. For every time I acted ungrateful, for making the burden on your shoulders so much heavier. You gave up everything for me."

"There's nothing to forgive. I would do it again. I love you. But I'm sorry for treating you like a child. I was scared. I was afraid I'd mess up and something would happen to you and I'd lose you. I was so afraid to lose you because you're my family. You're all I have, and I-I'm terrified to be alone, Aislinn." He exhaled and it was shaky. He was crying. I felt his silky tears beneath my fingers. "I don't know who I am without you. Without my role as your protector, your caregiver, who am I? I don't know who to be.

"You probably thought I had it all figured out, but I don't. When Mom and Dad died, I was lost. I didn't know who I was then either. I was just accepting that I was gay. I hadn't even told them. They never knew."

"Oh, Theo," I said, finding his hands on my legs and holding them, "they would have accepted you. They loved you."

"I know. I do know that." He sniffled. "I guess… I guess it's time for me to find myself. You've found you."

"I have."

"Do you love him, Ace?" he asked in earnest, using the nickname my friends had coined for me and the one our father had used when I was a little girl.

"I do. I love Finn, Theo. More than I can I tell you."

"Okay, then I'm happy for you. If he's who you want, then you should have him." He laughed a little. "I don't like admitting it, but… he's a good man. And it's clear that he loves you too." He sniffled again and let go of my hand to wipe his face. "I'll be honest. I'm a little jealous. You should see the guy. He's the hottest thing since—well, ever."

"Are you infatuated with my boyfriend?" I giggled, but I said, "I do see him, Theo. He's all I see."

His tone was wistful and sad when he said, "Yeah, I get that."

"You can have that, too, you know. If you'd let me go a little, maybe you could find your own Finn."

Laughing through his tears, he said, "I'm pretty sure there's only one of him."

"You know what I mean."

"Yeah, I do. And I'll try. Come here." My brother hugged me, and there was the loss of our parents still between us, but there was hope too. There was possibility where there used to be none.

———

Sitting in his lap, wrapped in a scratchy, wool blanket, Finn fed me crackers and made me take sips of ginger soda through a straw.

"Finn, I really am okay. I don't have the flu." I laughed. "And I really don't like soda."

"I know, but just eat the damn crackers and drink the damn pop, okay? You probably have low blood sugar or somethin'. If not, it'll just make you sweeter. Nothin' wrong with that. Just be glad it ain't orange flavored." He nuzzled my neck, inhaling and sighing. "Man, I missed you."

"I missed you, too, but I knew you and Billie would find me."

A deep and curt voice interrupted us, "Ma'am?" The man speaking wasn't someone I recognized.

"Yes?"

"Lieutenant Avett," he said. So, one of Theo's hired soldiers. "Ms. Washington has requested to speak with you. Your brother says it's up to you."

"Where is she?"

"Follow me."

Finn and Lieutenant Avett led me to a small room in the local sheriff's station, and I heard Shonda's soft cries as soon as we entered.

"Oh, Aislinn, I'm sorry. Please, will you forgive me? I just wanted to protect you. You're my family."

"No, Shonda. We're not family. We're related by blood, but nothing else. This is my family." I squeezed Finn's arm. "This man right here is my family. Theo is my family. Billie and Jay." I shook my head, feeling sad for her. "We could've been. You could have been a part of my family, and maybe someday I'll forgive you. I don't know. But right now, I don't.

"I'm not pressing charges." I could feel Finn's questioning gaze on my face, but I smiled up at him. "Because you're related to me, I won't. But I will expect you to get help. Your sister's in Boston. The police have her, and she's being taken care of until you can get to her. Blake Ormand is firmly in prison. He's not getting out and I'm not in danger. I'm sorry you're sad and alone, but that's something you'll have to deal with on your own. You can't force someone else to make things right for you. Trust me, I've tried."

"But, but, I—"

"No, Shonda, but nothing. Thank you for teaching me how to run an office. I do appreciate that. I'll use it. But for right now, that's all I want from you. I wish you well," I said, and I meant it. Tugging on Finn's arm, I turned and we left the room. We left the little town of McCann, and we went home.

CHAPTER TWENTY-THREE

FINN

WE'D BEEN HOME from Idaho and that whole mess of a debacle for a few weeks, and I'd never been happier. And not a fake, put-on happy, but a real genuine, satisfied happy.

Theo had calmed down. He was at least tryin' to live his own life. He was the mysterious buyer of ol' Jessup's buildin' in downtown Wisper. He'd bought it on a whim with hopes of turnin' it into a meetin' place, a haven for all kinds of people to go when they had nowhere else: kids without families, homeless people, LGBTQ folks lookin' for a little community in this harsh world. Anybody really, anybody lookin' for some of that down-home Wisper comfort that only us Wisperites could give.

Ace and I promised to help him get set up while he was lookin' for buyers for his business back in Boston. He admitted that he'd only kept it goin' for his dad, but he knew now that it wasn't what would make him happy. I wasn't sure he had any idea what *would* make him happy, but it seemed like maybe he would try to figure that out.

Ace was a little wary of Theo's decision to stay in Wisper. She wasn't completely convinced he wasn't doin' it to be close to her, but she'd decided to take him at his word, and so far, he'd given her the space she'd asked for.

Luuk and Kev had taken him under their wings, and they were all over the new center. Kev had already started takin' pics to hang up in the little buildin', images to make people feel at home. He and Luuk were gettin' ready to take another trip to the Netherlands to visit Luuk's friends there, but they were goin' sometime in the new year so we could all be together for the holidays.

It was fixin' to be a Christmas for the annuals.

Evvie was pregnant—surprise, surprise—and Jack was stupid happy about it. Apparently, he'd gotten to work tryin' to knock her up the second we got home from Montana, after we'd made sure Oly and the twins were okay. I laughed when I thought about just how many people were busy gettin' busy that night.

Dean and Oly were in baby bliss themselves, ignorin' the rest of us so they could play house and build their lives. I'd run into Oly's mama at the grocery store, and she was still cryin' over it. She hugged me and jumped up to kiss me on the lips!

Jay and Billie were all moved into their new house down the road, and any time anybody mentioned them havin' babies, Billie would pretend to puke and she'd scoff and roll her eyes, but when she didn't think anyone was lookin', she gazed at Fiona and Sara like the stars hung in their eyes. Which they pretty much did. She was an outstandin' aunt already, and she'd given the girls old computer keyboards to bang on when they were older. Fiona loved kickin' it with her feet. The clackin' noise seemed to make her happy.

Those babies were already spoiled rotten, and I knew Ma was lookin' down on 'em, watchin' over 'em, and keepin' 'em in line.

And speakin' of mamas, mine was the newest future employee at The Cade Ranch EveryBody Rides Barn. First of June was openin' day. We would be offerin' our equine therapy services to all kinds of people: kids, teenagers, and adults. And we were gettin' set up to open the house up to veteran clients, and they would stay and work the ranch with us while they were counseled and learnin' to live again, usin' our horses and our land as the bridge back to life. One of the therapists would be movin' onto the ranch, too, so she could be there permanently for any soldiers that needed her in the night. Theo bought some fancy Airstream trailer for her, and it would be delivered in the spring.

Ace and I would stay in the big house with the clients, too, like weird B&B owners, makin' sure they and the docs had clean sheets and good food to eat. I'd already moved into the downstairs bedroom with Ace after she'd forced me to clean my old room.

It took days, and I'd found shit I hadn't seen since I was a nose-pickin' seven-year-old—VHS tapes of *Power Rangers* episodes, little green army men from the dollar store, and a CD I'd made years ago with the first song I'd ever written called "My Brothers Eat Horse Shit". It was a punk song.

My mama's job would be to help with the cookin' and cleanin'. She planned to keep her job at José's diner, too, and whenever she talked about José, she got a little red-faced. Things between those two were goin' well, and they'd already been out to the house for dinner a couple times. We all liked José, and we knew he was a good man. Mama seemed happy and at home again, and I was glad for it. I was glad for her.

I was glad for us all. We were all happy.

And me and Ace? We were sexed up, blissed the fuck out,

and horny as a couple teenagers at a spin-the-bottle party in high school.

My woman was hot as shit, she was curious, and she was a *real* fast learner. Guess we both were.

"What'd you say?" I asked her when she whispered in my ear, beggin' for me.

"I said, 'I want you.'" She rolled her hips, seekin' contact with mine.

"No," I taunted. "That ain't what you said. C'mon. Say it again." Pressin' harder against her, I held her naked body to the wall in the foalin' room above the barn. My cock was trapped between us, wrapped in a condom, strainin' and dyin' to get into her. I gripped her delicate wrists in my hand and pushed 'em hard against the wall above her head, licked her bottom lip, then bit it. "Tell me what you want, Ace. Tell me plain."

She moaned and bit back.

"I want your cock in my pussy. I want it to hurt. I want you to fuck me so hard, I'll still feel you inside me in a month. I want your hips to leave bruises on my thighs."

I looked down at those smooth, quiverin' thighs, imaginin' just what she was beggin' me for. Well, who was I to deny the sexiest woman in the world?

Bendin' my knees and spreadin' her legs open with mine, I rammed myself inside her. One quick punch up into that sweet, tight body, then I pulled out just as fast and stared at her, marvelin' at the trust she gave me, the love, and the adventure she shared with me that poured outta every cell in her body.

"Finn!" she begged.

"Just hold your horses, baby. Don't you worry. I got plans for you."

"Oh, oh, Finn," she whined, sobbin' a little with need so

strong, I felt it in my DNA. "I can't take it anymore." She'd been writhin' and beggin' for me the whole hour I'd been workin' her up, but now it was time for me to give her what she wanted. I tried to act unaffected, but I was ready to come just lookin' at her.

Quick and efficient-like, I lifted her into my arms and tossed her onto the bed. She bounced and squealed and moaned so loud, I thought the horses in the barn below us would be embarrassed. But I was prepared. I knew what she wanted; she hadn't needed to say it.

Climbin' over her, I wrapped her wrists in the strips of fabric I'd ripped off an old shirt earlier and tied to the end of the bed, pulled 'em into tight knots, then I wrapped her long, lovely legs around my ass and pounded into her.

Oh, she was right—she was gonna feel me forever.

She pulled her wrists, pretendin' to try to escape, but I knew better. I knew this was where she wanted to be, trapped beneath me and held captive in my heart.

"You okay?"

Breathless, she said, "Yes."

"You sure? It ain't too tight?"

"Oh my God, Finn, fuck me!"

Oh, I did. I lifted her ass off the bed, holdin' her up like my very own golden-brown platter of perfection, her tied wrists keepin' her where I wanted her, and I fucked her so hard and good that I gave myself an ass cramp.

Her body glistened with sweat, sparklin' in the moon-light comin' in the window, her perfect, sexy, rosy-brown nipples peaked and beggin' for my mouth, and I was over-whelmed.

I slowed my hips, caressin' my hands all over her almost frantically 'cause, all of a sudden, I was afraid.

"Finn? What's wrong?"

Already, she knew me so well. Even though she couldn't see me, she could tell my mood had changed.

"I want you so much. I love you so much and it's so big. I've never felt this way before. You know?"

"I do. Untie me, Finn. Let me touch you."

I did. I pulled the knots out, and she lifted up to kiss me.

"I love you too," she said, and her hands explored my face, feelin' my smile and the crinkles at the edges of my eyes. Her warm breath washed over me, and I breathed her in.

"I waited so long for you. Now you're here, I can hardly believe it. And… and sometimes, it makes me sad you'll never see me. I want you to see the love in my eyes. Will you ever know how much I love you?"

She smiled, a gentleness colorin' her beautiful face, and pushed at my chest, urgin' me to lie back on the bed.

"I already know. Close your eyes."

I closed 'em while she climbed over me, straddlin' my legs, and she kissed my stomach. So soft, her kisses were breaths, but I felt 'em, and I felt the care and the love and the reverence in each and every one.

"Keep them closed."

"Mm."

"Feel how much I love you?" She stroked her fingers down my legs and back up and over my ribs, one at a time, and I focused on her breath and the slide of her skin over mine. Each new touch was different than the last. Each one was deliberate.

Climbin' higher, she kneeled with her legs on either side of my hips and leaned over me, runnin' her fingers through my hair. She was a little obsessed with my hair. Girl couldn't keep her hands off of it. I heard it slippin' through her fingers like a whisper, and she moaned softly.

Openin' my eyes, I watched her for a minute. Watched her

body flow in time with her caresses over mine. I loved the way she moved, like she was in total sync with me. When we were together like this, naked and open to each other, her body followed mine, like the magnetic sway of the sea.

She was feelin' me with her whole self, and it was the quietest, sexiest, most erotic experience I'd ever had. It was slow. And it was perfect. There wasn't any hard fuckin', no rope, no belts, no dirty words. Just two bodies, two souls becomin' one.

"Finn, your eyes are open."

How did she know?

I chuckled. "Sorry, but I can't not look at you."

She sat up. "Close them." It was a command and I followed her order.

When she was convinced of my compliance, she took my cock in her hand gently, and I moaned. I wanted to buck into her fist, but I didn't. I let her keep the control. I let her play my body this time, like I was *her* guitar. Like my body was the strings and she made the most beautiful song.

She moved higher, her legs squeezin' my hips now, and positioned herself above my cock. I felt her wet heat, and I moaned again 'cause I couldn't stop the sound.

"Feel me, Finn. See my love in your mind. When I touch you, when we breathe, do you see it?" she asked, and I could. It was like a colorless cloud in front of my eyes, but when I focused on it, it grew. It took over the blackness behind my closed lids. "See me?" she whispered, and she descended, takin' me into her body so slowly, so sweetly.

"Yes," I whispered, too, 'cause I was mesmerized by what I saw. Colors burst everywhere, and they overtook my vision, then my mind, and they traveled all throughout my body. And the places we were connected—our sexes, our breath, our hands clasped together, fingers threaded together—those places were bright points of light in my eyes. I could see 'em even though I wasn't lookin'.

"I see you. This is how you see me?"

"Yes. You are every color, every breath. You're everything."

She moved, rollin' her hips against mine, like that wave in the ocean I dreamed so long ago, and I gasped. It hurt like nothin' I'd ever felt, but the pain was so sweet in my chest. In my heart. In every cell inside my body. I was drownin' in it. I was lost to it, and I almost felt like I was floatin' away.

But she kissed me, touchin' her breasts to my chest, holdin' on to me like we'd both disappear if she didn't, and the contact grounded me. Brought me back to her.

"This is how I see you every day," she said. "You're the most beautiful man in the world, and I've never laid eyes on you. Do you understand?"

"Oh." It was all I could think to say 'cause her body gripped me so tight inside, and mine responded. The colors swirled and sparkled behind my eyes, and we came like that, quiet, almost still, and blinded by love.

EPILOGUE
FINN

"OH MY GOD! Does that kid ever quit crying?"

I laughed at Billie, kissed Ace's cheek, and lifted little Fiona into my arms. She was a good wailer, and I thought she would be like her Uncle Finn when she was older—a smartass and good at drivin' people nuts. I was proud of her for it already.

"It's time," Ace said. "Ready?"

It was June first, a warm, tranquil, summer day, and it was time to open The Cade Ranch EveryBody Rides Program.

"Yeah." Lookin' down at little Fiona in my arms and Sara in her cradle, I said, "We're ready. Jack? Jay?" I looked up at my brothers' faces. "Dean, Kev? You guys ready?"

"Fuck yeah," Kev said, smilin', and he wrapped his arms around Luuk's waist, huggin' him from behind, restin' his chin on Luuk's shoulder. I was so proud of him for bein' who he was, for acceptin' himself, and for lettin' us know the real him. I felt lucky to know my brother.

"Give her to me, Finn," Oly said, holdin' out her arms for the baby. "Go cut that imaginary ribbon,"

"I've got Sara," Evvie said, and she held quiet, itty-bitty Sara up above her own little baby bump, cooin' at her and talkin' baby talk. "The Cade women are ready," she said, tuckin' Sara (we called her Mitch—short for Mitchum) onto her hip, and she smiled at Jack just like Ma used to smile at her Mr. Mitchum, like she saw the world in his eyes. He winked at her and she melted, right there on the spot.

"Wait," Kev said. "Why didn't we get a real ribbon?"

Luuk laughed and kissed him, and Dean smacked the back of his head.

"Ow. Fucker."

"One dollar in the swear jar," Dean said, chucklin'. "Pony up, little brother."

"Alright," Jack said. "Let's go out there and at least act like we know what the fuck we're doin'."

"Hey!" Billie stomped her foot. "How come nobody yells at Jack when he cusses in front of the babies? I've paid at least five-hundred dollars to that damn swear jar. How much have you put in, Jack? A quarter? Those kids will have enough of my money by the time they're five to go to Harvard if they want." She rolled her eyes and scoffed.

"Mine too," Kev and I said at the same time.

Jack laughed, shruggin', and we all walked out to the porch.

Jay squinted, lookin' over the ranch. "You sure everything's ready, Ace?"

"Yes, Jay," she said. "We've gone over it. The appointments are all set for the next month. The paperwork's in order, consent forms are all signed and filed. Now, we just need cute little kid butts on our horses. Then, next month, we'll start the vet program. The first two men will be moving into the big house in three weeks. Everything's ready."

Jay nodded. "Thanks, Ace. I'm kinda not sure how we ever managed without you."

She chuckled, huggin' my side.

"Me either," I whispered, capturin' her mouth with mine when she pushed up on her tiptoes to kiss me.

Bigsy's orange clown car pulled up to the house, and he and Annie stepped out.

"Well, you fools ready? Annie packed steak in my lunch for my first day back to work, but don't you bitches be thinking you'll get any."

"Fine then," I called out to him, shadin' my eyes from the bright mornin' sun with my hand. "You can't have any of the brisket I'm makin' for the cookout. And just for that sneer on your face, I'm makin' you eat your cold steak in the barn, in a stall next to a big ol' stinkin' pile of horse shit."

"Finn!" Ace smacked my ass.

"Brisket?" Bigsy drooled like a dog, and ironically, or maybe rightly, Tony ran out the open screen door, jumped down the porch stairs, and stole the brown bag from Bigsy's hand. He took off, racin' to the barn to enjoy his spoils, and Iggy meowed in disapproval, perched on the porch railin', lickin' her paw while she watched Pepper chase after him. Pepper was the boss of Tony, and I was sure she'd eat Bigsy's steak while poor Tony watched.

"Son of a bitch! That's my steak, you mongrels!"

"I swear, you guys," Oly warned, "if the first words outta these kid's mouths is shit or bitch, I'm gonna start choppin' nuts."

"Do it," Annie said, rubbin' her hands over the bowlin' ball on her own stomach. "If Marcus knocks me up again, I'll kill him. I'm so uncomfortable, and I think my bladder's broken."

All the guys winced, Oly and Evvie nodded in solidarity, and I laughed.

"Alright," Isaac said, marchin' up the lane. "Let's get this show on the road. What are y'all standin' here for? Dr. Harris and two clients are waitin' in the arena for you." He looked like a different kid than the scrawny little bastard who'd shown up to the ranch a year ago. He was as tall as Jack now and just as strong as any of us. He'd graduated high school and was set to leave for his first year of college at the end of the summer.

"Isaac?" Jack said.

"Yeah?"

A chorus of voices called back, "Get to work. Shit ain't gonna shovel itself!"

"Whatever," Isaac smarted, rollin' his eyes, then he narrowed 'em against the sun. "Like I'm gonna listen to you. You all are like some ridiculous cowboy romance TV show, like my mom watches."

"Right?" Bigsy laughed. "That's what I said!"

The End.

If you liked the book (or loved it, I hope), please leave a review—even just a few words would help—anywhere you buy your books, Amazon, Goodreads, or Bookbub. Self-published indie authors rely heavily upon reviews to get our stories out to the masses. And thank you. I know it takes time to do this. I appreciate the time out of your day and the effort.

I feel like there should be a song playing now, like at the end
of some epic movie… Pick the one you hear in your mind
and then post it in the Facebook group, Wisperites Unite, or
tag me on Instagram. I'm dying to know the song you
choose!

WANT MORE?

Become a Wisperite!
Join my newsletter for exclusive stories, Wisper news, and
The Cade Ranch Sexcapades—naughty little interludes for
my subscribers ONLY!
Jack and Evvie's wedding scenes are there!
Sign up for your first FREE short story, Wild Heart: Welcome
to Wisper
Sign up on my website!
gretarosewest.com

I would love to hear from you, email me at
greta@gretarosewest.com.
I'll reply.
You can find me on the usual social sites, but I mostly hang
out on Instagram, Facebook, and Goodreads.

Join my Team!
Receive an advanced review copy of my next book. Join my
ARC Team, a wonderful group of people who help get the
word out when I release a new book!
Sign up on my website
gretarosewest.com

ABOUT THE AUTHOR

Greta Rose West was a floundering artsy flake until Jack showed up, knocking on the door of her brain, and then pounding on it, and then he just plain kicked it down. She lives in NW Indiana with her husband and her two precocious kitties, Geoff Trouble and Sally Mae Midnight. When she's not writing, she's reading and devouring music. She enjoys indie films no one else likes, and her favorite food is Aver's Veggie Revival pizza.

gretarosewest.com